BLOCK

BOYZ

BLOCK BOYZ

ISBN: 978-0-9992646-6-9

TABLE OF CONTENTS

CHAPTER ONE

The block had been jumping nonstop since early in the A.M. Hypes fiending for a fix ran up and down the avenue to cop that butter. The time was now 6 P.M., and Block and his right-hand man, Tree, sat posted up in an old broke down Crown Victoria that had been in the same spot for over a year. They passed some the finest gas back and forth, while taking a break from the hustle and waiting for the plug to deliver their re-up. They'd been doing numbers all morning since 6 A.M. Block had already run through a four and a baby, while his boy Tree was still cradling two ounces. But that was only because he'd dipped out the hood for a moment to go lay up with some thot he'd been tryna smash on for a couple of weeks.

"Man dis mutha fucka jumping like June Tenth," Tree announced, inhaling the levitating smoke into his lungs that had him feeling like he was out of space. "Fam need ta hurry up an' pull up so ya boi can catch da rest of dis doe out here, feel me?"

Block nodded in agreement. "Already my ninja." Block grabbed the blunt and took a pull. "Dis mutha fucka always doing numbers. You'd be knee deep in da money if you'd let dat thot wait wit'cha tenda dick ass." Block shot a slug at his boy, putting hoes before money. His priorities were asshole backwards. First you get the money, then you get the power, then you get the broads.

"Don't worry bout my dick. U need ta watch ur bitch, before I be swimming in dat trick. Right stroke, left stroke."

"Ninja, fuck dat trick, dat's community property," Block ragged on Wanda. Wanda was a thick ass chocolate sister from around the way he'd been pounding on. "Everybody den had dat. you'd just be adding your name ta da soul train line," Block said. Tree broke out laughing from Block's last statement.

"Tru dat, tru..." Tree stopped mid-sentence when Block's cellphone chimed "Harder Way" by Derez Deshawn.

"Wuz shaking?" Block answered without checking the screen display.

"Dawg I gawt dat lil info u ben looking fo." Pimp breathed deeply into the phone in his baritone voice. "Remember dat fuck nigga dat was talking out his neck u gawt into it wit da other nite at da club?"

"Yea, where dat clown at?" Block asked. How could he forget the clown ass nigga? Block and Tree had rolled with one of the homies off the deck named Dice, and one of his lady friends named Shay. It was Shay's birthday, and Dice wanted to take her out for a good time. They'd been doing that when the D.J. announced the last call for alcohol. Block made his way to the bar and ordered a bottle of Remy V.O.S.P. As soon as he popped the top, a fly, brown-skinned honey stepped between his parted legs as he sat on the stool and whispered some very freaky things in his ear about how bad she wanted him. Not looking or expecting any trouble, out of the blue it came. Block gently pushed the breezy away and did what any playa would do in the type of situation. "Don't check me, check ya bitch," he said. Homeboy didn't take to his suggestion and took off on Block. A mighty blow collided with his jaw, knocking his 20-carat diamond studded six-piece gold grill out of his mouth. A fight ensued between the two outside of Club Textures into the middle of the street. The fight didn't last long, because it was disrupted when one of his opponents rolled down and got to busting a semiautomatic handgun out the passenger side window of an old school 85 box Chevy. "How u so happen ta come by dat info?" Block questioned, taking a look in the rearview mirror. The image made him incense. He'd worn the grill, to hide the reasonable size gap between his perfectly straight white teeth.

"U act as if it's hard when des streets talk," Pimp replied. "I just kept my ear ta da concrete. Pull up on me wit dem stick's, so we can drop dat nigga off."

"Alright, I'll be der in twenty of em," Block informed, then hung up as he hoped out the Crown Vic.

"Wuz up Gee?" Tree asked out of skepticism.

"Nuthin," Block lied, tossing Tree the car keys to his all black 2000 S.S. Impala. "Remove da license plates," he informed before storming off.

Tree clutched the keys in confusion and placed the rest of the kush in the ashtray, before handling what was requested.

Block ran in the trap house, a house him and his team rented for the low from a clucker named Trish. Running in the backroom, Block grabbed the chopper they'd stashed in the closet. An A.K. 47 with a hundred round drum. Block ran out the house with the chopstick in plain view and hopped in the whip.

"So, u gone tell ya boi wat's going on?" Tree asked again. He wasn't buying that push offline Block gave him before.

"Put da peddle ta da metal," Block growled angerly, gritting his teeth. "Rememba dat bitch ass clown I got into it wit da otha nite at da club?" Block checked himself and let Tree in on the scoop.

"Yea, wat bout dat bitch ass nigga. Wat'cha you know where dat weak ass clown at?"

"Pimp gawt da drop on em."

With no further questions, Tree smashed da gas and the 454-engine floated down the block. This would be fun he thought. He couldn't wait to deaden that fuck nigga. As fare as he was concerned, he wished they could've blown ole boy shit off when the beef first kicked off. It had been a long time coming...

***

"I don't know why y'all fool ass niggas acting brand new like y'all don't know I gawt stupid hands," Stevo said to his two boys, Kilo and Chop. Stevo's young mind lived to impress. To prove how certified his hands was, he floats around like a trained boxer. "Float like a butterfly an' sting like a bee." Him and his crew laughed off his bad impression of Muhammad Ali. "Y'all niggas should've saw me da other nite when I almost knocked ole boy pussy ass out. I put my foot in dat nigga ass," Stevo lied. The black right eye he was rocking was suffice enough proof he had no wins. Only mark Block had was a minor cut inside his upper lip.

"Fuck dat shit," Kilo dismissed. "Dat's da same shish dat got'cha ass suspended from school last week." Kilo wasn't the average hood nigga. He was the pretty boy type that avoided trouble to chase them dollar signs. That was all that mattered to him. He didn't have time to be getting his light skin or pretty boy feathers scratched and lumped up. Kilo considered himself a chick magnet. His hazel eyes, wavy hair, and athlete physique had all the lil honeys going crazy and wanting to have his baby. "Shawty Bre was asking bout'cha too. U know shawty tryna lace u wit dat fiya toppin."

"Yo lil ugly ass thank u a mac," Chop playa hated. "How u know shawty gawt some fiya head?"

"Cuz she blessed ya boi, dat's how. Any more questions hoe detective?" Kilo ribbed his boy, causing them all to share a hysterical laugh. "U know des hoes luv making' ya boi toes curl. Plus, ya ugly ass just hattin, cuz dem hoe's give me da pussy an' nawt u."

Chop smiled smugly. "Now who da one hattin?" Chop countered. Chop knew his boy was flexing. He was far from ugly, quite handsome in the ladies' eyes. His six-foot, 200-pound frame covered in tattoos made women hot when he took off his shirt. His thug credentials drove women wild alone. Not to mention his dark skin tone, light brown eyes, designer braids, and mouth full of solid 20k gold added on to the ladies' infatuation. "U know ya boi a Ladies man," Chop rubbed his face and turned his head to show off his profile to substantiate his claim.

Stevo, Kilo, and Chop were all in the same age bracket. They all were 17 years of age and went to Custer high school. And just like any mundane teenager, they were able to obtain identification that gave them access to the bars and clubs where they normally picked up older ladies by cogently mesmerizing them with their mature looks and charming conversation.

"Hold on once," Chop interrupted. "Y'all know who da fuck dis is in dat car dat keep rolling thru da set?" he asked, pointing toward the black sedan that had cruised through their hood for the third time.

Stevo squinted his eyes to try to glimpse who participants were inside, but the tent was too dark.

"Dat's alright, next time a mutha fucka come thru here, I'm send some hot shit thru dat piece." Chop rose off the porch and went around the house to grab his Tech 9 equipped with a 50-round clip. He was always ready for action...

***

"Dats buddy soft ass right der fool," Pimp pointed from the back seat. "Dawg right der wit dem locks."

"Yea dat's dat bitch ass ninja," Block cocked the A.K. "Pull up right in front of em, so I can put dis whole hundit in em." Tree swerved up on the curb, and Block let his window down.

Bop, bop, bop, bop, bop, bop followed as Block let the chopper come alive. The first burst of rounds ripped through Stevo's abdomen and chest. Before Stevo's lifeless body could hit the ground, Kilo vamoosed through the gangway, quicker than Tom Hanks in the Forest Gump movie. Chop was a soldier who would die for the cause, so he stayed and fought like a man. Bullets spitting from Chop Tech 9 penetrated the Impala's fiberglass frame. The back window scattered at the blaze of gunfire. Pimp, who was dumping his Mac-10, ducked for cover to evade the ray of bullets that was sent in his direction. Block busted out the window like a wild man with no fear. He had already eliminated his target, but he had no plans to stop until everything moving was no longer breathing. Stevo was stretched out, body riddled with bullet wounds. It was a gory scene. Out of ammunition, Chop ducked along the veranda. He didn't possess enough ammo to continue or win this war, so he had to get out of there. Bop, bop, bop, bop, bop... Block unloaded the chopstick until the hundred round drum was empty. Nothing emitted after the weapon stopped jumping. The steal of day was upon, leaving nothing but a smoking rifle barrel as Tree smashed off the scene...

***

Wanda stood in front of a full-length mirror within her bedroom performing an examination of her naked body. She had a beautiful vassal; her petite frame was well put together. Her 34DD breast, slim waist, and fat ass was worth admiration. Most would argue she resembles Meagan Good, that's how fine she was, a dime from head to toe.

Wanda ran her left hand through her well-manicured pussy hair, then slipped a middle finger into her Milky way's center. She was extremely wet. Pulling her finger from her clit, she sucked the copious fluids off.

"Mmmmm..." she moaned out loud, savoring her own intoxicating flavors.

Wanda turned around backwards and looked over her shoulder to ogle her posterior. Giving it a light smack, it jiggled cutely. Wanda chuckled to herself, acknowledging her own perversion. Smiling, she bent forward at the waist, and parted her legs to view her cotton candy pinkness. Her dark chocolate skin made her center pop and stand out like a sore thumb. Facing the mirror straight on again, she took her right breast in the palm of her hand and circled the flaccid nipple with her hot tongue. It hardened instantly as a reaction of her thorough tongue action. She was on fire; she craved a man's touch to put out the raging fire between her legs. It had been two long days since she had her pussy tamed. Walking over to her vanity set, she picked up her cellphone and sent Block a quick text...

***

Block and his boys pulled up on their deck. "Dat's wat I'm talking bout," Tree proudly exclaimed when they stepped from the vehicle. "U let dem niggas have it. U sprayed da whole hundo." Him and Block shook up. "I bet'cha dat mutha fucka still hot ta da touch." Tree loved seeing niggas get smoked, so his gloating was just a reaction to his uncontrollable trill to what had recently occurred.

"Hold dat down," Block warned. Tree was quite loud, and Block didn't want the information to come into the wrong person's ears. "Hold on a minute, I gotta go stash dis bitch." Block went into the trap and placed the chopper back in the closet behind some old dirty clothes. On his way back outside his cellphone pinged with a text message. He read Wanda's jean stretching text, then replied with, "Keep it hot, B der in a jiffy."

Tree and Pimp were leaned against Block's car indulged in conversation when Block walked up. "Check it out y'all, I'ma bout ta head ta da promise land. Booty calls," Block informed, as if he hadn't just committed a murder moments ago. But that just how it was in the hood. Death was a normal occurrence. To Block it was just another day. "U need me ta drop u some ware?" he asked Pimp while showing both his boyz love.

"Naw I'm good. I'ma stay out here an' catch des dolla signs," Pimp answered. "Just be careful, u know it's hot out here an' u still in dis bad boi," Pimp said and slapped the hood on the car to demonstrate as to what he was referencing to.

"Got'cha, y'all be easy to out here." Block showed love a final time before hopping in the ride. Pimp and Tree threw up the rakes as Block pulled away from the curb.

Minutes later he was in front of Wanda's apartment complex. He parked, then sent a text for her to open the door. Wanda opened the door in her birthday suit. She pulled Block into the apartment by his shirt. As soon as the door shut, she was eagerly pawing and yanking at his True Religion button up.

"Dam shawty, slow down," Block gently eased Wanda away to admire her beautiful physique. Her nipples stood erect in the center of her huge sexy areolas. "We got time, so let's take it nice an' slow."

Wanda smiled at Block's suggestion then pushed him against the door. "I don't want it slow, I want it fast an' hard," she purred, sticking her tongue down his throat. Wanda was a nymphomaniac who loved to take control in the bedroom. Block couldn't have that. Taking control, Block pushed her back, dropping his pants in the process and pushed her to her knees. Without a word, she engulfed his ten-inch pole into her hungry gobbling mouth.

"Mmmmmm..." she moaned as she relished his meat like it was a full course delicacy. Taking Block's dick from her mouth, she licked up and down and around the length and width of his tool. She enjoyed the pulsating piece before slipping it back into her succulent mouth. Block was in seventh heaven on the receiving end of Wanda's superb head game. Wanda's eyes were closed in true bliss, enjoying giving Block the pleasure she was providing so tremendously. Wanda's head moved back and forth at rapid speed. Her toppings were so good, Block grabbed her head and leaned back against the door. He was on the verge of disgorging in her mouth.

"Shit gurl," Block whispered. "I'ma bout ta bust."

Wanda wasn't deterred by Block's warning. She determined to get him off and receive his tasty treat. So, she sucked him off with gusto until Block stiffened, clutching her head tightly, and shot down her greedy mouth. Wanda swallowed all he had to offer, not letting up, she sucked and swallowed until she had every last drop of his seed.

Once she released him from her lips, Block carried her to the couch and removed his remaining clothing.

"Come on daddy an' get dis pussy," she beckoned him, running her fingers through her wet clit. "I been waiting fa u to beat dis pussy ta it's sore, an' make it come fa ya daddy."

"U know I hold da title, I'ma beat da pussy up like fight nite."

"U promise."

Block pushed Wanda's legs up and locked them behind her head and penetrated her with his full length. Wanda cried out clawing at his muscular arms. She was extremely wet. So wet, that every time Block descended into her womb, squishing sounds were audible around the room.

"Dat's right baby, make dat kitty purrrrr..." she moaned. She loved every bit of Block's schlong stretching her out.

Block deeply patted while pounding in and out of her. In amidst their fucking, Block flipped her over and contoured her body to where her ass was stuck up in the air, and her face pushed deep into the cushion.

Wanda peeped over her shoulders as he slammed back into her. "Agghhhh..." she screeched. Block was putting in work, bringing her to heights no other man had ever achieved. She threw her ass back and matched the pace of his tempo. "Dat's right get dat pussy daddy," Moans and smacks of flesh emitted around the living room. The sound of their love making was animalistic. It sounded like two gorillas making love in the Congo. The heavy breathing between the two signified they were near to the edge. Wanda went over the cliff first screaming Block's name. "Block, yesssssss..." she yelled as she squirted all over his dick. The mix between her copious juices coating his meat, and her trembling orgasm, set Block off. He came pulling out shooting all over her back and ass...

CHAPTER TWO

Block floated his Impala down the avenue, not paying attention to his surroundings. Block was in his own world when, while searching through his playlist for "First Day Out" by Tee Grizzle, a dark figure materialized. Block slammed hard on the brakes causing the tires to squeal and slide across the asphalt before coming to an abrupt stop.

"Wat da fuck," Block snapped. "Watch where u going. U didn't see me coming?" He ranted on jumping out the car. Suddenly he caught himself. There, before him, was a ghost from the past. "My bad," Block quickly apologized.

Mary was astonished at Block's horrible manners. "Boi u almost cleaned my clock," she chastised. "U should be more careful. U could kill someone driving all erratic like dat chow."

Mary was an old soul from his past that he had great respect for. For as long as he could remember, Mary had always been true, caring, and respectful toward him. Back in high school, Block used to mess around with her daughter Kayla for a couple years. That was when he was 16 or 17 years old. He was now 23 and he was still head over hills in love with his high school sweetheart.

"Please forgive me Ms. Pickett. U know I'd never do anything ta hurt u." He crossed his fingers over his heart. "Cross my heart an' hope ta die." Block wrapped his arms around Mary for a hug, and she embraced him back, wrapping her frail arms around him. "How u been? How life been treating u?"

"I'm fine chow, blessed. How about yourself?"

"All u know I can't complain." Block smiled a warming smile. "Everything everything. How dat fine ass daughter of ur's?"

"Boi u still ain't changed," Mary chuckled to herself while shaking her head at the same time. "U still think u a playa, huh?"

"Nawt me ma'am," Block lied. "I'ma god fearin' man."

"Ummhhh." Mary twisted up her mouth and moaned. She hoped Block didn't actually believe she brought that nonsense he said about him being a man of God. She was born at night but not last night. "Chow u still da same as I remember. I guess somethings never change. But to answer ur question, Kayla doing alright. Everything starting ta fall in place fa her."

That was good news to Block. He had never forgiven himself for how he had dogged her out. Back then he was young, dumb, and full of cum, and he didn't quite appreciate that he had a diamond in the rough. He had a girl that would ride with him to the end and go through hell and back. She was with him as thick as thieves whether rich or poor, but he had cheated on her with numerous girls. One of those girls being her best friend. One night at a house party, Block got caught red handed in his infidelity. The only excuse he could produce was, "U an' I ain't fuck'.

When they were younger, Kayla was the good girl type. The type that didn't believe in copulation unless marriage was purposed.

"She got any shorties?" Block inquired, hoping what slim possibilities he possessed to rekindle the relationship, wouldn't be stopped by children complications.

"Nah chow," Mary exclaimed. "I don't even think she'd have anytime fa dat. U know she studying ta be a doctor."

"Nah, I didn't know dat." Block was glad to hear how goal orientated Kayla's life was. "U know I ain't seen ur daughter since high school." So much had changed Block thought. It made him feel as if he was being left behind.

"Chow, I gotta get out of here," Mary said after taken a brief glance at her watch. "I'm sorry chow we ain't gawt more time ta catch up, but I'm already late." Mary was supposed to pick up her best friend so they could have a girl's day over brunch.

"No need ta apologize, I understand. Just take my number down an' tell Kayla ta get at me," Block informed pulling his iPhone from his pocket.

"Nah chow, I ain't gone be able ta do dat," Mary declined crushing Block's heart as soon as the words left her mouth. "But I'll give u hers an' u can dial her up."

Block punched in Kayla's number feeling as if he was on cloud nine. All these years of building castles in the sky, his dreams were finally coming true. The heart wanted what it wanted, and his wanted Kayla.

"Alright," Block said coyly, not trying to sound over elated

"U take care now," she said, hugging Block a final time. "U be safe out here in des streets." She turned Block loose, adjusting her spring jacket before waving goodbye.

"Same to u."

When she was out of sight, Block hopped back in the ride and headed toward the hood. Before Block's dopeboy Air Max 95s could grace the sidewalk, cluckers was already approaching his car door. A hype named Gerome ran up to the whip. "U good yung blood?" he asked, scratching his neck and arms. Gerome was fiending badly. Gerome was one of them funny type hypes every hood had, u know the type the neighborhood made relentless fun of. He reminded Block of one of the T.V. characters Martin Lawrence played on the 90s television show "Martin." He was lost in the sauce. He still wore leather pants, half unbutton polyester shirts, with a tired ass 1990s Jerry Curl. His whole style was played out, just like his pathetic image. Gerome was a character that believed in his mind he would blow up and make it out the hood by becoming a R&B artist. It was a real-life hype dream.

"Nah, I'm out right now unc," Block referred to him in a slang the hood had coined to addressed the customers; and vice versa, the clucker called the dealers nephew. "Holla at Tree, he round here somewhere."

"I ain't seen da nigga all day nephew, an' I need a hit bad. Don't do me like dat, I always spin good money wit'cha."

"Dat's to bad Rome," Block snapped. Block had shit to do, and he didn't have all day to watch Gerome stand in front of him fiending and begging for a hit. "Come back bout an hour, I'll be straight den."

"Cool yung blood," Gerome agreed, then scurried up the sidewalk.

The hood was deserted. Compared to its normal functions, it was empty. All the hustlers were nowhere in sight, but all the fiends crowded around like the television series "Walking Dead." They were waiting on their first hit so they could come alive.

Block detached his cellphone from his belt and hit up Tree.

"Wat's up," Tree answered groggily, yawning, and rubbing the crust out the crevice of his eyes.

"Where u at family?" Block queried walking into the trap house. "Don't tell me your tenda dick ass laid up wit some lil slut bucket when its money ta be made?"

"Nah, wat time is it?" Tree yawned for the umpteenth time. "Me an' dat nigga Pimp went out last night an' a nigga head spinning like crazy from all da Hen dawg," he explained.

"Fuck all dat sentimental shish. Its eight in da morning an' da block lit like da Rockefeller Christmas Tree," Block dismissed Tree excuses. He didn't have time for that type of nonsense. To him it was sucker shit. Wayne Dwyer once said, "the only thing worse than a lie, is an excuse." Pondering that philosophy ninjaz could save the game for their bitches. "Get up an' get'cha self together I'ma bout ta swoop down an' pick u up," he ordered.

"Alright, one," Tree obeyed.

Hanging up, he clicked over and called the plug.

"Yo," G-Ball answered.

"Wuz up?" Block inquired. "I'm tryna get right. Pull up on me."

"Yea, well," G-Ball replied unconcerned by Block's request. "U should've been round yesterday when u had me ride way cross town, den u an' your men pulled dat lil Houdini act." G-Ball was annoyed by the situation, and he had cogitated the option to cut Block off. But the dilemma wasn't logical. Block and his people spent good money, and Ball didn't turn nothing down but his collar.

"T.P.," Block apologized. "Don't hold me ta dat doe, something came up dat had ta be takin care of wit no delay."

"So wat!" G-Ball snapped, losing his patience. "U handle personal matters on your own time, not on mine nigga. U got da game fucked up," he said while asserting his position in the game. "I'ma boss, an' time is money. So as long as we do bizness, don't ever waste my time. U got it?"

Block didn't reply. He bit his tongue in spite of the pain and let G-Ball talk out his neck. Block knew how to handle clowns like G-Ball, and it involved letting them guns talk.

"I hope u hear me loud an' clear, cause dis da last time I'ma tell ya," G-Ball continued. "If u want ta get right, u know ware ta find me," he offered then hung up.

Block looked at the phone in his hand, he couldn't believe the nerve of G-Ball. Block was a gangsta, and G-Ball was violating him with a high level of disrespect. Block couldn't believe G-Ball had the audacity to try to check him like he was one of his groupies or foot soldiers. G-Ball had fucked up thinking he could address Block like a bitch. For now, Block would give G-Ball a G-pass for his condescension and sideways talk, but only momentarily. Once

Block found a new connect, he would take that heat to G-Ball front door. Block pulled up in front of Tree's home and honked the horn.

"What's cracking my nigga?" Tree asked hopping in the passenger seat. "What's da word?"

"It's simple." Block put the car in drive and pulled off the curb. "Money, my ninja," he emphasized, smiling with confidence. The hood was rocking with junkies, and Block hadn't seen a penny of the circulating money. He knew he could blame no one for his slim pockets, but himself. He felt like a walking paradox. The behavior he'd been portraying in the streets, was equivalent to the kind he was always on his boyz ass for. Block knew he had to shape up in order for his team to follow suit. Leading by example was the only way to obtain the results he was expecting. "Money is da word every day. Money make da world go round. An' ta be honest, it's time we boss ourselves up, an' get a new connect."

"Why, wuz wrong wit da one we got now?" Tree questioned Block's motive. They already had a connect, and Tree had a blind view as to why they needed a new one. "Don't tell me u in ta fixing shit dat ain't broke."

"Everything wrong wit da one we got now. We still penny pinching like bottom feeders, when we supposed ta be making bigg boi moves." Block was right, they'd been small time hustling since high school. "It's time ta graduate G. Da world constantly turning an' we standing still watching dis money fly by, when we should be changing it." Quite frankly, Block was tired of a couple bands here and there. That was a game for the lil homies, not big dawgs. "It's three type of people in dis world," Block preached. "Those dat make it happen, those who watch it happen, an' those who wonder what happen. It's up to u ta figure out which one u want ta be. Feel me?"

Tree honestly felt what Block was proposing. He was right, it was time to get a head of the game. They'd been stuck in neutral mode for way too long. The game was in motion. Bricks were being shipped across the Atlantic Ocean daily, and they hadn't even touched a whole thang. "Fam I feel ya on dat tip, straight up." Tree lit up a Newport 100 and inhaled the menthol into his lungs. "Ya boi wit'cha ten toes down, but what's your plan ta get things in motion?"

"I'm working on dat right now. One thang I know fa'sho, is we gotta move dat bitch ninja G-Ball round. He getting to big fa his britches," Block enlightened. Block was tired of G-Ball's high ass prices on the snow tip, and his bumping off at the gums. "Plus, we gotta get dis show on da road before Six come home." Six was their ace. He'd got knocked a couple years back on some trumped-up charges when the police had received an anonymous tip that Six had been involved in a reckless endangerment. The Milwaukee police department had kicked in his front door without a warrant. Six was booked and charged on possession of a firearm and reckless endangerment of safety charges. Currently, Six was awaiting on the Federal courts to make a ruling whether to vacate his sentence for violation of his Fourth Amendment. "Speaking of fam, did'cha send homie dat bread?"

"Fa'sho, I sent dat asap," Tree informed.

"Alright." Block made sure he kept Six's books fat for canteen and any other necessities or accessories Six needed. That's what real ninjaz did, they broke bread with those they came to the table with. "I wonder if Pimp still pushing up in da guts of Ball main dame?"

"Who u talking bout, Kesha?" Tree inquired, nodding his head while blowing cigarette smoke out the passenger window. "Yea, he still smashing on shawty every blue moon. U want me ta holla at em bout putting da bug in her ear?"

"Like yesterday." Block saw the opportunity to stain G-Ball. Block had responsibilities. His mother was sick, and in debt up to her neck with mortgage. She'd developed lung cancer due to her excessive cigarette smoking. And since she couldn't afford chemotherapy, the avarice doctors prescribed her a bunch of pills to prolong her pain and suffering. Plus, the childhood house Block's mother had raised him in, was on the verge of going into foreclosure. Block was providing what little money he could to try to savor the home his grandmother had left behind to his mother after her passing when he was only twelve. The pennies Block was chasing just wasn't enough to cover the fees. The bank continued sending daily foreclosure notices, warning she had 90 days to come up with 30,000 dollars. So, Block had a cake to bake. On the other hand, his boy Six was on his way home. Block had to make sure when his boy returned, he had a king's welcome. They were down bad, and it was left up to Block to make it happen and put the family on. "Tell Pimp ta start grooming her."

Pimp was just the man for the task. He had the gift of god and women went crazy over his Midwest drool and swagger. Plus, Block knew Pimp and Tree were brothers from another mother. Therefore, it was best to have Tree holler at Pimp about coaxing G-Ball girl Kesha to set up her man.

"I'ma get on dat asap," Tree announced as they pulled up in front of G-Ball trap house...

***

Meanwhile, Kesha was bent over the Hilton Hotel love seat receiving a ferocious pounding of her life.

"Aaaagghhh!" she screamed out as a climax tore through her. She was loving every inch of Pimp's ten-inch dick that was slamming into her from behind. Seconds after she had coated his stripper pole with her copious cum, he followed suit, filling her pussy with gallons of spunk. She shuddered as she was sent over the edge once again. Dropping to her knees, she took him into her mouth and cleaned him off. The mixture of their cum mingled in her gobbling mouth, and it tasted amazing. Enjoying the delicacy, she found herself caught in the moment. Pimp stood still, with his head tilted back as Kesha gobbled his dick down her throat. He wondered if she gave her man the same treatment. The head was so good, that it could be considered none other than a luxury. Pimp grabbed the back of Kesha's head with both hands, and face fucked her wet succulent lips. She received his monster down her throat with no problem. It was as if she had no gag reflexes. She deep throated him as he rapidly positioned back and forth in her mouth. Like a pro, she sucked him down her esophagus, and at that moment, Pimp tensed up and spewed his unborn children down her gullet.

"Dam gurl," Pimp moaned. Kesha stayed on her knees nibbling around his bulbous head and licking him clean. "Dude know u gotta lil Karine Stephen in ya?" He joked.

"Shut up stupid," she laughed, slapping Pimp on the arm. "Dat's special treatment. Everyone isn't entitled ta dat. Dat's fa u an' only u."

"Don't I feel special."

"U better," she playfully warned before heading off to the suite's bathroom.

Pimp watched her backside as she walked off. Her naked behind was a sight to see. Kesha was beautiful, an aesthetic work of art. A redbone with a 34DD-25-36 measurement that weighed 125 pounds and stood 5'6. A Goddess is what she was—God's gift to man. Her Rihanna facial features had captivated his attention from the moment they'd meet. Pimp didn't love her, but he loved everything about her. Her mind, body, and sex game were on point. Whenever she could sneak away from her man, she came to please, and she left him satisfied with no complaints.

"Hurry up back out here, so I can beat dat thang out da frame again," Pimp called after Kesha. "U know dat's wat'cha like."

Kesha stuck up her middle finger up over her shoulder.

"Dat's wat I'm tryna do, if u hurry yo fine ass back."

Kesha shook her head and closed the bathroom door. "U a freak!" she yelled from the other side.

"Take's one ta know one," Pimp riposted, searching his Coogi jeans for his lighter, so he could blaze up a blunt of that Moonrock. He was tryna get lifted before he blessed Kesha for the umpteenth time. He'd been ravaging her since the A.M. after he had bumped into her at the night club. Kesha was a nymphomaniac, who couldn't get enough of sex. Every time he'd bust, Kesha's talented mouth would instantly get to work to revive him. Even when Pimp felt he had no more energy to burn, ice and menthols seemed to always do the trick for another round.

Pimp found his lighter just as Kesha came out of the bathroom still in her birthday suit and sauntered over to the bed. Pimp fired up the bag and inhaled the weed smoke into his lungs. He held it in for six seconds before exhaling through his nostrils and blowing it back into the atmosphere.

"Daddy, when we gone make dis thang official?" Kesha asked, laying her head on Pimp's sweaty chest. "U know I been feeling u since we was kids, but u never showed me no interest until I started fucking wit da bitch ass nigga Ball." Kesha trailed her finger lightly around Pimp's nipple while she verbally expressed her affection for him. "So wuz up, we gone do dis thang or wat? Cause I ain't tryna be Ms. Lamont. Dat shit ain't fa a bitch like me." Lamont was G-Ball's government last name. "I can't spin da duration of my life laid up being dat phony ass nigga wifey."

"Ma, I need time." Pimp was feeling Kesha in a major way, but not in such a way where he felt it necessary to add a nomenclature onto what they shared. To him, what they had was special enough, he didn't want to complicate things. "I need time ta focus on dis grind," he said, attempting to let her down easy. "Nawt dat I don't see you in my future. I just wanna make sure everything straight on my end before a nigga get ta claiming." Pimp kissed Kesha on the forehead to assure a sensibility.

"How much time?" Kesha curiously asked. "U know ole boi clown ass proposed ta a bitch da other day?"

"Wat'cha tell em?"

"I told em I gotta think about it," she informed him while setting her chin on the back of her pedicure hand that laid flat upon Pimp's chest. Kesha stared him in his eyes while Pimp listened and enjoyed the gas he was on. "To be honest, I haven't gave it dat much thought. My soul don't align wit his. When he kisses me, der is no fiya. Wit u its different, my heart flutter an' sends me sailing on a river. U make me fly sky-high wit wind beneath my wings. No other man has ever made me feel dat way."

"Me neither shawty." Pimp sat his half-smoked blunt in the ashtray upon the nightstand, and kissed Kesha. She reciprocated, moaning and purring in sync. Pimp was tired, but he knew the only way to shut up her love-struck conversation, was to stuff her with dick. "Let me slide up in dis."

"It's all ur's daddy." Kesha rolled on her back smiling up at Pimp as she set herself out. "Aaagghhh!" she cried out loudly as Pimp shoved his meat into her and started pounding away...

***

Chop pulled up in front of his boy Kilo's momma's crib and parked his smoked gray 84 T-top Cutlass at the curb. Chop was angry and emotionally distraught. Last night he had lost his best friend all over some punk ass, weak ass hoe, who couldn't keep her legs shut. She would open them for any Tom, Dick, and Harry she thought had a little paper. Now his boy was laid up on a slab in a morgue, and the vamp Connie was nowhere to be found. Chop had tried to contact her. Even dropped by her crib to let her know Stevo had been killed. Deep down inside, Chop knew Connie wasn't the one to blame for Stevo's death. Chop had warned Stevo multiple times before that Connie was a slut, but he would take heed to none of it. If it wasn't for Stevo's sucker for love shenanigans, he would still be alive. Chop recognized ole boy who had shot and killed Stevo. Why Chop was covering behind the veranda, he'd gotten a good look at the assailant, and he remembered him from a couple nights prior.

Stevo had gotten into some beef over Connie with him at Club International on 60th and National. Chop had rolled down and emptied the whole 32 shots out on him and his crew. Regretfully, Chop wished he had flat lined Block. Rather it be him than his nigga. At least Chop wouldn't be burying his friend. It would be the other way around. Instead, Block's family and boyz would be lowering him in the dirt. Soon it would be an eye for an eye. Chop was plotting revenge to avenge his boy's death. It was a matter of time before he gathered the information that he needed to know about the subject responsible for Stevo's death. And when he did, Chop would execute his plan, and teardrops and close caskets would be the results.

Chop rung Kilo's mother's doorbell.

"Who is it?" Grace bawled from inside her home.

"It's Chop, Ms. White," Chop replied, utilizing his manners. "Is Kilo in?"

Grace cracked the door a bit, leaving the chain attached as she peeked around, the badly chip wooden door. She was cautions about who she opened her door for or who she welcome's into her home. Living in the ghetto, you could never be too careful. Bullets didn't have no name on them.

"Oh, how u doing der boi?" she queried about his well-being why simultaneously taking the latch off the screen door. "He up in his room. He been depressed all day. What's wrong wit em?" she expressed her concerns.

"I don't know," Chop fabricated. He didn't want to trouble Grace no more than he assumed she already was. The look in her eyes told him she was worried, and possibly stressed out. "Can u tell Kilo I'm out here?"

"Kijana," Ms. White corrected. "U know I don't resonant wit dem made up names u boy's go by des days. I named dat boi Kijana." Ms. White refused to recognize her son none other than the birth name she'd giving him. When she was born in 1965, men and women referred to one another by simple names. Nowadays, that wasn't enough. The young people had to have some catchy street name to gain recognition. She couldn't understand what perception the generation was aiming for.

"Forgive me, Ms. White," Chop sincerely apologized.

"I'll go get Kijana for u," she said, walking away toward the stairs where her son resigned upstairs.

Chop respected Ms. White. She had always treated him like a second son back when Chop and his mother couldn't see eye to eye because he had chosen to follow in his father footsteps. Because of his choice of lifestyle, his mother had kicked him out the house at thirteen, and Ms. White had taken him in as one of her own until Chop was able to get back on his feet. If it wasn't for Ms. White's caring, nurturing embrace, Chop would've been down bad on his luck.

Moments later, Kilo stepped outside onto the front porch. "What's good," he asked. Depression wore heavily on his facial expression, unlike his normal self. Normally, he was upbeat and cocky. Today his head hung low and his voice was nothing more than a murmur. "Mom's city told me u wuz out here."

"Let me holla at'cha back here." Chop stepped off the porch and flounced toward the backyard. Kilo was in tow, still sagging his head like a sad puppy. When they rounded the corner, Chop did the unexpected and walloped Kilo with a right hook that knocked him against the house. "Why u leave us on stuck like dat wit'cha scary ass?" Chop hemmed Kilo up by collar.

Kilo held the side of his face looking bewilder. "Wuz up fam?" he asked out of shock rubbing his jaw. "Wuz dis shit all about?"

"Yo weak ass left me an' family ta die," Chop growled. "Yo bitch ass ain't got no heart. Because of ur cowardice, Stevo lost his life."

"So wat, u gone kill me now?" Kilo struggled out of Chop grip. "I didn't have no heat, an' I dam show wasn't bout ta stand der an' let buddy em smoke me too."

"Shut dat lame shit up. Your pussy ass alwayz supposed ta be strapped up," Chop muffed at Kilo. "I ain't gone body yo azz. I got too much respect fa yo ole gee fa dat, an' I gawt to much luv fo yo weak ass. I'm just mad as hell, cuz I can't understand how u can run off an' leave us in combat, when u know we a die fa yo ass. Stevo showed his loyalty in death." Chop always knew Kilo wasn't a fighter or a shooter. Kilo was the type you had to force in a corner like a cat before you got a reaction out of him. Chop wouldn't apologize for hitting him in his shit. Kilo needed to learn the game, it revolved around more than fashion, money, and hoes. Kilo was in the way if that was his reality. Niggas was hungry in the streets, and in order to feed their empty stomachs, they would eat any weak link in their way. Kilo would be the prime candidate on the roster of blood thirsty wolves roaming the streets. "Yo ass just need ta realize dis game ain't fa da weak. Dis real life, not one of your virtual video games."

"U outta order my nigga. You ain't da only one grieving da lost," Kilo sniffled, trying his best to hold back tears. While alone, he had done nothing but cry. Mourning the loss of his friend, he knew it was gonna take the man in him to conquer the insanity. "U don't need ta lash out at me, I ain't ur enemy. You don't need ta put your hands on me, I would've never rolled on u like dat."

"Look, I ain't sorry bout dat shit. Somebody needed ta hit'cha in yo shit. If u feel some type of way bout it, take off, an' we can settle dis like man. Otherwise, shut up with all dat soft shit," Chop dared, leering at Kilo straight in the eyes as he spoke. Realizing Kilo wasn't looking for a fight, he resumed the conversation. "I got major luv fa ya ass, u just need ta tuffin up. Dis shit real out here in da battlefield. Get'cha shit together."

"I ain't tripping bout dat shit." Kilo changed up the topic of conversation. "Let's go holla at Stevo brotha an' see how he holding up."

Considering Kilo's suggestion as an armistice truce, Chop and his boy headed off to their destination...

***

"Nephew let me get four fa da 35?" Johnny Pack requested. Johnny Pack was one of the neighborhood's cluckers.

"Run dat." Block dug in his pocket and fished out four dime bags from the open Zip'loc bag where he hoarded his crack. "U fuck wit me, I fuck wit'cha back."

Johnny Pack handed Block a bunch of crumbled up singles and two five-dollar bills.

"Be back in like an hour yung blood." Block could count on that. Johnny Pack was one of his best customers. Throughout the day, they exchanged hand to hand transactions at least ten times a day. Johnny always spent 30 or better. His money was always good, and Block never questioned Johnny about where his loot came from. Block felt it was none of his business. As long as the money was good, Block would provide.

Tree was on the other end of the block hustling. After they'd reed up, they both hit the block hard with that ready rock. The fiends was loving it. Block had run through three and a half ounces in all dimes, in a matter of hours. It was only 2P.M., and he knew he had to re-up soon to keep the money flowing.

Out the blue, Pimp pulled up in his hoopty, a 1971 Chevelle SS with a 454 under the hood. It was a show quality Cortez, with a black stripe down the middle. It was worse than it sounded. The frame was rusted, and the exhaust was loud. You would swear up and down on this and that, when the car rolled past, that someone was shooting.

"What's cracking?" Pimp asked out the window while parking at the curb before hopping out. Pimp was fly. He dressed smart in a Robbin fit. "Let me get some of dis cash wit y'all."

"U know u alwayz welcome ta eat wit'cha boi," Block pronounced, locking racks with Pimp. "Plus, u need ta fix dat bucket dat's pollutin da environment," he ragged on Pimp's ride.

"Man, fuck dat trap," Pimp laughed. "It's bout time I upgrade anyways."

Tree made his way down the block while Pimp and Block was rapping. "What's good my dude?" he greeted. Pimp and Tree had major love for each other. They had known one another since diapers. They had come from the same orphanage home. When Tree's mother passed away of natural causes, and Pimp's mother abandoned him on the front steps of an unknown civilian. Tree and Pimp had ended up at the same place, at the same time. A family had adopted the duo, taking them both in as their own. So technically, they were brothers from another mother. They just didn't literally identify themselves as such.

"Shit out here tryna catch these coins," Pimp replied.

"Dawg, I'ma bout ta head upstairs an' hit Trish with a couple P's, den hit up da liquor store," Block informed his boyz. "Yall want something from the store?" he asked Pimp and Tree.

"Yea, bring me back like foe of dem Wet Mango wraps." Tree tried handing Block a twenty-dollar bill which he rejected.

"You know ur money ain't no good here homie," Block pushed Tree hand away. "I got'cha my ninja."

"Aright, grab me a Snapple grape juice too," Pimp added in addition to his list. "Since u buying an' shit."

"Don't even lean on it. Just handle dat bizness we discussed." Block headed off leaving Pimp and Tree to it. Tree needed to holler at Pimp anyway, and hip him to the plan. So, Block bent off. Block could feel it in his bones, soon him and the team would be on. It was just a matter of time.

CHAPTER THREE

Bando filed out of Holy Redeemer Church of God & Christ at the end of his brother's funeral service. Burying his little brother didn't sit well on his heart, he felt somewhat responsible for Stevo's murder. Bando had introduced Stevo to the dope game. Mainly because they had no other means of support. Their mother was strung out bad on the crack pipe and growing up wasn't easy in the projects with no source of income. The welfare checks his mother received from the government every month always lined the pockets of the neighborhood dealers, instead of filling the refrigerator with food, or keeping the electricity on. Bando and his brother Stevo were constantly ragged and ridiculed by neighborhood kids for their raggedy clothing. So, when Bando was old enough, he took to the streets like a duck takes to water. After Stevo had begged him to let him make some bread, he had given in and let Stevo hustle. Now he wished he hadn't been so weak and would've enforced another alternative. But now it was too late to cry over spilled milk.

Bando entered the Lincoln limousine in the company of his lovely fiancée. Bando couldn't stop his mind from pondering about her. Something just didn't sit right with him. Here he was burying his brother, and he couldn't do anything but wonder about the skeletons in Shay's closet.

During, the service, everyone that passed by his brother coffin to pay their respect and greet Bando to convey their condolences.

"Sorry fam," Chop apologized as he passed by Stevo's open casket. Bando could tell Chop felt somewhat responsible for Stevo's death just as much as he did. "Dis shit fucked up. Dat should've been me, not fam."

Bando removed his Cartier Buffalo Bucks that he had been hiding his puffy eye's behind all service. Putting his face in his hands, he wept. Shay placed her arms around his shoulders to console him. Regaining enough strength to compose himself, he wiped his face. That's when he noticed a look of dismay that covered Chop's face. It looked as if he had seen a ghost. The analogous, appalled look was upon Shay's face also. Bando made a mental note to check that at a later time.

"Why was dat nigga Chop looking at u like dat?" he leaned over and whispered in Shay's ear as the limousine trailed his brother's hearse...

***

Block rolled out of bed and slipped his feet into a pair of Deebo house shoes. Rubbing the crust from his eyes, he picked up his cellphone to review how many missed calls he had. Afterwards, he strolled his call log, and stopped upon Kayla's number. He pondered the thought to give her a call. It had been ages since they had last spoken, and their departure wasn't what you would refer to as peachy. There was roadblocks and obstacles Block knew he had to overcome before reconciliation. That was factual. He couldn't see his life knowing he hadn't tried to reconcile. So, he hit send and dialed her number.

"Hello," Kayla answered on the third ring. "Who is dis?"

"A man dat would find u thru 1,000 words an' 10,000 lives," Block smoothly said. You're your high school sweetheart."

"Bentley?" Kayla blurted. A state of shock washed over her. Her and Block hadn't spoken since their break up, and there was no reason for them to. Block had played the game of chess wrong, and it had cost him his queen.

"None other."

Kayla rolled her eyes on da other end of da line. "It seems like da ghost from da past always come back ta hunt u," she cynically retorted.

"Dat's how u greet an old friend?" Block reproached. He was a bit deterrent by Kayla's unenthusiastic greeting. "I thought you'd be happy ta hear from me."

"U thought wrong. U got some nerve calling my line after wat'cha did ta me. I know u don't expect me ta greet u wit open arms." Kayla eyes started to tear up, and thinking of the retrospective pain, her voice began to crack.

"It would be a start," Block returned. "I thought time heals everything. I didn't call ta upset u or start a fight. I simply called because I was thinking of u, an' I was hoping da feeling was mutual."

"U was thinking of me, huh!" she said sardonically. "Let me guess, u finally realized I was da one an' u couldn't live without me." Kayla was fuming and it was becoming harder by the second to contain her building anger. "How did'cha get dis number anyway?"

"Your moms gave it ta me," he answered. "An' don't put words in my mouth. I didn't call wit no bullshit such as u quoted."

"Don't call my phone an' tell me wat an' wat not ta say," she snapped. "You're not at liberty ta do dat no more. U lost dat privilege, remember?" Kayla had lost all her patience to logically deal with the situation. "Look, I gotta go. Don't call dis number no more, lose it."

"Before u go," Block made his final plea. "Remember u don't find da meaning of life alone, but wit another."

"Fuck u Bentley!" she loudly soliloquized before hanging up.

Block stared at the phone in confusion. It seemed like everyone was hanging up in his face lately. That hadn't gone as well as he had expected it to. In a way, he felt like calling back and going hard on her. But instead, he utilized his better judgment and dismissed the thought. There was no way he would let his emotions get the best of him. That would ruin what slim chance he did have to get her back. What he needed was another avenue to charm her and get her attention. Block wanted Kayla in the worst way, so he wouldn't let a little anger and animosity hinder him from accomplishing his goal. When there's a will there's a way. He just had to will the way.

Thirty minutes later, after cleaning up, he was dressed to impress and ready to go. He cruised his Impala through traffic bumping "Rico" by Yo Gotti out the sound system. He was turning down 35th and North Avenue when he had a collision. A red 2018 AMG ran the light and collided headfirst into the passenger side. Unfazed, Block grabbed his Glock 40 from under the seat and hopped out...

***

Tree was in the kitchen wrist twisting like its stir fry. Trish came stumbling in while he was whipping up yola. She had been on an all-night crack binge. Her hair was a mess, disheveled and matted up like she'd been sleeping under the mattress, and she smelled of dried cum and promo smoke.

"Hey," she greeted while smiling sheepishly. "I didn't think no one would be here. I lost track of time." For some odd reason she felt the need to explain for her actions, as if she was a child. "I ain't got no money but I need a fix. Get me right nephew."

Tree hated when she did that. Anytime he was cooking up dope, and she was around, she felt as if she was entitled to a blast because it was her house. Every two weeks, Block, Tree, and Pimp made sure Trish was straight. Between the three, they all broke her off an 8ball a piece. Three 8balls every two weeks was more than the average D-boy paid for rent. She ran through them like Water then stuck her hand out requesting more. Tree had a solution for her problem.

There would be no more gratuitous highs provided from him. Trish would have to perform undignified duties equivalent to any other dope head bitch if she wanted something from him.

"Me too," Tree decreed turning off the eye on the stove.

"I didn't know u got down," Trish naïvely replied.

"Nah, but u do." Tree unzipped his Trues and pulled out his semi-hard dick. "Come ova here an' suck dis dick," Tree commanded.

Trish took a look at the fresh batch of dope, then back at Tree who was leaning on the stove with his dick in his hand. She needed a hit, and it wasn't like she had never given up some toppings for a fix before. So why not give Tree what he wanted? His chocolate ass was handsome, and if she had her shit together, she would be riding his dick every chance she got. Weighing in her options, Trish dropped to her knees and engulfed Tree in her mouth.

"Dat's it, suck dat dick," Tree moaned out in pleasure. He needed to relieve himself, and what better way than the filthy slut Trish greedy gullet. "Dat's it gurl, suck dis dick," he repeated.

Trish gobbled Tree's fuck stick down like a witch's treat. Dick sucking was her talent. For fifteen years, she had swallowed the cum of man to support her junky habit. So, if Tree wanted to play in her mouth, she would give him his money worth.

Tree grabbed hold to her head with both hands as he humped his hips to the tempo of her bobbing head. She slurped his piece fast but gentle, treating his meat like a lollypop.

"Sssss," Tree hissed through his teeth. Her moist mouth was vicious, never missing a beat as he fucked in and out her mouth at lighten speed. Her saliva coated him, and the inside of her mouth felt like velvet. Tree was near. When he came, he didn't slow his pace. He kept bucking rapidly while shooting globs of cum down her throat until he was drained. Trish didn't gag. Her reflexes were used to the kind of treatment. She received his load, cleaned him up with her pouty lips, and rose to the occasion.

"I got u right, now get me right," she requested licking her lips and sticking out her hand.

Tree zipped up his pants and cut Trish a half of hooper from the clump of dope sitting on the saucer plate. "I might need dat mouth of your's later," Tree informed.

"Anytime daddy," Trish licked her lips once again to make a show of it.

When Trish was gone, Tree finished what he was doing—chopping down Oz's, weighing, and bagging. Once the task was completed, he hit the block. It had been slow all day, but it was to be expected, it was hump day. Since things were slow, Tree decided to head to the gas station to get a gangsta meal. A gangsta meal consisted of a microwave preserved burger, a bag of chips, and soda. The hood had coined its name after long days and nights of hustling with no real food to fill their stomach. So, they became accustomed to junk foods.

"What's hood my dude?" Block called rolling up alone side of Tree. "Where u headed?"

"Bout ta hit da G-station an' get some munchies an' shit ta snack on," Tree rubbed his belly. "Wat da fuck happen ta da ride?" Tree inquired about the sizable dent that caved in the passenger door.

"Da shit da story of our life. Get in an' I'll tell u bout it."

Tree got in and rolled the window up to keep the AC in. "Lace me wit dat track," Tree said, adjusting his seat. "Cause I'm tryna figure out why your ride look like Godzilla chew toy," he jested.

"Dawg I was on my way ta da hood when dis red Benz collided into my whip," Block verbally reenacted the scene. "Mad ass fuck, I hopped out wit my llama ready ta spit. An' guess who popped out da other whip?"

"Who nigga? U know I ain't wit all dat suspense shit."

"Dat ninja Niko."

Tree gave a confused look regarding the information. Tree couldn't pinpoint or put a face on it.

"You know Niko. U know Rock lieutenant, ole boi dat be slanging all dat yayo thru da city." After realizing it still wasn't registering with Tree, Block continued on with what he had to say. "Anyways, buddy left me wit his number an' told me, get at em." Block had every intention to do just that. Especially with the dept his mother was in. It was time for Block to help her relieve the burden. "I'ma get at ole boi an' see what's shaking an' set up a meeting, so we can start eating."

"I'm all fa dat, a nigga hungry," Tree rubbed his stomach again. He was hungry two ways, literally and financially. "Mutha fucka starving! It's about time we get da ball rolling an' da trap jumping. It's money ta be made."

"I feel ya fa real," Block assured. "What's up wit Pimp on dat other tip? Everything everything, or dew we gotta come up wit another solution?"

"Nah, everything gravy. Pimp picked shawty mind, an' she spilled da beans. She fed up wit dude fuck ass just as much as us. So, u know how dat go." Tree rubbed both of his hands together. "She ready ta wipe ole boi down fa a real nigga. Pimp said she think Ball's bitch made anyways."

"Alright, u an' Pimp start laying on him an' let me handle dis connect," Block degreed. "We gon get dis shit jumping like a six fo, so we can feed dat," Block said while pointing at Tree's stomach.

"Speaking of feeding, let's go get something ta eat. I'm hungry as a mutha fucka," Tree half-joked, patting his belly.

With that, Block smashed the gas to the whip, and headed to McDonald's...

***

"Oh gurl, dis shit right here fly," Kayla's best friend Connie exclaimed. "If u wear dis ta da club all da D-boyz gone be on ya fine ass." Connie held up a magenta Dior dress in front of Kayla to measure her figure. Connie was overly excited. Whenever it came to shopping, she got like that. Kayla just shook her head at her best friend ignoring her suggestion. Connie knew she couldn't afford the luxuries of designer brands. All of her money went toward tuition and bills. "Look at'cha self." Connie pushed Kayla in front of the full-length mirror.

Kayla imagined how she would look in the dress while smoothing the expensive fabric out. She knew without a doubt she would look elegant in the dress, but it was too expensive for her frugal budget. "I can't afford dis gurl," she winced as she took a look at the price tag. Knowing she couldn't afford it, she placed it on the dressing room door.

"U gotta live a lil an' treat'cha self ta some nice shit every now an' then." Cogently, Connie tried convincing Kayla to spend money she didn't have.

"Dat's eazy for u ta say when u got a man dat buys u everything." Kayla had Connie's number. Her boyfriend was a baller, and whatever Connie wanted, she got. All she had to do was bat those pretty little mink eyelashes of hers, and money would rain with galore from the skies. "I don't have no man who dropping knot after knot in my lap."

"Dat's hurtful," Connie played, appalled and mortified by Kayla's accusations. This caused both of them to laugh, because they both knew the real. "But u know wat? U getting dat dress, my treat. I can't have my gurl out here looking all ratchet an' shit."

"Gurl, please, u full of your'self," Kayla waved her hand in Connie's face. "I'm too fine to be ratchet. An' I could get a man in my pajamas." She strutted back over to the mirror and posed as a model.

"Yea, den why u don't u have one?" Connie became cynical. "Ta get a dude wit money, u gotta look like money. U know how da saying goes, it takes money, ta make money. Ur body is a money maker, so use wat'cha got ta get wat'cha want."

Kayla pondered on her friend's words for a moment. The reason she didn't have a man was on the tip of her tongue, and she almost blurted it out. The reason Kayla didn't have a man was because Connie couldn't keep her legs closed. The last man Kayla had, Connie had fucked. But instead of trudging up old demons, Kayla kept her lips sealed and her comments to herself. After all, Kayla had forgiven Connie for her treacherous and mischievous deeds that happened in their high school years. Kayla kind heart was able to look beyond the ultimate sin Block and Connie had committed against her. But the pain seemed to resurface when Block had contacted her out the blue earlier that day. Kayla had thought those wounds had closed and healed, but they had burst back open at the seams after hearing Block's voice.

"U ain't gone believe who I heard from today," Kayla said.

"Who? St. Francis nursing home?"

"Nah gurl," Kayla giggled at Connie's joke. Although, she had been expecting St. Francis to contact her for the certified nursing assistance nightshift position that she had applied for a few weeks prior. Kayla needed the extra money. The job she had, and between classes, wasn't fronting the piled-up bills that had accumulated in the past months. "Bentley called me out da blue."

"Bentley!!!?" Connie exclaimed. Her once gleeful pleasant smile had turned upside down to an astonishing look of shock.

"Yea, Bentley."

"Wat did he want?"

"I don't know." Kayla grabbed the Dior dress off the stall hook and went into the dressing room to try it on. "I hung up on em before he even got a chance ta tell me."

Connie smacked her lips before replying. "Wat'cha dew dat fo? U didn't even hear him out? At least after all y'all been thru, u could've giving' him dat much courtesy."

"Dat's why I couldn't give em a chance" Kayla explained. "After all we've been through, I didn't want em trudgin up old demons."

"Old demons!!!?" Connie exclaimed. "Dat's wat ur concerned bout?" Connie observed her friend's face. "Oh my gawd, u still in luv wit em aint'cha?" Connie expressed her concerns. "Dat's why u didn't want ta talk ta em. U felt dat if u let em get close ta u again, you'd get hurt."

"Nooooo..." Kayla spoke shyly.

"Gurl don't lie ta me, I know u like a book. My mother alwayz told me only time a woman shows any kind of emotions toward a man, rather it be joy or unhappiness, is unless dat woman has feelings for him," Connie elucidated. Her philosophical analogy had struck the nail on the head. Deep down inside, Kayla was still deeply in love with Block, but she would rather die before she admitted her deepest secret. Especially to the home wrecker that destroyed her and Bentley's relationship.

"What's it ta u?" Kayla lashed out. "Ain't like u ever gave a fuck bout da feelings I had fa him. So why does it matter now?"

"Ok, I see we hitting home where it hurts. Since we digging up old scabs, let me put something on ya brain," Connie rolled her neck. "I apologize fa wat happen between me an' Block when we were teenager's. But even doe we both did u wrong, dat boi alwayz had a soft spot for u. An' ta be honest, wat we shared would've never happen if u wasn't being stingy wit da kit kat." She slid an untimely awkward joke in. "Dat boi loved u, but we wuz yung, an' our hormones wuz raging out of control, an' we made a mistake. I'm sorry fa dat, but don't keep allowing da past ta destroy your future happiness."

"U know wat gurl, u right," Kayla gave credit when due. "Let me apologize. I should've never blamed u for something dat happen when we were kidz."

"It's ok gurl," Connie accepted and comforted her friend with a hug. Kayla found solace in Connie arms. It felt good to know someone understood you. Although Connie had done her wrong as a kid, since adulthood, Connie had been the only true friend she had. She had made up for her past actions everyday by showing he loyalty. "U know u my gurl no matter wat, I love u like a sista."

"Wat should I do?" Kayla asked for advice. "I don't want ta get hurt again, or for him to think I'ma push ova. He needs ta know he just can't run over me an' get away wit it."

"I'm pretty sho he won't think dat, it happen so long ago. He probably wondering why u still hate him." Kayla giggled in Connie shoulder. She knew Connie was telling the truth. "But u need ta make a decision an' figure out wat will make u happy. I can't tell u wat u should do, but I can tell u I think u should call him. Its ur final call. I'ma be by your side regardless wat conclusion u come to." Connie disengaged from their mutual hug and gave Kayla a warming smile. "Come on now, let's pay for dis shit, so we can tear down da shoe store before it close."

While purchasing their dresses, Kayla gave a long hard thought about what Connie had said. Kayla knew there could be no harm done in calling Bentley to see what was on his mind.

CHAPTER FOUR

"Hello," Shay answered her phone groggy. She'd just woken up from a peaceful sleep. "Who is dis?"

"Never mind who I am, just know I am da one ta turn your world upside down if u don't comply with my demands," the mysterious voice on the other end threatened.

"Wat? U have me sadly mistaken for someone else. Please stop wasting my time. I have things ta do, so I'm hanging up. Bye bye now." Shay was on the verge of pressing end to disconnect the call, when the phantom spoke.

"I wouldn't do dat if I was u." The minatory made chills run down her spine. "If u do so, I'll inform your fiancé Bando u wuz at da club wit da enemy da night his brother got whacked, an' your da cause of his death. An' I don't have to say what'll happen ta ya, cuz u know dont'cha?"

Shay froze, her heart stopped, and a sense of panic washed over her. She feared what she didn't know. Whoever the person was on the other end of the line, had just threatened her livelihood with false accusations that put her life in peril, especially if the information was to so happen to fall in Bando lap. Bando would kill her even if he thought she was the reason his brother got killed.

"What do u want from me?" she asked naively. "I had nothing ta do wit Stevo's death. Please leave me alone," she pleaded. "There's no reason ta bother me, I don't know anything or have anything ta give." Shay was frustrated but feared hanging up. She feared the unknown male might do as he threatened. She couldn't take that chance to see if he was bluffing. This was a life and death situation.

"See, dat's ware u are wrong. U have everything I want, an' I will get it or else your head goes on da chopping block." Shay shivered in belief of what could happen to her. "Tonight at 9, u will meet me at da Ambassador Hotel wit 10,000 in cash. An' don't be late."

"How will I get my hands on dat type of cream in such a small amount of time?" she asked, baffled. She had never been so frightened in her life. She didn't know what to do. How would she accommodate the man's request?

"I don't know, an' don't care. U have ta 9 o'clock to find a solution, or else your secret will be exposed."

"How do I know who I'm meeting."

"I'll know u," ge warned, then the line went dead.

"Hello, hello!" Shay screamed into the phone, but the strange man was gone. She checked the display for a call back number, only to discover it had been blocked. She was scared and confused. What secret? She questioned herself. She didn't have anything to do with Stevo's death, nor did she arrange it. She had been out with some friends on her birthday and they had gotten into a physical altercation with Bando's little brother, but that was it. Dice and his friends wouldn't murder Stevo over some minor misunderstanding. But then again, it wasn't minuscule. The situation had escalated into a major one the moment gunplay came into effect. So maybe she was more responsible then she assumed. Dice and his boyz would definitely turn it up a notch after the occurrence that left everyone scurrying away for their lives. But still, how would Dice crew know where to find Stevo and his crew?

Shay didn't know what to do, she was trapped between a rock and a hard place. She didn't know rather to comply to the stranger's invitation, or not show at all. There were options to be weighed. Shay knew if she didn't show, she had everything to lose, and she was taking a risk of her dirty laundry being aired. If Bando found out she wasn't at her mother's house sick on her birthday like she had claimed, he would kill her. But if she did go to the hotel with the money, she had everything to gain. She could keep her secret that she had been out cheating, and her and Bando's relationship would continue on fine and dandy. She would take a financial lost doing so, but money could be replaced. She had stashed away some money for a rainy day. Being petrified shitless, she decided it was time to dig into those funds, to keep a happy home…

***

Bando and his boyz gathered around the trap house loading up ammunition. Since his brother's death, they had started exterminating all their foes on a mission to avenge the sudden death of Bando's brother. Someone had to be held responsible, to hold true to those words, Bando decided to kill off those that had ever posed a threat.

"Pass the bottle," Bando requested, loading up the S.K.S with a magnified scope. His leather glove fingers loaded round after round into the two fifty-round banana magazines. "Y'all niggaz up in here hoggin all da liquid courage." Bando normally loaded himself with an enormous amount of drugs and liquor before riding out. He was the prime example of a juiced-up coward; He wasn't a shooter; he couldn't do that shit without no molly. Bando had money, therefore he had shooters. Usually when there was beef, they were the killas on frontline blazing that heat, and reporting the message back to him when the heat was squashed, why he laid low sipping liquor like a bitch.

"Man, ain't nobody hoggin up da drink," Chop replied sitting at the kitchen table that was loaded with assault rifles. Uzi and Moski, a couple of the team hitters, that were always present at war time, sat along with Chop preforming the same task. Chop tilted a bottle of white Remy to the head, taking a huge gulp, before reaching across the table passing it to Bando. "Here my nigga."

"Where dem trees at?" Uzi asked. "It's dry as fuck in here. No cronic blazin', des shit lame. Put something in da air."

"I ain't got no blunts ta lite up," Chop exclaimed.

"Don't worry bout dat, I got my half if u got da filling," Uzi assured. "Moe, get dem B's out my hoody ova der on dat chair."

Moski set the drum on the table and grabbed Uzi's hoody and threw it to him. Moski was the quiet type, he rarely uttered more than two words a day. A real killer is what many referred to him as. His guns did the talking for him. Moski felt talking was for hoes and chumps; he was neither, so he had no verbal words for people. If he left something on your brain, it would be a bullet.

"Dam nigga, I said hand da blunts not give me da cotton field." Moski hunched his shoulders at Uzi comment, as if to say, "So what, get it how you get it."

'Fuck all dat shit!" Bando vociferated. "Let's go roll on des mutha fucka's. We can smoke out later." Jamming the clip into the chopper, he cocked it, and tossed a molly into his mouth. "Let's roll out."

With no debate, Chop and Uzi attached their hundred round drum to the H&K rifles, and Moski did the same to his M-16 with a laser beam, and then followed Bando outside to an awaiting stolen Grand prix and chop 85 box Chevy he had used to spray down the club a couple weeks prior. The maroon Grand Prix and dark blue Chevy cruised through the streets. Hitting 41st and Brown, Bando spotted his target; Sco was right where one of the hood hoes from around the way named Shuana said he would be. Sco and his right-hand men posted up in front of their trap house, leaning against his triple black 2010 Audi S-5 Cabriolet Convertible, waiting on the workers to run the weekly collection out. Bando Grand Prix came to a halt, tires squealing across the pavement. The sudden noise drew the attention from everyone, even Sco and his man Blaze turned their heads simultaneously over their shoulders, only to be confronted by rapid gunfire. A spray of gunfire erupted from Bando's chopper muzzle, scattering Blaze's face. Multiple 7.62 slugs ripped through his dome; blood spattered all over the hood of Sco's Audi. Bando hopped out of their respective vehicle squeezing the trigger on any moving person. *Bop, Bop, Bop, Bop, Bop, Bop,* mingled with loud screams tumultuously drowned out the peace on the block. The shock of Sco's homies head busting open in his face drove him to his knees. He ducked behind his now riddled car; blood specks of his guy matted his face and button up. He knew he was in peril danger as bullets ricocheted and penetrated his ride. His gun was in the car in the stash box, and there was no means, in anyway, he could get to it. Uzi took one to the shoulder as gun fire erupted behind him. One of Sco's workers on a porch, across the street from where Sco had stood disbursed rounds from a Czech scorpion machine gun. The piercing bullet forced Uzi's chopper out of his grip, he cringed in pain attempting to repossess his weapon, when another round tore through his back. An all-out war had ensued, and Bando started to panic, ducking behind the Grand Prix for shield. Moski rushed over to aid his boy Uzi, who huddled on the ground in harm's way. When he dragged him to safety, Chop riddled the porch where the participant who had shot Uzi stood. *Bop, Bop, Bop, Bop,* bullets struck the panel in loud thumps. As bullets struck, the target dived, jumping over the railing to flee through the gangway. But it was too late for that; Chop followed on foot, walking him down with the assault rifle. Numerous slugs struck him in the back, sending him face first into the concrete, dead before he hit the ground.

'Let's get out of here!" Bando shouted, jumping into the car. Sirens wailed loudly, drawing nearer by the second.

"Help me wit Uzi!" Moski yelled, dragging Uzi across the rough road by his armpits, Chop helped. Together they got him into the backseat. Moments later both cars darted in and out of busy traffic.

Moski took his shirt off and tossed it in the back seat. "Apply pressure my dude." This had been the first time Moski have ever uttered more than two words. Normally, he was quitter then a church mouse, but the circumstances were different now. He feared for his homie. "U gotta keep pressure on dat wound, or u gone bleed out."

"Dis shit hurt like a bitch," Uzi cried, softly applying the shirt to the exit wound. The bullet had gone straight through the back and out the front. "AAAggghh!" roared from within. So much pain surged through him, he felt as if he would pass out. Drenched in sweat, he gasped for breath.

"I know dat shit feels like a hornet sting, but'cha gotta take dat shit like a gee. Feel me?" Moski and Uzi had known each other for about five years now. They'd met while doing a bid up north. Their history was a classic story; they'd been the worst of enemies, always bumping heads and colliding with one another point of view, mainly, because Uzi thought Moski was a soft nigga because of his quiet reserved mannerism. One day in the dining room at supper time, Moski had enough of Uzi's jacking antics. Uzi was jaw jacking with a few of the inmates, being his normal self, sharing his war stories about how much iron he be slanging on the streets, and how much money he be getting, when Moski blew a gasket and told Uzi to shut his hook ass up—a coined term that's disrespectful to vice lords.

"Weak ass clown, wat u just call me?" Uzi barked defensively. "Dis ain't watcha want, so I suggest ya watch yo mutha fucking mouth before I dig in it."

"U ain't gotta keep fronting, U heard wat I said. If u got a problem wit it, we can slide up in one of des cells and handle dis shit like man, pussy," Moski flexed and stared Uzi's so-called home-boyz down. Moski couldn't call it with Uzi, but he knew for sure, his pack was soft as cotton and didn't want no smoke. They wouldn't squish grapes at a vineyard.

"Don't meet me der, beat me der," Uzi huffed marching off toward his cell. Uzi and Moski did their thang like two wild animals fighting for territory. Moski lost, but stood his grounds like a man, leaving the fight with lumps, bruises, and blood all over him. He had to eat canteen for a couple of weeks in his room to avoid being seen by the correctional officers. The battered injuries he had sustained would've landed him in segregation under investigation. Uzi, on the other hand, had sustained a black eye, and a broken hand. He had to mendaciously tell the authorities it happened while playing ball. After the dust had settled down, both men felt their disagreement had been handle in the physical altercation, so they wiped their hands clean from the matter. The hands-on battle brought them closer somehow, and for the remainder of their time spent behind bars, they we're thick as thieves.

"Hang in der my dude," was the last thang Uzi heard before he started floating in and out of consciousness. Cold chills ran through him as he lost the ability to stay awake.

"Wake up dawg!" Moski yelled, slamming on the brakes on a back street. "U gotta stay awake. Fight it fam, u gotta fight it." Moski did everything he could, even cradling his boy's head in his arms, but it was too late. Uzi took his last breath and then his body went limp like a wet noodle....

***

"Check shawty at three o'clock," Pimp informed Block and Tree, nodding in the direction of a fine yellow bone, sashaying their way. "Damn shawty bad."

"Ah dat's just Lisa," Block said nonchalantly. Block paid her no mind. As far as he was concerned, she was nothing more than any average sack chaser tryna get in his pockets. He had other things on his mind, Kayla had been running rapidly through it lately. Not able to shack her freely, marijuana in his lungs helped ease his mind day and night.

"Damn shawty, wat it's gone take fa a gee like me ta get to know da lady in dem jeans," Pimp spit when Lisa got close enough.

"Boi please," Lisa popped her lips frowning up. "I don't fuck wit no nigga dat still refer to women as shawty. I'ma lady, until u can approach me as such, get used ta ya hand," Lisa clowned. Block and Tree busted out laughing

"Dat never happened, my hands to busy counting bands, trick I'm da man," Pimp tried redeeming what little confidence he had left.

Lisa smacked her lips once again. "Anyways, wat's up Block," she spoke, tryna get Block's undivided attention. Block jerked his head, silently returning her greeting and continued staring off into space. "Uggghh, u make me sick acting all stank-stank," her nose crinkled up, expressing her disapproval. "When u gone let me slide thru an break your hammer like Helen in Ragnarok?" Lisa licked her lips in a teasing manner.

"I'll break your heart," Block broke his silence. "I'm sorry dat's wat's thugs do."

"Daddy, I just wanna ride dat dick, not fall in luv and shit," Lisa exclaimed. "I mean, who needs a heart when a heart can be broken? I don't do emotions daddy," she assured. Lisa wasn't no dime piece; she was the whole hundred in the looks department, and she knew it. Her mulatto heritage gave her a distinctive look. Lisa's mahogany ringlet hair hung down the middle of her back, and her greenish hazel eyes complimented her beautiful high yellow complexion. Standing 5'5, 36-24-35, and 120 pounds, she was petite, thick, and conceited with a reason. As bad as she was, she could have any man she wanted; but Block had always caught her eye. His brown skin and riddled tattoo body looked good enough to eat. She would let Block have her any and which way he wanted her.

"I hear u, but I'm busy right now chasin des dolla signs," Block let her down easy. "Maybe some other time."

"U know where to find me when u ain't scared of pussy," Lisa said, trying to shoot at Block's belt, but he was confident in his title and had nothing to prove. "see you later daddy," Lisa said while walking away and putting a little more twist in her walk cause she knew they was looking.

"Dam shawty bad, u ain't blessed dat yet?" Pimp asked tapping Block on the shoulder. "I would've been smashed dat."

"Fuck Lisa, she ain't my type," Block said looking at his Samsung screen." I ain't into dat high yella shit, I like women chocolate wit no cream."

"All…. Let me find out u scared of dat pussy like shawty said." Pimp and Tree shared a laugh at Block expense "Tell me it ain't tru, u scared of dat cookie box?"

Block ignored Pimp's ridicule. Pimp and Tree sensed his seriousness and stopped laughing.

"Wuz up folks?" Tree asked, sincerely concerned. For the last couple weeks, he had been witnessing his boy drifting in in out of happiness. "I'm worried bout u dawg, wat's on ya byrd?"

Block shook his head. "Nothing, just thinking bout dis meet." Block had set up a meeting with Niko and Rock. They were supposed to meet up soon and discuss a business proposition to get the trap jumping, "U strapped up?" he asked Tree.

"Always, twenty-four seven," Tree replied. Blocked looked in Pimp's direction and patted his waist to cure Block's curiosity,

"Let's ride out. It's time ta see what dat real money like," Block hopped off the front stoup, and headed to his Impala at the curb. Once they were all seated, he put Gucci's song on, "All White Bricks." He blurred through the six by nines and tweeters, as the bass pounded from the L7's in the trunk. While in traffic, Block's cellphone rang.

"Hello," he answered

"Hello," Kayla replied. "Is dis Block?"

"Dis he. Who's asking?" Block asked, peeking at his screen. A smile washed over his face. Just when he had thought all had failed, Allah had answered his prayer.

"Dam really, how many ladies be hitting dis line?" Kayla replied, a bit hurt that her voice wasn't rememberable. But after all, it was fair, they hadn't spoken in years. "Maybe I'll call back another time," she continued, playing her role as if she was fomented by the situation. "Hold on, be easy. It ain't nothing like dat," Block tried easing the tension. "Just surprised u hit me back. Ta be honest, I don't wan't ta argue. Dat's a game fa fools. Makin up an' brakin up. We not kids anymore. You called, speak ya mind." He put some perspective between their feud.

Kayla respected his request. Although she was quite shocked, he had spoken with so much prestige. In their younger days, Block would have lost his composure, precision of language would have went out the window, and he'd become belligerent. Now he was more humble, respectful about thangs. His response caused Kayla to check herself and put the childish behavior behind them. "I had a chance to dwell upon wat u told me," Kayla referred back to their brief conversation. "Ur right, we don't find da meaning of life along, but I'm nawt tryna find da meaning of dis," Kayla said, applying a coating of lipstick. She was getting ready for class while she spoke with Block. "I'm tryna gather why u choose to get at me after all des years. Wat is it, u just tryna cram me, like I'm some wham, bam, thank u ma'am; or u looking ta build? Let me know now, so I don't waste my time Bentley." Block took in everything she said, the words registered in his mind, and he had no intentions of what she was claiming. Block respected her as a lady, not some fluzzy he got his rocks off and never saw again. This was more than that and he had every intention to show her how important she was to him.

"Let me put something in perspective. I'm not sure wat kind of dude u been out here dealing wit since us," Block spoke calmly in his smooth deep voice. "Dats not who I 'am, I'll be lying, if I told u I didn't have any intentions of blessing dat fine ass back side." Kayla giggled briefly. "But dis is more den dat, in my eyes u da most exquisite lady dat ever graced my site." Kayla was an extremely beautiful woman. Even way back when they were younger, Block believed she was super model potential. She reminded him of his actress crush Nicole Bahairi. Her chocolate skin tone, and light brown eyes drove him wild. "I want nothing but da best fa u, I want ta see u happy, even if it ain't wit me. From da moment ur ole'gee gave me your digits, I started makin plans." Block was being one-hundred percent honest. He saw them the long way, and he would prove it if she allowed him to. "Look actions speak louder den words, so why don't u let me take u out dis weekend as a token ta an inception of our relationship. Is Sunday at six o'clock straight?" he asked.

"Dat's fine," she assured, excepting his proposal. "I just hope u ain't still da same dude u was in high school. I don't have time for games. I have too much on my plate an' I don't want u stringing me along in your games. My trust is something dat has to be earned, not given." Block turned his car into the Sam's Club parking lot Niko had arranged they meet. "I'm not asking u ta let your guards down an' just trust me. I don't want to move too fast; I want u ta take your time, an' determine wat u feel is real from my actions, all I ask is u let me prove myself ta u. Will u let me do dat? If u don't approve after dat, I'll leave u alone, an' u'll never hear from me again!"

Kayla closed her eyes and breathed in and out, lingering over her decision making. Listening, she wanted to give him the benefit of the doubt, but her instincts told her no. It wasn't a gut feeling or woman's intuition, it was more fear of being hurt again. She wasn't up for that depression right now. Stuck between a rock in a hard place, she let her intellectual side override her emotional state. Everybody deserved a second chance, after all, was she the same person she was a decade ago? No, she had change in many ways. Taking that into consideration, her decision was much easier.

"Ok," she agreed. "I'll give u a chance. Please don't play wit my heart Bentley. Like I said before, I don't have time for childish games," repeating herself to make sure her point got across. "I'll be ready at six, don't be late."

"It's a date…" he stated before hanging up.

"Check lover boi out," Pimp joked when Block hung up the phone. "It's a date," he mocked. "U sound like one of dem preppy white college boys." They all laughed.

"U must have drunk your hater rade dis morning," Block shot back. "Yo ass been hattin all day Mike Epps." Block referred to Pimp as Day-Day off Next Friday.

Two off white 2017 Lincoln Navigators pulled up in the lot and slid into two empty parking spaces right behind Block Sedan. Three Cubans descended stepped out scrutinizing the area, before hitting the roof of the truck, to inform Niko everything was good. Niko rolled down the window, and signaled with his trigger finger for Block, liked they had arranged. "Yall stay here," Block informed his boyz. "Keep an eye on thangs, if it jumps off, yall ninjaz know wat ta do. Set it off in dis muthafucka, feel me?" he asked rhetorical.

Block headed over toward the truck. Upon his arrival, one of Niko's boyz opened the back door, and Block got in. Block observed the three participants inside the navigator. There was Niko seated next to him in the luxury vehicle, a driver, and a passenger Block didn't know. A sense of nervousness washed over him, he felt a bit out of his element being surrounded by a group of strangers.

"I see U are still in dat hoopty," Niko stretched every syllable in his raspy accent. Niko was born and raised in Cuba. At the age of fifteen, his mother and father had American dreams. So, they illegally paid a coyote to help them escape across the border and enter the United States. Soon after, his father caught a federal case under the Rico act, and he was sent to Leavenworth for a 30-year stretch. When his father's departure came, Niko was 17, and he had big pants to wear being the man of the house. He had to fulfill his father shoes and the position he held in the cocaine trade.

"Can't afford new wheels right now," Block was struggling like any low poverty citizen, striving to make a dollar out of fifteen cents.

"Plus, I felt it was easier to be identified in da wreckage. U wouldn't have known who I was had I would've swung thru in one of my homies joints."

"U shouldn't worry yourself wit such small shit." Niko blew smoke from his Romeo and Julieti Cuban cigar. "I've did my homework on U an' your two partna's. I could have spotted U from a mile away." He pointed his finger up ahead as an indication of a mile. "U see, in dis bizness U can't afford to slip, u have to leave no loose ends. Everything must be as tight as Fort Knox. If no, U leave yourself open to fall victim. Do u know wat I mean?"

Block nodded his head and stared out the window momentarily. He knew exactly what he meant. In this new age and time, the world was overpopulated with male and female inhibited with a crustacean mentality. They were nothing more than crabs in a barrel, waiting to pull the next person down cause they failed. Block expected Niko to check his jacket, he expected nothing less. It was too much at stake for Niko, and Block knew he wouldn't risk it for no small fish.

"Yea, I know exactly wat u mean." Block turned his attention back to Niko. "But it seems as if u have some concern. Was up?"

"There u go again' wit mediocre non-sense." Niko coughed harshly from the strong cigar smoke. "Excuse me," Niko said after his air waves was clear. "U see, if der was some type of concern, we wouldn't be here mingling. I would have had u eliminated quicker den u can say one, two, three."

Niko words were chilling to Block. Block searched Niko's eyes for some hint of humor, but there was none. Niko's cold words were intended maliciously. Block knew from Niko's look, that the stories he had heard in the streets about Rock's lieutenant were true. Niko didn't get rich by playing Mr. Nice guy. He ruled with an iron fist, smashing any competition that's in his way. Murder was easy to him, to kill another person, made him feel like a god. Watching the light disappear from someone's eyes was a satisfying trill. Block knew if he fucked over Niko, he would be no exception to Niko's ruthless trigger finger.

"Now dat we have dat clear, let's see if we can get u dat new car," Niko eased the tension in the air with a wry joke that opened the door for business negotiation. "In this bizness, there is no breaks to parlay in the shade an' sip Hawaiian-punch." The man occupying the driver seat laughed, but no one paid him any mind, everyone was to focus on the tete-a-tete conversation at hand. "Dis gig is around da clock, 24/7. I want to know if I can rely on u to get da job done?"

Block cogitated what he was being asked. He knew if he excepted Niko proposal, it came great responsibility. Deadlines he would have to reach with no excuses, great links he would have to overcome with assumed expectations. This was risk you had to take on the road to success. Climbing robust mountains to achieve a goal. This was his chance to shine, and he refused to continue to watch everyone else eat, why he starved of malnutrition; figuratively speaking. "Check it, u don't know me other den da artificial intelligence intel you've found on data," Block conveyed with direct eye contact. Block was trying to send a message that would not be misunderstood, and let Niko know he had the potential to strive for betterment as much as him, if not more grind. "I'm out here in these streets day and nite grinding ta da sun come up wit what lil I got," he gave the routine of his life. "Not ta say u a lit, but until u gave me da opportunity ta make dreams come tru. Takin da notion dat I'm out here cherry picking into consideration, is enough ta say I'm starved an' do wat ever it take ta eat a healthy plate. U fuck wit me, me an' my team gone make it do wat it do; rain, snow, or sleet."

Niko put his cigar down in the door panel ashtray. "Dat's wat, I like ta hear my friend." Niko smiled showing his diamond studded fronts. "So I'ma fuck wit'cha, ta give u a chance ta put some major ends in your pocket. Nothing major, let's say 20 kilos," Niko offered. He didn't want to burden Block wit an astronomical number like 50 or 100, because he wasn't sure if Block and his boyz could handle that kind of numbers at the moment. 20 kilos, Niko pissed that, so taking a minor lost as such wouldn't put a dent in his pocket. "Do u think u an' yours can handle dat?"

"I'ma take da bull by its horns an' ride it ta victory," Block quickly replied, returning the smile. Block had cliental lined up ready for pure fish scale to drop and lock up in the pot. "My only concern is price's, wat da number's we looking at? Are dey reasonable."

"Very reasonable," Niko assured, contemplating a satisfying price that would be considerable for both of them. "How bout a two-hundred thousand even? Dat's ten a key. That leaves enough room for both of us to eat wit no complaints." Niko gave dirt prices. He could have went to the roof with numbers. Niko and his people had the purest form of cocaine on the streets of Milwaukee, at 72%, u could hit it with a eighth and still be potent enough to kill a monkey. Plus, he couldn't lose, tons and tons were shipped or flown in monthly. His only concern was seeing if his customer could pull his weight. "As our business continue, I'll flood u wit more and more weight, an' prices will get better depending da quantity u'll be responsible for. Sounds good?" Block was gracious. He wanted to celebrate his accomplishments, pop a couple of bottles. But that had to come later, right now he had to focus strictly on the grind. Once the money rolled in, they would have a chance to live it up and party. "When should I be expecting da first delivery?"

"Here, take dis." Niko reached in his pants pocket, pulling out a cell phone. "Dis is an untraceable phone." He handed it to Block. "Only one numba is programed inside, my business line. That will be da only numba u need," Niko warned for the safety of both of them. Niko didn't need the government poking their nose around where it wasn't wanted. "When u or I need ta contact one anotha, dat line will be our source of contact. When I'm ready, I'll hit u wit da drop point."

Block cradled the phone in his hand before slipping it in his pocket.

"U'll be hearing from me," Niko assured extending his hand. Block took it they shook to seal the future deal. "Nice doing bizness wit u."

"Same here," Block returned, then exited the vehicle with hopes of skies the limit, as he perambulated back over to his prospective vehicle....

***

Shay entered the Ambassador Hotel's lobby, dressed casual in a pair of white air force one's, a pair of blue Zara jeans, and a white spaghetti strap tank top. Observing the lobby, she noticed different faces of all races, but none of them seemed familiar. Looking at her fit-bit, she noticed it was 9 P.M., so she had to make this quick. Soon Bando's antlers would go up and want to know her whereabouts. Right now, she didn't need that kind of drama, or energy, so she hoped whomever the mysterious voice had belonged to, would hurry up. Her prayers were soon answered when a startling hand tapped her on the shoulder. Uneased, she turned around to confront her harasser.

"U don't seem happy ta see such a handsome face," Chop said. Chop's conceited remark rubbed Shay the wrong way, leaving her feeling some type of way. She wasn't sure how to respond; whether she should cry, scream, or just keep quiet. Whatever she decided, she knew nothing would heal the open wound in her heart. "Follow me, I already reserved us a room. We'll need it as we get more acquainted." There was a sotto voice in Chop tone that made Shay feel more uneasy than before. She didn't even know this man standing before her. Her instincts told her to run, but common sense told her to stay. Conflicted, her feet lead the way, trailing Chop with a mind of their own. "Make yourself comfortable," Chop offered while opening the hotel door.

With unease playing a major factor in Shay's state a mind. She scurried into the room, jumping a bit as the door shut behind her. "Relax," Chop rubbed her back. "Ur so tense. there's no need ta be, u in da best hands in da city. With women, I believe in pleasure before pain."

"What do u want from me?" Shay curiously asked, removing herself away from Chop's touch. There was no way she could be comfortable in this kind of predicament she was in; her circumstances didn't justify her being at ease. "Did Bando put u up to dis, because if he did it won't work. I remember u from Stevo's funeral, your one of my man's friends." Shay remembered him, because he was the sole reason she and Bando had gotten into a heated squabble after Stevo's funeral service. A debate between the two that had gotten so far out of hand, Shay thought it would escalate into a violate situation. Bando had never struck her before, but the way he'd flew off the handle in the limo, made her feel there was a first time for everything. "If Bando didn't arrange dis ta try an' catch me up, maybe I should tell him your tryna blackmail me, so he can kill your damn ass."

Chop let out a hearty laugh. Shay's idol threats were flattering. He was impressed Shay tried to deter him, but slayed in humor at the same time, because she believed getting him whacked would free her of the matter altogether. "Believe me, it won't be dat eazy to get out of da hot seat you've planted your ass in." Chop headed over to the bar and fixed them both a libation. "U see, to every action, there's an equal reaction. If u rat me out, I spill da beans an' let Bando know u was in da club wit da same niggaz dat killed his lil brotha." Chop wasn't bluffing, he had witnessed her on da night before Stevo's murder, in Julian's Hall and Lounge hugged up with the enemy. Of course, Chop didn't know her at the time, not until Stevo's service. "He will kill u. Hell he might spare me, an' have me put u out your misery. Believe me, I'll enjoy every bit of your life seeping from your eyes.

Chill's ran down Shay's spine, she couldn't believe she was in an enclosed area with a maniac. This man was insane, and there was no doubt why Bando kept him around. Shay wasn't naïve to Bando's street dealings. She knew he kept gun slingers on deck for immoral purposes. The man before her was a mere pawn of those purposes.

"Ur crazy," Shay judged.

"Well isn't dat da kettle calling da tea pot black?" Chop took a seat next to Shay, setting their glasses of cognac on the stand. "I'm not da one fronting like my shit don't stank. Your no rose bush your'self." He slyly saw through her retrospective transgressions in her face. Her heart cringed at the truth; the truth was known to hurt. "See me and U have more in common den u know."

"Me and you are nothing alike," she retorted. Angered by his assumed comparisons, she took a deep breath to calm her nerves. "Ur a bottom feeder an' I'm at the top, looking down on u crustacean," she insulted Chop, hoping she could make him feel as bad as she did at the moment. He laughed her condescended comment off.

"U think because you spread your legs, your a boss? U screwed your way ta da top. Bein' flat backed doesn't qualify as putting' u in work bitch." Shay was appalled by his choice of words, a part of her wanted to bite his head off. Some audacity he had. He wasn't at liberty to speak to her in such a manner.

"Let me put u back in your place." Chop grabbed his phone, pulling up some photographs he had of her indiscretions. "Take a look at your 'self. Dis is da reflection of a whore," he pushed the screen in her face. An indecent picture displayed her in V.I.P knocking Dice back. It was something she had done at her own risk, but risk is what turned her on. She had sucked Dice's dick right there in the V.I.P section while his girl was in the club.

"Wat do u want?" she managed to ask through cotton mouth. Here she was supposed to be marrying the love of her life, and her freaky nature had come back to haunt her. Some photos capturing her like some low-class porn star were being held over her head as leverage.

If her cards weren't played right, the souvenir could get out and destroy everything she'd ardently worked for.

"I'll start by taking da money I requested." Chop calmly took a sip of his scotch on the rocks, while she reluctantly fidgeted in her purse for the bank roll she so desperately thought she wouldn't have to pay. "I own U, you are now my slave. U do whatever I tell u ta do. If I say jump, u say how high. Do I make myself clear?" Chop asked, taking the money from her hand.

Shay didn't want to obey, but she was in no position to disobey. Either it was this or go back to the slums, and she refused to back track. She'd come too far to look back now.

"I said do I make myself clear?" Chop repeated.

"Crystal," she found herself saying. With no hope for freedom, she somehow could relate to those behind bars. Empathically, she felt analogous to their pain. "I'll do wat' ever u say. Just please keep dis between u an' I?" she begged with the last ounce of dignity she possessed.

"Good gurl, dat's wat I like ta hear." Chop set da money and his glass down. "Fa ur first task of obedience," Chop unzipped his Coogi jeans.

"What are u doing?" she blurted in disbelief.

"Introducing U," he replied, pulling Shay's head into his lap.

CHAPTER FIVE

Wanda prepared her make-up in silks night club dressing room, making sure it was to perfection. Proper preparation prevents poor performance.

Her performance was always live. She had no time to perform anything poorly, her body was a money maker, and she would shack her protuberant ass until she got rich. Besides the normal letting the bills rain all over her body, she had an itch to fulfill between her legs; picking up her phone, she dialed in her fixer....

***

"Don't stress, I'm on my way." Block spoke into his cellphone maneuvering his vehicle through traffic. "I just hit da interstate, just be easy and I'll be der in a jiffy."

"Alright, just don't leave me waiting forever." Kayla anxiously awaited Block's arrival. Over the past week they'd had ample time to settle their differences. They had spent long hours on the phone late night speaking sweet nothings in one another's ears. Kayla couldn't lie, she felt bubbly inside, and she was looking forward to their date. "U know time is money, right?"

"Please, don't try ta hit me wit dat old hustler line, time is on my side," Block counter attacked her cliché. "I'll be blowing da horn in two," Block assured, hanging up the phone. As soon as he ended their call, his line rang again. Glancing at the display, he chose not to answer. It was his bussit-baby, but he had shit to do, so he would get at her a little later. Minutes later, he pulled up in front of Kayla's duplex and hit the horn. She came out dressed casually in a matching Dior fit and a Fendi purse thrown over her shoulder. Block got out of the car to open her car door like a gentleman should.

"Thank U," she conveyed her gracious appreciation.

"Don't mention it," Block coyly said. "Dis only da beginning."

Block rounded the car and hopped in the passenger seat and seconds later the whip was heading toward their destination.

"By the way, u look exquisite," Block complimented his date, who wore red Dior pants coordinated with a white belly button shirt with Dior emblazed across the front in bedazzle red. She looked amazing in her Manolo red bottom pumps that set her fit off.

"Thank u," Kayla received Block's admire with joy. "An' you look extremely comfortable," she joked like the peculiar V-neck tide laundry detergent commercial, indicating Block wasn't at his best.

"Huuggghh," Block faked laughed. "U funny." He popped the collar of his True religion button up. "U know u lyin, I'm already fly when I walk thru customs dis shit should be illegal, cause planes can't get on planes." Block popped the rim of his collar. "Oh boy!" he imitated E-40.

"Whatever I see. U still silly as always," Kayla gave Block a once overlook from head to toe. Much hadn't changed in his look department; he was still incredibly handsome as he was the first time she laid eyes on him in high school. Come to think of it, their meeting had been like a fictional tale out of a fairytale novel. Some lame had called himself ragging on her appearance because she wouldn't give him no play. When she had told him she wasn't interested, instead of him pushing on like true playaz do, his ego became bruised.

"U silly lil bitch, I know u don't think u can do better den me. Look at'cha yourself he barked, putting his finger in her face. She had done her best to ignore him. She was shy at that age, and didn't like conflict; so, she tried by all means to avoid it. "U should be lucky a playa like me givin u da time of day," he had said and much more, when Block overheard and intervened into the situation.

"Playa push on, can't see da lady not interested? Don't play yourself out like dat, it's not a good look," Block said, stepping between her and the boy.

"Why da fuck is u sticking your nose ware it don't belong?" Her bug-a-boo pumped up his chest. "I suggest u point it in another direction before it get broke homeboy."

Block gave a sly smile to the nonmoving threat. There wasn't an ounce of fear in his demeanor; he stood his ground, not budging. In that moment, Kayla admired him, he was the definition of a knight in shiny armor.

"I'm da one u don't wan't to fuck wit," Block calmly warned the boy. "U don't really wan't dis beef bro, it'll spoil your stomach."

Through the unsuspecting huddled crowd on the bus stop, two other males appeared. "Wuz up my dude, u got a problem?" they asked, starring viciously at Block's opponent.

"I don't know," Block replied with questioning eyes. Block watched his potential challenger, hoping that he didn't force him and his boyz to party pack him. "Do we have a problem?" he asked. "Nah," the boy said and deflated his chest. He had been reluctantly defeated. "U can have dat bitch. U an' her deserve one another," was his last response, before departing through a bunch of adolescents.

The heartwarming introduction would forever be incised in her memory bank. Block had been so strong in the face of the enemy but so kind to the embrace of her. Kayla had to admit, from the very first time they had met, Block was the only guy she had envisioned long term.

Block pulled up to their destination: The Farmhouse Paint and Sip, a place where you could eat delectable fried chicken, drink remarkable libations, and play Pablo Picasso with paints. The atmosphere was chill and relaxed. A place one could go to get away from the hustle and bustle of everyday life.

They ordered a buffalo chicken tender platter and took a seat toward the back of the establishment while they awaited their order.

"Dis a nice environment," Kayla gave her approval. She was already enjoying herself watching other couples and families get their hands messy with paints. This was her type of setting, she felt as if she could be herself, without all the imbuing judgment of mankind. It became tiring after a while; people just wanted to be themselves and live without the stigma others automatically assumed certain cultures was supposed to live by. "Where did U find displace? I've never heard of it." She could see herself returning in the near future. "One day I saw their advertisement on Fox-Six news," Block explained, picking up a purple bottle of paint off the table to read the ingredients. "An' I thought of u, I remember u love to paint in your spare time." Kayla was flattered. She couldn't believe Block still remembered that. It wasn't anything she did regularly she did it as a hobby. That made an even more of an impression. The fact it wasn't a main priority, but something she indulged in more as a recreation, let her know she had never been pushed to the wayside. She had always been a factor in his mind. "U still paint don't'cha?"

"Not as much as I used to." She grabbed the bottle from his hand, and he playfully snatched back.

"U ain't gone hoe me out dis bottle, get'cha own," he joked. Kayla laughed at his silliness. For some reason she felt comfortable around Block. It was if they had never been apart.

"Nah, but seriously doe." She grabbed the bottle back from him, seductively grabbing his hand in the process. Block didn't protest, just gave a hungry eye look. Like he would devour her right there in the public place if she allowed. "I don't really have da time anymore, between school and working, most of my free time is spent counting sleep." Most of her time was consumed, she couldn't remember the last time she had to herself to paint a canvas. How she missed it, it was something she enjoyed. To be honest, she hadn't experienced the peace she once knew when she zoned out to slow music and messy paint. "I miss it doe, I wish I had more time."

"Wat about right now?"

"Right now?" she asked, shocked.

"Yea, right now." Block grabbed her by her hand, pulling her off the stool.

"I see no reason u can't enjoy yourself."

"But I don't have a change of clothes." She complained following Block.

"Clothes can be replaced, but once in a lifetime moments are irreplaceable." Block stopped and pulled her close. His lips were so close, she could feel his breath on her ear. "Let's make dis moment memorable," he whispered gently.

Kayla's heartbeat became irregularly. The scent of his masculine cologne and the mixture of his deep voice made her melt like butter. She found herself trying hard not to collapse in his arms, she couldn't make it that easy for him, no matter how irresistible or delicious he smelt. "Ok."

Block smiled down like sunray upon her. Thank god she was blessed with dark skin, because she was blushing something terribly, feeling all mushy and gooey inside. She found herself agreeing to terms by a nod of the head. Block took her hand again, and just like that, she was enraptured in his mid-western charisma….

***

Moski walked up the ave smoking a Black-a-mile and sipping out a Sprite bottle he'd filled to the rim with Patron. Lately he'd been consuming more alcoholic beverages than usually in a tipple fashion. Hope on the rocks drowned his sorrows. Intoxication was the only solace he could relate to. In a matter of weeks, two of his boys had been wiped off the face of the earth. Taking a swig of the drink, his red glazed over eyes focused on a familiar face he guessed he would never encounter again. There, across the street, was a milestone he vowed he'd kill if he ever saw them again.

Diamond had just entered the store. Diamond was an old hood rat Moski used to fuck on regularly, until she had pulled a snake move and cuffed a couple of his jewels one night while he was on some squirrel chasing a nut type shit. He hit up Diamond though so he could knock them walls loose. She gladly obliged beckoning to his needs, or so he thought. When she arrived at his spot, one of her friends was in town. Diamond explained a disarming reason why another woman was tagging along with her with no intentions of a ménage-a-trois. Naïvely, he let the excuse ride and proceeded to knock Diamond down in the back bedroom. It wasn't until long after Diamond had long gone that he noticed two Rolex, a 32-inch gold chain, and a pair of supermen cut diamond earrings were missing in action. Trying to be rational, Moski contacted Diamond by phone. Futile, because she told him fuck him and charge it to the game. So, Moski measured the 31,000-value lost as fair exchange for her life. It was then he pledged to put her in the dirt. That was three months ago, now here she stood in the flesh.

Moski dropped a half empty soda bottle into the gutter at the curb and clutched his 32 revolver in his pants pocket. His Black-a-mile still dangled at the corner of his lips, that he took a pull form every so often as he headed across the street.

Diamond came out the store carrying a gallon of milk and a plastic bag concealing her other purchase. As she tossed her purchase into the car, Moski walked up and tapped Diamond on her shoulder. When she turned to face him, he sent two through her face, leaving her slumped against the passenger door. He ran up the block, and jumped into his 2000 Porsche Boxster and fished tailed off the scene...

***

Kesha rode Pimp's manhood like an equestrian. Pimp firmly gripped her ass while she did her thang; gyrating round and round, up and down. Kesha was a beautiful sight to see impaled upon his pole. Every time she descended down his pole, her voluptuous breasts did a sensual dance of their own. Perspiration poured down the center of them. Her mouth opened wide and she called out as her umpteenth orgasm tore through her.

Pimp was in seven heaven. The pussy was feeling so amazing. It made him want to deny taking control, but he had to. Pimp flipped Kesha off of him and placed her on all fours before burying his bone deep inside her tunnel. Her walls invited him in with no resistance.

"Mmmmm," Kesha made a hearty moan in her throat. Pimp was so deep, he was hitting her G-spot making her wrench at the sheets and gasp for breath. She felt amazing like a newborn virgin all over again.

Pimp jack hammered in and out of her womb with great velocity. He emitted flesh slapping against flesh echoed throughout the room, while Kesha tried muffling her cries into the pillow clenched between her teeth. "Ooooooh Pimp, shit fuck dat pussy!" Kesha ululated as another orgasm erupted. At the moment of her release, Pimp spilled forth filling her with his copious cum.

Pimp laid molded to Kesha's back side a moment before walking across the room to fix himself a drink.

"Dam nigga, u be stretching a bitch out like I'm given birth," Kesha complained while rolling over, displaying her fresh bikini wax. "I do have to return home an' my man know he didn't create dis gappin hole," she explained letting her hand venture between her thighs. Her fingers drifted into forbidden territory and she played with her clit.

"Not for long." Pimp took a seat on the edge of the bed and took a sip of his drink why letting his lingering words cogent Kesha into a decision he knew she wanted.

"Not for long... what are u saying?" Kesha crawled across the bed, draping her arms loosely over Pimp's shoulders and kissed him on the neck. "Are u suggesting wat I think."

"Wat I'm suggestion is u can do wat ever u like." Pimp grabbed Kesha's hand and kissed it. "Dis amerika, an' u have da right ta do wat'cha please."

"So, where do we go after dis move u an' your friends are puttin together?"

"Like I said, ware ever u want ta go." Pimp pulled Kesha into his lap. "Skies da limit," he coaxed, planting a soft kiss upon her lip...

***

A cocaine white 2003 Mercedes SL 500 convertible with peanut butter insides pulled up on Bando and his squad. Chop bailed where the roof go to rap with Bando.

"I gotta holla at'cha." Chop showed love. "Wuz popping Creep, Duck, an' East-side," he greeted the rest of the squad.

"Wuz good my nigga?" Duck returned. "It's been a minute family, I ain't seen u round des parts. In a minute wat'cha been up to, how u livin?"

"I can't complain," Chop pointed at his Benz sitting on 24inch chrome Dalvens. "But let me holla at Bando, an' I'ma get at'cha later. Cool?"

"Fo'sho." Duck went back to mingling with the rest of the homies.

"Wuz up?" Bando inquired.

"I got dis lil shawty dat want stay off my tip," Chop lied. "She wuz up in Julian's da nite dat drama popped off. She claimed she know ole boys an' em from round da way." Chop withheld Shay's identity for the moment. He had no intentions of keeping her anonymous for the long haul, just for the moment. He needed her for the time being, because she was a vital source to what he was planning. If everything went as planned, he would be the head honcho. He just had to make sure all his ducks were in a row.

"Do u trust her, is she trustworthy?" Bando was ready to ride. The information he'd just received was the best he'd received in weeks. His trigger finger had been itching badly to squeeze on the fools responsible for his brother's death. But to do so, he had to be sure who the assailant was. And from his perspective, that was like tryna find a needle in a haystack with no directional purpose.

"I don't know bout being trustworthy, but she did tell me bout dis dude off da tre's named Block." While explaining, Chop pulled a pack of Newports from his pocket and patted a loose cigarette into his palm. "Da detailed description she gave fit da nigga I saw come thru blasting da next day."

"Dat's all I need ta know. Let's ride."

"Wat, right now?" Chop asked dumbfounded.

"Yea right now. Wat'cha think I'ma wait on Christ return?" Bando became cynical, patronizing in a way. "U said u know ware buddy em at, right?"

"Yea."

"Den wuz da problem? Let's ride out. We need ta peep da scene a message to whomever ouch dat mutha fucka, feel me?" Bando headed to his 2013 Porsche Cayenne AWD Base and grabbed his AK 47 equipped with 75 round banana clip from the trunk. The gun looked like something straight out the Rambo movie. Moments later Bando was riding shotgun in a dark maroon Tahoe while Chop whipped and clutched a Tech 9 on his lap...

***

Block stopped in the midst of him and Kayla's stroll through the park.

"I want ta thank u fa wat I've ben missing," Block sincerely conveyed, looking her directly in her eyes. His tone and stare captivated her soul, in a sense, she felt hypnotized. "All da joys I've been missing is right here wit u." They had recently had a wonderful dinner that included equal conversation.

Kayla had to admit, she hadn't felt so relaxed and compatible with any man in a long while. She wanted to pick up the pieces where they left off but couldn't allow Block to play with her emotions.

"Bentley, I feel da same an' I hope dat u sincere in your words," she explained, hoping her candor wouldn't come back to bite her in the ass. She was a firm believer that people could change. But on the flip side of the coin, there always were wolves in sheep clothing who possessed an agenda on their minds to destroy others. They were like predators who preyed on the weak. "I can't... No, no, no, dat's wrong," Kayla corrected herself. "I won't allow u ta string me along in your games. I won't be led on like we in a monogamous relationship, when I'm only a side piece. I don't have time ta be out here in des streets fighting wit no other bitch. I have too much on my plate fa insignificance. If u can't be man enough ta respect my dreams, u need ta part ways right now why there is no hard feelings."

"Come fly wit me, an 'be da woman of my dreams. It's your name in a blimp I envision." Block tried his hardest to make Kayla see life through his eyes, to see what he saw. "I see us together ta da end of times. I know we didn't start off on good terms, but I want I atone for my childish mishaps an' give u da world."

"I don't need da world," Kayla declined.

"I know, but dat still doesn't discourage me from trying ta give it ta ya on a silver platter." Block pushed her stylish bang away from her face then stroked her cheek. She had a bob style that contoured perfectly with her profile. "It's u an' I against da world."

Kayla believed everything Block was saying. It was something different about him; something much more mature about him then when they dated. Here he was standing before her as she had always dreamed of him. He was caring and sensitive to her needs as a woman and not an object. It was if he understood she had feelings also that had to be attended to before any dude could get to her Milky-Way. Kayla overwhelmingly wrapped her arms around Block, then withdrew them as quickly as she had unconsciously hugged him.

"I'm sorry, I'm all covered in paint," she complained about her messy state, self-consciously wiping her hands on her shirt.

"Don't worry bout dat. Material things can be replaced," Block soothed Kayla by wrapping her back in his warm embrace. "But des moments shared wit u can't be replaced." Block's every intention was to show Kayla she meant the world to him. The only other woman he had loved so deeply was his mother. There was a reverence for both women. "Come on, let me get'cha home before da clock strikes twelve."

"Shut up stupid," Kayla laughed at his joke and swatted his arm. "My name ain't Cinderella fool," she playfully snatched away from Block's embrace, crossed her arms, and pouted as if she was mad.

"U look so cute when u mad," Block teased, flicking his finger over her stuck-out lips. "Come on let's roll." He took Kayla by the hand. Half an hour later, they pulled up in front of Kayla crib. Block helped her out the car like the ever so gentlemen he was.

"Thank u, I had a good time," Kayla expressed her gratitude by surprisingly kissing Block upon the lips. Block reciprocated her affection. "Ooooooh we... Let me get in here before u start a ragin fiya between my legs," Kayla murmured and fanned herself off when they broke apart.

Block smiled mischievously. "Don't sound like a bad idea," he replied, pressing his groin into her abdomen.

"Maybe not," she agreed. "But now not da time. I'm gonna give u da chance ta show me u been real wit me, an' if u play your cards right, I'll ride u ta da sun come up," she seductively promised kissing him.

"I'll rather u be bout it an' show me."

Kayla wiped her lip gloss from his lips and opened her front door. "Trust me, I will," she assured smiling. She peaked Block on the lips one last time before waving him goodbye and close the door.

Block rubbed his chin, smiling internally. He hopped in his whip and smashed off to Silk night club. Block had unconditional feelings for Kayla, but he had to get the monkey off his back. Kayla presence had left his jeans stretched.

Entering the establishment, Wanda was just coming off the stage from finishing her set when he grabbed her by the hand. "Hey daddy!" she exclaimed, jumping into his arms and wrapping her legs around his waist. "I called u earlier. I missed u," she excitedly expressed her affection in between kisses.

Block didn't respond. His silence spoke volumes, and she knew what he wanted. Lowering her back to her feet, he dragged her off to an empty stall. Closing the door and locking it behind, Block unbuckled his Saint Laurent belt, and slid to the promise land. As he stroked away, he thought of Kayla...

***

"There go one of dem bitch niggaz right der," Chop pointed out to a young male posted upon the porch of Block's trap house.

Bando took a good look at their prime target, cocking his AK in the process.

"Pull up right der on da corner. We gone walk dis clown down."

"Wat?" Chop asked astonished. "U can't just walk down unfamiliar territory gunz blazin like dis da wild-wild west." Chop had concerns regarding Bando's plan. They didn't know the hood they were in from Adam and Eve, and Chop wasn't sure how organized Block and his team was. As far as Chop was concerned, they could be walking right into an ambush. Plus, there was no telling what a bitch would do in distress. Shay could've told ole boy and e'm that Chop and them would be gunning to avenge Stevo's murder. Especially after what he had done to her. Chop had done some real freaky indescribable things to her. The part of their escapade he enjoyed the most was when he had fucked her mouth at full velocity, then shoved his dick down her esophagus as he came, making her choke as his cum spewed from her nose. He found sadist pleasure in treating her like the slut she was.

"Dis ain't a democracy, do as your told," Bando barked an order as if Chop was in the army. That was the type of shit that pissed Chop off. Bando was always talking out his neck like he reigned over niggaz persons. Bando didn't view people as his equal, instead he saw them as subordinates beneath his ruling. Chop wouldn't put up with Bando Poor attitude for much longer. Soon Bando would know when you play with fire you got burned. "Now pull up over der like I said."

Bando and Chop hopped out the car with Bando leading and Chop in tow. A malicious thought ran through Chop mind; there, it dawned on Chop to execute Bando right there on the spot. Just drop him off and hop back in the ride. But that was too easy. Before Chop put the iron to Bando, he wanted to make sure he stripped him for everything he was worth. Once he had his wealth, he would easily put him out of his misery. Until he could properly play the card he had up his sleeve, Chop would have to let Bando play boss. Really, Bando was nothing more than a puppet being controlled by a puppeteer. Chop was the real boss. The one on front line making all the moves. Chop's next move would be his best.

"Dis fo Stevo," Bando alerted, standing ready in the middle of the street. The chopper erupted in a blaze, and a hell of gunfire spilled from the muzzle. The target dived off the front porch in a panic, spitting the double mint gum he was chewing in the grass. As bullets struck the home, *bop, bop, bop, bop, bop*, Tree took flight through the gangway.

"Come on let's rock dis nigga ta sleep an' get up out here," Chop announced, attempting to run after him, but Bando stopped him by grabbing his arm firmly.

"Nah, let em go," Bando requested slowly turning heading back in the direction of their respective vehicle. "Dat was just a warning before da real fiya works."

"Dawg u must be nuts." Chop ran back to the trunk with a look of disgust plastered across his face. "U just put dem niggaz on alert an' we won't get another chance like dis again."

"Dat's exactly wat I want, dat way I kill two byrds wit one stone." Bando tossed his hot chopper in the backseat as Chop smashed the gas and burned rubber off the block. "I want der niggaz ta line up like dominos, so I can knock dem aw down in a sequence."

Chop didn't respond, he thought the plan was insane. Bando acted as if they were playing Grand Thief Auto, and they had lives to be wasted. Pondering that notion, Chop knew he had to put his diabolical plan in effect, and fast. If he didn't, there was a possibility Bando would not only get himself killed, but also everyone riding with him..

CHAPTER SIX

Six jumped off the top bunk when his door popped. He was unaware to why the sergeant had buzzed his door, but he put on his green uniform to report to the officer station and discover the mystery.

"Bout time your lazy ass raised up off dat cot." Six's cellmate, Nut, announced while in the mirror shaving. "I thought u was never gone depart from dat bitch."

"Insha Allah," Six praised Allah for his will. "I hope des dem courts gettin back at'cha boi'. I'm tired of been caged in like some animal." Six slipped in his fresh pair of Air Max 95 tennis shoes. "Dis shit fo da Byrd's. It's time fo a gee ta grace dem streetz again." Six had been down two years going on three. He didn't like being housed like stock and cattle while waiting on the federal courts to make a ruling to overturn the circuit court decision on his botched conviction. "Wuz up?" Six asked, approaching the Sgt. cage. "U popped k-49, so wuz up?" Six expressed a bit of attitude after the sergeant frowned up dumbfounded as if he didn't know as to why Six was approaching the officer station. Inmates didn't have keys to their cells. Waupun was a maximum institution where convicts was confined to their rooms 23 and 1, so it wasn't like he could open his own cell door. Six hated when the guards acted ignorant. They possessed tendencies like broad that forced niggas to go upside there wigs.

"What cell are you in sir?" The Sgt. smugly asked.

"For da second time, k-49," Six stressed. "Dam, pay attention."

"Ok calm down," the Sgt. tried to defuse the situation before it escalated. They were familiar with Six's flaming hot temper. They knew he would snap out at any giving moment. Some guards threw fuel on a raging fire, but others stayed at bay because they didn't want to provoke a fight. Six had never put his hands on a correctional officer, but he had given a few of the inmates a taste of night quill. Employed officers had witnessed his handy work, and they didn't want a piece of what he was serving.

"Sorry Mr. Stokes. You have legal mail," Sgt. James picked up a pile of mail and flicked through it. Legal mail had to be opened in the presence of an officer to make sure it possessed no contraband. "Wat's your D.O.C. number?"

"Fo-eigh douba oh," Six conveyed his six-digit identification number. The guard compared the number to that upon the envelope, then opened, searched, and distributed.

"Here youu go sir."

Six took a glance at the envelope, it was from the Eastern District federal courts. Hoping the mail held the information he'd been waiting for, he sped back to his room.

"Dats wat I'm talking bout!" Six shouted ten minutes later jumping off his bunk. "Y'all den up an' done it."

Nut assumed the news was good, so he turned to face his boy. They'd been bunked up for a year now, and in the short course of time, they'd gotten tight. Disregarding the fact they was from two different sides. Six was from the tres, while Nut was on the other hand was from 6th and Burliegh. But that didn't hold any weight, because the real embraced their own no matter what walks of life you were from. Nut loved Six like a brother and vice versa. They rolled for one another. Six and Nut was niggaz and no one would or could come between their loyalty.

"Dat's wat'cha been looking fo?" Nut inquired, turning off the switch on his Philips Norelco. "Wuz up? Speak up nigga," he attempted to hype his boy up. "Dat's shit should have u turned up."

Six was stuck in an unbelievable trance. He wasn't the loud type that displayed his business all over the tier. He just let the overwhelming joy download slowly like bad internet service. Nut expected his boy to react in the manner he'd said he would when his case got overturned and bust his flat screen TV and WR-2 on the floor. But Six could only contemplate how it had been a long time coming. He was on his way back to the streets, and in all reality, he was more depressed then joyful. Why? Because he was leaving behind a gang of real niggas that didn't deserve to be behind cell bars. For instance, his celly Nut. Nut was one of the real ones. To have niggas like Nut in the kind of predicament Six was luckily escaping, let the real know that life was a bitch, then you die. Unfortunately, Nut would die in the confines of a prison if the traditional system didn't rule in his favor and overturn his first-degree intentional homicide conviction from over a decade ago. On the bricks, Nut and his team ran an extortion ring. But business had went downhill when one of the niggas decided he had enough. On pick up day, the store owner in their neighborhood had told Nut to go fuck himself and whomever he came with. Being the boss Nut was, he sent one of the blood thirsty wolves to go collect. When the owner refused, his goon put a hole in Gus chest big as the equator. Everything was cope esthetic until the little homies got knocked and told the police about a chain of murders and robberies Nut and his boyz had committed throughout Milwaukee. Nut down fall was the prime example about getting licked in the face if you played with puppies.

"My dude, I'm turnt. Believe me I am," Six admitted. He reread over the court's order to vacate his sentence. His freedom literally laid in his hands, but his mind was clouded with despair for all the real niggaz that had lost their life to the white man's jacked up system. "I just can't help but feel some type of way leaving my nigga. U suppose ta be out der wit da team, nawt stuck here in da land of suckaz."

"Fuck all dat shit real talk," Nut dusted his trimmed facial hair off his chest and threw his gray T-shirt back on. "Wat u gotta realize is real niggaz adapt ta der living arrangements. We don't repent an' reform, we adapt an' over come in da jungle," he explained. "This shit right here da jungle an' I'm swinging on branches like George. Apes run under my proxy. This right here can't break me, believe me I'ma be alright just get out der an' hold it down fa niggaz like me an' keep me in ur prayers. When da trumpet blows, da gates gone open up fa ya boy." Nut walked over and placed his hand on Six's shoulder. Nut was only a few years order then Six. At 30, Nut possessed infinite wisdom, an esoteric of sort. He envisioned the world as if he had been there before and came back around.

"How u expect me ta pull dat off?" Six asked. "When I gawt niggaz up in here living life thru a pen waiting on an appeal. That shit fucked up."

"Da way u been balling." Nut informed. "Only deference now, is u have da best of both worlds. A reality check ta keep u grounded when u feel yourself slipping. All u gotta do is look back an' picture yourself in my shoes. Dat should be enough ta help u make your decision's wisely."

Six lingered on Nut's words for a minute, and he knew what he had to do. By all means, he would keep it real and reach back for the real ones trapped in the belly of the beast.

"U know I got you on da other end."

"U ain't gotta tell me dat, I know when I'm in da grace of a tru one," Nut assured. "Just get out der an' make it do wat it do. I need cha out der mo den I do in here. So, stack dat paper an' den make boss moves."

Six nodded and shook up with Nut. "I got'cha playa."

"Dat's wat I'm talking bout," Nut applauded.

It would take 72 hours for the warden to verify his release. While patiently waiting, Nut exercised his mind and went over his game plan. Soon, he would touch down and make it do what it do...

***

"So, u sure it wuz dem clowns we wet up?" Block asked. He was trying to put everything his boy Tree had just said in perspective. Block, Tree, and Pimp were all gathered around the trap house living room. Block felt it was urgent to arrange this meeting after what had occurred to Tree. They didn't need the drama at the moment. It was too much at stake, so Block had called a meet so they could come to a conclusion to do away with the unnecessary conflict. Beef was bad for business. You couldn't be in the middle of warfare and chasing dollar signs at the same time.

"Yea I'm sure," Tree confirmed. His tone of voice said he was frustrated by Block's interrogation. "I just told'cha dem niggaz tried ta kill me. Wat'cha don't thank I can see? Wat kind of shit is dat?" Tree was raging with anger toward the situation. Talking only pissed him off more, he was ready to strap up and ride out. Someone had to pay for the attempt on his life.

"Be easy my nigga."

"Fuck dat shit!" Tree snapped. "Dem bitch ass niggaz ain't being eazy. So, wat we gone do bout it? I know we ain't gone sit on our hands an' talk bout dis shit all day why dem bitch niggaz get away wit dis shit."

"Dat's exactly wat we gone do," Block confirmed Tree's worst fear. Tree was about that action, and he didn't let shit go. Ducking action wasn't in his DNA.

"Wat?" Tree jumped out of his seat so stunned that he knocked over the chair he occupied in the process. "I don't think I heard u right. I know u just didn't agree dat we gone let dem fuck boyz get away wit dat foul play ridin thru our hood like they desperados.?"

"Dam ninja, let me finish wat I have to say before u fly off da handle wit'cha hot ass temper." Block tried clearing the elephant out of the room. The thick tension in the air clouded around like cigarette smoke. "It's only momentarily. We got to much on our plate ta be focus on small shit."

"Excuse me fa dis, but my lyfe ain't small shit. My lyfe a major factor an' I ain't bout ta let no fuck niggaz take it from me."

"Tree right," Pimp seconded, siding with his boy Tree. "Dem niggaz violated by ridin thru here setting it off like dey Queen Latifah. We gotta body dem bitch made niggaz."

"Dat's wat I'm talking bout." Tree excepted the notion, gladly shacking up with Pimp. "Dem niggaz gotta go G."

"An' dat's gone happen. Just not at da moment," Block informed. They could no longer make inexperience puerile moves at any spare moment. Escapades were rash, and they couldn't be moving erratically. If they made one false move after Niko's work was in their hands, it could cost them their lives. "We gotta start using our heads in a major way. We no longer small fish. We bout ta start playing wit keys ta doors in a boss world, so we gone have conduct ourselves on a boss level. Bosses don't have to handle matters of dis caliber, dis a duty fo da hitters. Feel me?"

"Right, right," Tree agreed.

Pimp said nothing. He just stood in the corner pulling slowly on his cigarette.

"I gotta plan, I just need ta know if y'all wit me. Cause I can't do dis alone. We a team an' we in dis thang ta win it together." Block awaited a response from his boyz.

"So, wat's da plan?" Pimp questioned speaking up.

"First, we gone catch des Byrd's an' fly in any weather..." In the middle of Block's lecture his untraceable cellphone rang and he pardoned Pimp and Tree to answer. "Hold on a sec." Block put his finger up. "Speak," he spoke into the receiver.

"Meet me at Brewers stadium," Niko informed on the other end. "An' drive something big enough ta fit da family. I got da children wit me." He coded the bricks as kids.

"Got'cha," Block replied, then hung up. "Come on let's ride out," he directed his boyz. "Tree go grab dat body dropper out da closet."

"Why, wuz up?" Tree was confused. Just a few minutes ago, Block denied them the satisfaction of burning Stevo's guys block down. Now all of a sudden he was demanding him to grab the chopstick. "Wat'cha change ya mind? U gone let me do dem bitch niggaz in?"

"Nah," Block declined. "Da byrdman just arrived. Come on, let's be out, an' we takin your whip too." Block grabbed his 9 Biretta off the table and stuffed it in his waistband. After Tree grabbed the flat liner, and all three men set off in Tree tomato red 2002 Dodge Durango. When they pulled into the Brewers' stadium parking lot, Block noticed it was deserted except for a few scattered cars, which probably belonged to employed security.

Block spotted Niko and his entourage immediately. He was in the Escalade they done business in. Beside him was a black caravan occupied by three man, one which stood leaning on the side panel as a lookout. Tree pulled up next to the van and Block hopped out.

"How's it going my mane?" Niko greeted. "Are u ready fa da beginning of your new lyfe? Dis here is serious bizness. Are u sure dis is da road ta rich's u want ta pursue?" Niko forewarned Block. Niko wanted Block to understand he was selling his soul to the devil. Once you were in, there was no out. No blood in but blood out was the only way Block would ever be free if he signed the verbal contract.

"I'm sure," Block excepted without giving Niko proposal a second thought. He knew what came with the game, and it was where he wanted to be. On top was the mission. And if drugs wrote his vision in the sky, then he had no choice but to reach for the stars. "I've dedicated my lyfe ta da mighty dolla, an' I refuse ta turn back now. I spent nites dreaming of moments like dis so I could feed da supreme team. Dis all I know. I was bron in da streetz an' I'ma die in da streetz."

"Alright." Niko excepted Block's endeavor as sincere expectations. There was a bit of himself in Block's eyes. His determination, ambition, and drive reminded him of how he was when he first got involved in the drug trade. In those days, Niko was hungry. And being the head of the household after his father departure, he was forced to provide and put food on the table for his family. The grind became his life day and night to fulfill his duties as a man. "Come, let's get dis show on da road." Niko smiled and patted Block on the back.

The two boxes of merchandise were loaded in Tree's trunk in a matter of minutes. Once the task was complete, Niko made a circling motion with his finger and the van sped off.

"Der is one thang I want u ta know," Niko informed before his own departure. "My boss is el senor de los cielos. Which means da lord of skies. Please don't violate our agreement. B'cuz I would hate ta have to send u ta da skies." Niko paid close attention to Block's face. Block's smile quickly diminished into a blank stare. "Don't let your emotions get da best of u. Dis is only bizness. An' if u hold your end up, I'll stand loyal ta mine." With his words lingering in Block's mind, off in the wind Niko went.

Block took heed to Niko's warning and hopped back in the truck. Block was uncertain how to feel. But he was certainly sure Niko would protect his investments at all cost. Block would do the same to secure his loot. With an understanding, Block reclined and enjoyed the ride...

***

Kayla was the first student out of her class. She collided with another girl in the hall, the impact almost sent her textbooks spilling on the floor.

"I'm so sorry," The other girl apologized.

"It's ok," Kayla assured over her shoulder while continuing through the hall at an amble pace. She was limited for time. She couldn't afford tardiness, only promptness was required for her next class. The quail of dealing with the dean threaten to snatch her tuition was too much to bear. Picking up her pace, she made it to class on schedule, and seated herself in the front. While the class filled to its full capacity, Kayla awaited the professor's boring lecture that was similar to a church sermon. Staring off in space, Kayla's mind began to wander back upon her and Block's last date. He had showed her a wonderful time. Block had given her a break from the routine she was accustom to and taken her on a jubilant adventure. It was nice for a change, to remove her head from the books and live for a moment.

Block had been running rapidly through her mind all night. His charm was distracting her from her priority functions, distorting her focus with visions of him. Everything about Block was compelling, and she knew she couldn't continue rebuffing his advances for long. Forbidden fruits were the sweetest, and his temptation was getting stronger and stronger. Putting her face in her hands, she tried her hardest to dismiss Block from her thoughts and focus on her schooling...

CHAPTER SEVEN

"Were in da monies," Tree joked, singing the old theme simultaneously rubbing his hands together. Tree, Pimp, and Block had been held up in the kitchen for days cooking, cutting, and wrapping pigeons.

"Be eazy, dis just da stepping stone. We still have to orchestrate a foundation by laying da groundwork," Block warned. "Dis da beginning but be ready tonight. Dis da take over. Tonight, we ride an' take dat nigga Ball bitch ass down. Make show all dis shit good, I'ma bout ta go rap wit Dice."

"Let me put something on your brain." Pimp placed his Newport filter in the ashtray. "We just hit a gold mine wit all dis work, an' we back tracking on some Robbin Hood fairy tales? Wat's really good? U just got on our case a few days ago bout making immature muv's. Well my nigga, dis muv equivalent."

"My ninja, u epitomizin horribly. Thank outside da box, there's a bigger picture den wat'cha closed eyes seeing." Block was right, Pimp was focusing on only what he could see, not what was on the other side of the door. "Dis move here bout expansion. I know u don't think buddy gone just lay down an' let da customers become da provider's wit out tryna shack us down. Look how ole boyz be acting now, he be on plain bully shit." There wasn't a chance in hell to move forward without moving the bolder from out front of their path. G-Ball wasn't the ordinary street chemist. He wanted things his way, if it wasn't his way, it was the highway. It was no doubt Ball would try to take them out, claiming they was on some communist counter revolutionary tactic nonsense. "Its best ta eliminate da threat, before it becomes a problematic issue. Plus, we need da territory. We get rid of e'm, den we can move in on da open land. It's fair game."

"I'm wit dat," Tree added his two cents. "I'm tired of homeboy anyways. It's bout, time we dump his hoe ass down." Tree lived for the thrill to kill. His trigger finger was always itchy for the opportunity to body somebody. Block had to keep him on a short leash, otherwise he would run wild like Billy the Kid, killing everybody. "We should've been laid dude bitch ass down long time ago."

There was no argument to that, Tree was right. Long time ago he should've dropped Ball's weak ass like a bad habit. Only reason G-Ball still was breathing was because he was the only provider Block had on the dope tip. Although Block had to jump hurdles to get the white, he didn't complain; because above all money was the motive. But now, there was no excuse. They had a direct connect and Ball's time had expired.

"Look I'm bout ta go rock wit Dice an', see if I can start flooding him an' his team. I'll be back dis way bout an hour." Block rose from the table. "Make show y'all ninjas don't put no extra cuts on dat shit." They'd already been getting an extra one and a half keys off one brick of pure powder. That gave them a 30-key profit for themselves. So, there was no need for avarice. "Hit my line when dis shit ready for distribution," he requested showing his boyz love before bouncing.

"I'm glad dat bitch Trish ain't round wit her beggin ass," Pimp said after Block's departure. "Where she at anyways," he inquired.

"I don't know. Fuck u asking me for? I ain't her man," Tree replied nervously. He felt some type of way regarding the queries. It made him feel as if Pimp was secretly implying something. Knowing in his heart no one knew he was dope dating Trish, his guilt still played on his mind, and it was getting the best of him.

"Dam nigga, get'cha panties out a bunch."

"Fuck u nigga." Tree barked sticking his middle finger up. "Weak ass nigga, I'ma G, an' I don't wear no mutha fucking panties."

"Den act like it," Pimp countered. "I just asked cuz we don't need da bug eye bitch snooping round tryna hit us up. I'm tryna get rich an' u jumping down my throat..."

***

Block had just hit the main ave on his way to Dice's spot in his hooptie when his cellphone rang "Keeping It Gangsta" by Geto Boyz. Block squinted at the display to see who was calling before answering.

"Who dis?" he stressed. The screen read blocked. Someone had hit his line star 67 on some old James Bond shit.

"Wuz good my nigga?" Six asked. "I see yo ass still ain't changed a bit." Six knew Block hated it with a passion when people disguised their number. Normally he wouldn't entertain the caller by answering, he would've ignored the call. "Wuz happening fool, u still der?" he inquired after the receiving a pregnant pause.

"Yea, wuz hood my ninja?" Block eased up recognizing the familiar voice. He hadn't heard from his hitter in about a week. Circumstances had forced him to assume his boy was going through one of his moments or in segregation for touching a nigga up. Normally that was the case when Six didn't hit the trap phone. Why u calling three way? It's coins on da phone. Matter fact, I just juiced up da line a couple days ago."

"Nigga I ain't calling u on no three way, I'm calling straight thru." Six had been out the joint for about a week and he had kept it under way and didn't let anyone know. There were things he had to get in order before he could enlighten the team they had rolled out the red carpet for a boss.

"Wat'cha den knock one of dem broads an' got'cha self a phone," Block asked. He was confused, cause Six had never before hit his line on three way, now all the sudden he was calling straight through. Therefore, there was only one factor to assume; and that was his boy came up on a little breezy. "If so, tell shawty ta pull up an' holla at'cha boy. I gotta nice package fo ya."

"I appreciate dat, but no thanks," Six declined. "I'm out here wit'cha on da bricks running like a mad man again."

"Quit yankin my chains dawg. I ain't gawt time ta waste." Block hit the brakes at the red light. "I'm out here tryna make away so when u touchdown u got it made. So, my dude, respect da game an' stop playing games. U know dis shit bout dat money we makin."

"Nigga look in da mirror," Six informed.

Block adjusted his rearview mirror and took a glance. He couldn't believe his eyes. Behind him in a forest green Chrysler 300 drove by a Scarlett Johansson look alike. There in the passenger seat sat his guy since knee high. Block hit the gas and his car leaped forward. Nearly causing a collision as he sped through the red light. Other drivers honked their horns. Block ignored the honks and pulled over at curb once through the intersection and hopped out. The 300 parked in front of him. Six jumped out fresh to death in Gucci from head to toe. They locked racks a brief moment. It had been quite a long time since Block had seen his homies.

"Dam dawg, its been a minute. I can't believe my eyes." Block gave Six a once look over. This had to be a blessing from above. The streets hadn't been the same since Six got knocked. Six had been truly missed. Now here he was in the flesh right where he was supposed to be; back on the bricks where anything goes. "When u get out dat hell hole?" Block asked.

"Bout a week ago. Da courts over turnt my shit."

"Why da fuck u didn't hit me up sooner?" Block couldn't believe Six had kept him in the dark about his release. "U know I would've swooped u up wit a bad bitch in da ride."

"I know, but let's not cry bout spilled milk," Six enlightened.

He was aware Block would have done just that. Him and Block went back like four flats in a Cadillac. Time and time again Block had shown and proved his loyalty. Six and Block had started kicking it real tough in middle school, their eighth-grade year. Six had brought a bag of rego and asked Block to match. From that moment, a bond was established. One day Block took Six over one of the other homies crib off his deck. Six was from the other side of town-across the bridge south side bound, while Block was north side until he D.I.E. Block had introduced Six to the old heads, and they had sat around smoking, laughing, and drinking tequila. Everything was good until this dime breezy walked into the apartment. Six was unaware she belonged to another, so he let his raging hormones control him and he shot his shot in the wrong direction, which almost got him into a heap of trouble. Block's big homies Twain felt disrespected that Six had the audacity to spit at his ole lady right in his face. Twain poked his chest out, and his boyz followed suit planning to party pack Six. But Block intervened, warning Twain and his wolfpack off. Block had mad respect for them, but he wouldn't allow them to jump on his right hand. From that moment, there was no reason for Block to prove his loyalty. His actions had spoken for themselves, and Six knew where Block's honor laid.

"I just had ta get somethings straight on my end," Six informed. "Plus, lil ma got'cha boy. She been going hard wit me since da beginning. Shawty a rider." Six tilted his head toward the vehicle he'd just gotten out of.

"I feel ya," Block acknowledged. "Look, why don't'cha come ride wit'cha boy? I got some bizness ta attend to, an' I wanna put'cha up on how things out here is now."

"Alright, hold on a sec," He pardoned Block then leaned over in the car window. "Snow, I'ma bout go take a ride wit my manes, so I'ma have to get up wit'cha later."

"Hold on," she asked while getting out the car and running around to Six.

Block stood mesmerized in the process. His eyes almost popped out of his head watching this fine dime dressed down in a Gucci dress and matching heels. The dress contoured to her ass that set up like Serena Williams, with a slim hourglass waist.

"U be careful babe, alright," she said standing on her tippy toes to kiss Six. "U watch after him." She placed Six's care in Block hands.

Block smiled his Denzel Washington academy winning smile. "Don't worry, ya boy in good hands."

"See u later." Six smacked Heather on her phat ass making her giggle.

"Alright, watch out now. Don't start nothing u can't finish," she warned, swatting his hand away and sashaying back around to the driver seat.

"U know I'ma claim dat title later," Six stated.

"We'll see. Keep your eyes open out here," she smiled, blowing him a kiss before getting back in her respective vehicle and pulling off.

"Dam ware u catch Coco at?" Block asked as they hopped in the ride. "Shawty bad."

"All dat an' some," Six agreed. "I caught her thru my celly back up north. She his lady best friend." Nut had put Six in the car one afternoon after he'd just gotten off the phone collect with his own lady. She confined in Nut that her friend was tired of the many lame ass dudes she was encountering on the outside. She needed a real man in her life that knew how to treat a woman. Nut being the real nigga he was, he plugged Six in. "She one hundo too, an' she fuck wit'cha boy da long way."

"Dat's wat's up. I like ta hear shit like dat, it really warms my heart," Block joked, cuffing his right hand over his left chest. They both laughed. Block was always ridiculing Six for his sentimental side. It was all for kicks and laughs. Block knew it was a wonderful thing when two people joined together and could love each other beyond their faults. "I know u ain't seen Dice in a lil while. But I'm bout ta go holla at e'm, so u'll be able ta catch up. Pimp an' Tree back at da spot makin it happen. U know how dat go."

"Already."

Block pulled up behind Dice's candy painted T-top firebird sitting high on 28-inch chrome D'Vinchi's. The car resembled a match box Hot Wheel. Hitting speed dial on his Samsung, Dice picked up on the first ring.

"Back door," he informed then hung up.

"Come on. Let's slide up in dis piece." Block got out and slammed the car door behind him, then activated the alarm. Although there was no need to secure the death trap. The whip was a hooptie that got him from point A to B. It was only force of habit for him to hit the alarm. "A lot den change since u been gone. Allah gotta work in mysterious wayz, cuz u was released by da grace of god." Block became religious momentarily. Usually, he based life occurrences proved on scientific bases only. But in this particular case, there was no other logical explanation for the release of Six. So, he gave praise to the most gracious and high. "U right on time too. Ya boy just copped a plug an' I'm knee deep in dat white."

"U serious aint'cha?" Six asked.

"When have I ever played wit'cha bout some real shit?" Block was serious as a heart attack. He never played about money. There were many things in life he found humorous, but cash ruled everything around him and that was no joking matter. "Dis shit real. We got dat cake better fa da phat boys. I'm just orchestrating properly ta get dis shit ta all da real niggaz."

"I know a couple mutha fuckaz," Six offered. Being in prison had provided him the opportunity to mingle with other go getters. Some of those contacts were now out on the streets. "Ya know yo boy alwayz got something up his sleeve." That was factual. Ever since Block could remember, Six always had his way in the game. He was fit for the streets. He knew how to manipulate any situation because he'd mastered the art of socializing. Therefore, he was amiable, and cherished by most hustlers and robbers.

"Fa'sho, keep dat under your hat. We gone utilize dat when da time is right. But right now, I'ma bout ta see ware Dice head at"...

***

Chop laid reclined back on the headboard with his head propped upon several pillows in nothing but his boxer briefs. He was being entertained as Shay stood over him in the nude dancing very provocative. Shay had become Chop's personal sex slave, hence to the agreement that he kept her dirty little secret from getting out. It was some price to pay, but well worth it on Chop's end. Sad, she had sold her soul to the devil in return to be a servant. She was dumb, at least that's how she felt. She felt degraded, the lowest of the low, like scum.

"Open it up," Chop demanded. "Let a G see wat gifts up in dat cookie box." Chop treated her like an object instead of a human being. He forced her to do degraded acts like open her pussy and spread her ass cheeks for his own sexual gratifications. "Yea, just like dat. I like it when u do nasty thangz dat'cha mutha could never imagine not even in her wildest dreams."

Chop had a perverted mind. He thrived off dominating women, making them submissive to entertain him with no back talk made him feel invisible. He could do away with the lip. The way he saw it, bitches had one job, and that was to put his meat log where their teeth parted. Mouth and lip service were what he required. "Shut up bitch and do what you are told" was his model. "I need you to do something fa me." Shay immediately dropped to her knees. "Naw, not dat," he objected, grabbing Shay by her shoulders. "Not right now, I need u ta do something else. Something mo sophisticated."

Shay froze, she was confused. Normally, when he wanted something, it involved her down on her knees polishing his knob.

"Wat do u want?" she asked, resuming her dancing routine in the center of the soft mattress.

"Dude u blessed wit dat flity lil mouth in da V.I.P. section, I need u ta have a talk wit em."

"Bout wat? Wat could u possibly want wit him?" Shocked by Chop's request, she turned in the opposite direction and rolled her hips and posterior seductively to Chris Brown's single called "Wet." "If its for wat I think, he would never go fa dat. He don't fuck wit new cats. He prefers ta keep his circle small like gulf balls." Shay was right, Dice didn't operate on that level. His team was all he needed. He'd learnt long ago, that new niggas were bad for business. Usually, when a new person placed himself into what had already been started, it always went downhill from there. Because either that person was the boys in blue or was on some shyster, sneaky, snake shit to set niggaz up. Dice wasn't born yesterday, and therefore, niggaz in the game wasn't to be trusted.

"Dat's fine, cuz dat's on u," Chop said. Shay had a job to accomplish and it involved whatever Chop employed her too. "I need'cha ta tell ole boy Bando responsible fa dat attempt hit an' ware ta find em at."

"Wat?" Shay asked shocked. His question had stunned her to no avail, leaving her mouth ajar. "I can't, I mean I won't do it. U must be crazy. Bando would kill me if he found out I plotted in gettin em whacked. Hell, Dice might just kill me for laying dat kind of info on his brain."

"First an' foremost, u don't tell me wat u not gonna do. Wat I say goes an' dat's final," Chop checked Shay. He didn't know where Shay got off thinking she had any authority to call shots. She wasn't at liberty to decline his orders. "I might kill your stupid ass if u ever fix ur mouth ta tell me wat u not gonna do." Chop snatched Shay legs from beneath her, and she tumble to the bed. Chop climbed above her, and before she knew it, his hands was around her neck. As his grip tighten around her neck, she felt her breath slipping from her body. "Do I make myself clear."

Tears wailed up in her eyes and streamed down her face. Petrified, Shay quickly nodded her head in agreement. She feared what might happen to her if she didn't do what was recommended of her.

"Good." Chop breathed into her ear and released his death grip from her neck. "Now save dat moisture fa dis dick." Chop laid back against the pillows. "Dis wat'cha should be choking on." He slipped his dick out his boxers, and Shay crawled in position. Tears still clouded Shay eyes as she took him into her mouth...

***

Meanwhile, Trish was bent over the kitchen table with her face smothered in piles of Ziploc bags while Tree hammered at her from behind. Half of the crack supply was on the floor as a result of the tremendous fuck.

She hadn't been in the house but twenty minutes, and she was already taking a pounding to get high. Pimp had received a call and left when she arrived. Pimp didn't really care for her, and she knew, but didn't care. The only thing she cared about was getting high at any means necessary.

"Oooooooh shit, hit dat pussy!" she shouted over her shoulders. Tree loved dirty talk, so she gave it to him. She wasn't in it for her own pleasure, she only wanted a fix. They both were getting what they wanted, so the way she saw it, fair exchange ain't no robbery. "Dat's right, fuck dat pussy ta it's sore." Her language was filthy just the way Tree expected. The filthier the better. "Oooooooh go, dis pussy yours, make it cum, make it squirt babe."

That was it, Trish's last words sent Tree over the edge. He grabbed harshly at the nap of her neck as he shoved himself to the halt and let loose inside her walls.

"Dam bitch, u got dat fiya," Tree grunted, filling her with his spewed seed. When done, Tree pulled up his jeans. "Here take dis, an' get up out of here. I got work, ta dew." He gave Trish a hooper and sent her on her way...

***

"So wuz good wit'cha an' lover boy?" Connie asked, prying into Kayla business. Curiosity had gotten the best of her, and she was dying to know how her friend and Block were getting along.

"I don't know," Kayla honestly replied. She really didn't know. She was conflicted between mind, body, and spirit. Although she had strong feelings for Block, she was fighting her hardest not to give in to his temptation. She wanted to be with Block, but she didn't trust her feelings. "He hasn't called me since da nite he took me out."

"Are u blushing?" Connie asked. Kayla's brown cheeks were a tad bit rosy.

"Nooooo..." Kayla answered nervously, placing her hands over her face to hide her embarrassment. "Why would I be blushing? There's nothing ta blush bout," Kayla lied through her front teeth. Kayla knew as well as Connie, Block had always made her feel all fuzzy inside like some teenage girl.

"Oh, I doubt dat last statement ta be true. U an' I know better den dat. Don't try ta deny how u feel inside, dat's where da realness is." Connie took her friend hand within her own. "U ain't gotta hide your true feelings from me. Ever since we were kids, Block always made dem panties of yours wet," Connie joked, making both of them share an infectious laugh. "Shit, dey probably drenched right now,"

Connie continued. "If u feel for him, call em. Ain't no shame in going fa wat'cha want gurl."

"Even if he ain't call me?" Kayla asked. She was reluctant to take Connie's advice. "Isn't dat a bit desperate? I thank I'll just wait ta he holla at me."

"See, dat's da problem as a black race. We always worried bout wat other people thank of us."

"Says da one gotta have all her clothes from high end stores," Kayla countered, changing the topic of conversation. "Gurl u worst den a socialite."

"I didn't say I was perfect." Connie felt the need to defend herself. The truth hurt, and Kayla was showing her a mirror. She always had to brand herself in the latest brands, as if clothes made her. The great Malcolm X once said, "if you wear other cultures names on your chest, you are a chump, and they're laughing at you." Like many young people, she hadn't yet come to terms with his notion. She was under the false impression that expensive fashion was the way to keep a baller. In her twisted mind a man wouldn't love her in rags. If she didn't dress to make him remember her, he surely would forget her. "We all have our vices, an' fashion is one of mine. But gurl, despite my faults, u know Block one if your's. He in your system like a virus in da blood stream."

Kayla smiled to herself and put her chin on Connie's shoulder. There was no use in faking the funk, Block had her heart. Hell, she couldn't even conjure the last time, if ever, that there was any other man she ever held precious in her heart besides Block. There was an effect Block had on her. Like the way her heart melted, or the butterfly flutter she got when he was near. The chills he gave her told her it was real, and that was something she couldn't deny.

"Alright, I'ma call him," Kayla agreed.

"Dat's my gurl!" Connie excitedly hugged Kayla. "Go get'cha man gurl. I know he would be happy ta hear your voice."

"U think?"

"I know," she enlightened. "Dat boy just ass head over hills for u as u are fa him."

Kayla felt at ease and was able to let her guard down after the understanding conversation she'd just shared with her best friend Connie. She was no longer trapped in between feeling what's wrong and right. If loving Block was wrong, then she didn't want to be right...

***

Hours later, G-Ball posted up in his main trap house. He was waiting to collect the weekly money once his workers got everything in order.

"Come on, get da ball on da roll so I can get up out here," G-Ball rushed Quan and Black along. "Bag dat cash up. Time is of da essence, an' I ain't got non ta waste."

"Here, dat's da rest," Black informed, stuffing the remainder of the dope money from the living room sofa in the book bag, then handing it to G-Ball. "Everything straight. Da trap been doing numbers like Count Dracula."

"Come on nigga, I'm to street fa Sesame Street," G-Ball shot down Black's bad analogy. "Dis street life to real we out here living. Leave da underage reference fa da babies. Dat shit ain't real nigga. Feel me?"

"Early," Black replied with a one-word reference that said already.

"Alright den, let's burn rubber. Let's get dis bread ta da safehouse." Ball grabbed the bag and tossed the strap over his shoulder. "Quan hold down the trap ta Black get back. U thank u can do dat?"

"Its nothing me an' my rusty 9 can't handle. Y'all be easy out der," Quan confirmed while showing them love.

Outside, Ball jumped in a guerilla lifted burnt orange 69 Pontiac GTO sitting on 30-inch Forgis. In traffic Black trailed inconspicuous in a midnight blue Mitsubishi Outlander. Black was on security detail; he was the decoy car in case the police got behind him. Black would side swipe the squad car so Ball could get away. Moments later, they pulled up in front of the safehouse and Black followed Ball inside.

"I gotta hit da can my nig," Black announced as Ball headed to the safe to secure his wealth.

"Nigga u know ware da bathroom is... Upstairs ta da left," G-Ball pointed out.

Black had been knowing Ball forever, and he was the only man Ball trusted enough to have information to where his safehouse was. Up in the bathroom, Black was draining his bladder when a loud crash came from the front of the house. Black jumped frantically, zipping up his pants, why reaching for his cannon.

"Get'cha bitch ass on da flow," Block ordered, jamming his pistol in Ball's back. "Looks like we hit da jackpot," he said, gazing at the bundles of money stacked neatly in the safe. "Bet'cha den thank I'd be da one shacking yo clown ass down, did'cha fuck boy?"

"U a dead man," Ball threatened.

"I hear ya, but I don't feel ya," Block smacked Ball over the head with the Mac. "Now shut da fuck up an' tell me ware da rest of da shit at, before I dead'n ur bitch ass." Blood poured down Ball's face from the open gash Block had created over his left temple. "Let's get dis doe. Put dat shit in da bag," he ordered his boyz.

Pimp stuffed the crispy bills back into the Nike bag next to the safe. Tree on the other hand went off to search the house for drugs, guns, and money. Downstairs was useless in regard to the particular, so Tree headed upstairs. Upstairs he stopped at a suspiciously closed door. He twisted the knob, but the door didn't budge. Jiggling the doorknob, a fusillade of bullets ripped through the door frame hitting his cavalier vest. The impact knocked him to the floor. On his back, Tree aimed his AK-47, and fired a burst of rounds threw the door. They crashed through the door like a tank to a brick wall. *Bop, bop, bop, bop, bop, bop.* The 7.62 basically tore the door off the hedges, leaving a ridged shattered hole in the center.

"Go check dat shit out!" Block commanded Pimp when he heard the exchange of gunfire erupt.

Pimp rushed up the stairs to discover Tree laid out clutching at his chest and stomach area. His chopper was still smoking at his side.

"U alright?" Pimp, concerned, rushed to Tree in aid and assistance.

"Yea, check da bathroom G," Tree pointed at the riddled door.

Pimp kicked in the door. Black was stretched out with numerous gaping bullet wounds. He was still alive gasping hard for breath through his lungs. Pimp kicked his 45 away from his grip, then let his Mac finish him off.

"Here's a breath of fresh air." Pimp sent ten hot shells through Black's chest, killing him instantly. "Come on my dude, we gotta get up out of here," he said, helping Tree to his feet. "U sure u good?"

"Yea I'm straight. Just a lil pain, but I'll live."

Pimp and Tree headed back downstairs. Block was still looming over Ball with his heat pressed against his temple.

"Fuck u nigga, I ain't got shit for u," Ball spat, keeping up his tough guy act. He was persistent in turgid even in the face of death. "I'ma see your Bitch ass again, an' I'ma get at'cha small time ass."

"Nawt ware u going," Block laughed and pulled the trigger letting his Mac hiccup in Ball's face. The bullets splashed his brain matter all over the safe and bedroom curtains. "Come on let's be out." Block grabbed the book bag and off they went...

CHAPTER EIGHT

"Come on gurl, u still ain't ready in der?" Connie impatiently shouted outside Kayla's bedroom door. "I'm tryna get up in der an' snatch me up one of dem ballers before dem other bitches get em all. Now hurry up so we can go." Connie had convinced Kayla on a girl's night on the town. Kayla wasn't big on clubs, but to shut Connie up, she had reluctantly agreed.

"Get'cha panties out a bunch, I'm ready." Kayla opened the door dressed down in Dior. Her feet fitted in matching red bottoms, and the fragrance of "Jador" by Dior made her smell fantastically delectable. "Dont'cha already got'cha self a baller? Now u just being insatiable." "Gurl please," Connie replied insouciant. "U can never have too many. Da more da better."

Kayla shook her head at her friend's sumptuous greed. Connie was unbelievable sometimes. Her whorish nature always overrode her reasonable decision making. It was if she was never satisfied with what she had. The more the merrier was her motto.

"I don't know why u shacking ya head. Ain't no shame in my game," Connie asserted. No one could argue with that. She was a gold digger; gold digging was enough to store treasures in her heart. She wanted the finer things in life. It was money that made her cum, dick wasn't pleasurable without a M to back it up.

"U playing wit fiya," Kayla warned. "U know if Dice catch your ass, u grass. He most definitely gone put a foot up your ass gurl. U better stop playing."

"Please spare me," Connie cynically blew off her friend's worries. "All I gotta do is put dis ass on him." She turned putting her derrière on display. "Dis dat get right gurl. Just give em a dose of dis, an' he'll be alright," she added, twerking her ass.

"U such a slut," Kayla cackled at her friend's incorrigible ways. Connie lacked inhibition; it was outrageous. It made Kayla wonder why Connie wore Christian; Connie was far from holy; the devil had his claws wrapped around her soul. "Come on wit'cha slutty ass, let's go," Kayla said, grabbing her purse.

When they arrived at the club, it was packed. So packed, Connie couldn't manually park her 2018 F-Type Jaguar, so she activated her auto park to squeeze into the tight spot between a Navigator and Beamer.

"Gurl look at all des ballers out here," Connie squealed. "Look at dis crowd," she beamed proudly like a kid in a candy store. "Here, take my keys," she offered, tossing them to Kayla as she took in the scenery. "I know I'm going home wit somebody tonight. Since u gone need a way home, feel free ta drive yourself home."

Kayla detested when her friend sold herself to the highest bidder. She was like an episode of The Price is Right. Her pussy was an ATM machine, where dick went in, money came out. Kayla was surprised that as much as Connie screwed around, she hadn't contracted any STD's, or worst, the HIV virus.

Kayla wasn't really up for waiting in long compact lines. She would rather be home studying for her finals, but that was out of the question. Her options of priority diminished the moment she decided to go out with Connie. Now she was a dependent. Kayla had to check herself, normally she wasn't a demimonde; after all, she was with the whore of the century. She wouldn't be surprised if Connie knew the bouncer.

"Come on gurl, we ain't finna be standing out here with these low life's. I know da bouncer." Connie's assurance didn't shock Kayla one bit. She just smiled as they strolled passed the waiting bystanders...

***

Bottles of Dom Perignon, Rose, Louis XIII, you name it, was there in the VIP section. Block and his team were living like there was no tomorrow up in VIP. Everything was benevolent on their end, and skies were the limit. They were up and living the American dream. Finally, they had gotten a piece of the pie, and were moving on up to the East side like the Jefferson's. The clique's last lit had put them in a high rise. They had come up on seven figure-$300,000. It was like the old saying, taking candy from a baby. Three-hundred thousand divided four ways between Pimp, Tree, Six, and Block was a nice slice of the pie. They all had $75,000. Block would have it no other way, he ate with the team he came with. Round table or not, real niggas brake bread.

"S'up?" Block asked. He and Six were sitting in VIP, and Block was sipping on a bottle of Dom Perignon and smoking a blunt of Kesha. A haze of smoke surrounded them. "Ur pockets lined wit doe, an' u just touchdown. But der still a hundit yard dash ta da big lead," he calmly spoke taking a swig from the bottle. "I don't want ta push u into something u feel ain't for u. Even if u chose not ta rock wit da team, u still my NFL." NFL was an acronym for niggaz for life, but in Block's case, ninja for life. He had a problem with identifying one another in a derogatory term such as nigga. In his opinion, the word should be extirpated from the whole world's dialogue. A man could get no respect if he didn't respect himself. In order to change the world, it had to start in his best interest to choose better dialect. "We tackle foes, fumble hoes, an' touchdown money like da pro's. So, wat's it gone be now dat u back on da bricks."

"Look u ain't gotta run no spill on me," Six informed Block. In all honesty, he was feeling a bit insulted that Block tried to convince him with something that was in him, not on him. "I'm still down. Just cause I had a bit of down time, don't mean I ain't still rocking wit da team. I'm still in ten toes. I'ma thug an' I wouldn't change dat fa da world" Six was hoping his boy understood things. No prison could run him from the life he was accustomed to. He bled, slept, and ate the streets. It was in his veins; a street nigga by heart was how you could describe him. As long as oxygen was in his lungs, in the streets was where he would be. He was a rolling stone.

Block observed the club's surroundings, it was an electrifying atmosphere. Ballers were everywhere, and some of the finest top-notch females from Milwaukee graced the scene.

"Plus, I had a chance ta rap wit dem people I had lined up," Six enlightened. "An' dey said dey a take a fever ta start wit. If everything straight, dey'll take ten every week after dat." Block tried passing Six the gas, but he declined. "Nah!, I'm straight. I can't get hit wit dat shit in my piss. U know I gotta go see my P.O." Six was still on papers from his prior offence, a reckless endangerment he'd caught several years back, and he wasn't going to take the risk going back to prison for a measly dirty U.A.

"Thousand pardon. I completely forgot about your situation," Block apologized. To be aware was to be alive, but he was dead, because he'd lost consciousness of his homie's circumstances. Here it was, Six was on probation, and he had offered him something that which would most definitely effect his freedom. Like Jaime Fox, he did what came naturally and blamed it on the alcohol. "Dis liquor got me buzzed. Dat's my fault."

"Don't lean on it. Its water under da bridge," Six swept Block's mistake under the rug. There were more important things to focus on, so there was no need to focus on something so small. Mistakes were a part of life; you live, and you learn. "Let's enjoy dis nite. We can talk bizness another time; right now, let's party an' do what our boyz out der doin'," Six suggested.

Pimp and Tree were out on the floor getting their mack on. Tree was on the dance floor with some freak getting his grove on. The scene they were creating was like a scene straight out the Basic Instinct movie. To the naked eye, it appeared their PDA had turned to full fledge fucking.

Pimp on the other hand had a more mellow approach. He was rapping with some fine ass yellow bone with large breast and a fat ass by the bar. The nubile appeared to be engaged in his conversation. She was laughing and rubbing her hand down his arm ever so often.

Block was on the verge to reject Six's proposal. In his book, it was business before pleasure. But he almost ate his unspoken words when he saw Kayla standing across the room looking beautiful as ever.

"U right. I'ma get at'cha later," Block agreed. He rose from his seat and headed toward Kayla. Her vision was magnetic. Block felt as if he was floating instead of walking. There she stood in the presence of her friend Connie in deep conversation. She looked like a beautiful nymph associated with aspects of nature. An element of a mixture of earth, wind, and fire described her best. "Ur so beautiful, an' if dis world was mine you'll take my hand an' we'll fly away," Block whispered in Kayla's ear, creeping up from behind. A smile creased her lips, but she didn't turn around. She knew that smooth deep voice from anywhere.

"Where would we go?" Kayla played along. Connie said nothing, she just stood there smiling and giving Kayla a knowing look. What Block couldn't see was Kayla melting at his touch. The mixture of Block's captivating presence, intoxicating Cologne, and baritone voice had a major effect on her.

"Skies da limit," Block answered. "But right now, I just wanna get lost in your eyes an' take u ta da moon."

"Ur game is tight," Kayla complimented, facing Block and smiling ear to ear.

"Sho u right."

"Dat's my Q, y'all gettin a lil ta lovey dovey for me," Connie interrupted. "U got my keys just in case. See u later." Connie hugged her friend and headed through the crowd.

"I see u an' Connie still rocking tuff," Block inquired when Connie was out of earshot.

"Yea we still thick as thieves, dat's my gurl," Kayla assured. Her and Connie had no animosity between them. They'd let bygones be bygones. "I didn't expect to see you tonight."

"Same here."

"Let me find out U stalking me," Kayla joked playfully pushing Block by the shoulder.

"By da way, your furniture look good from da window." They both shared a mutual laugh.

"Eew," she replied. "U a predator."

"Only ta those worth praying on." Block stepped closer to Kayla. "I wouldn't mind makin u my prey wit'cha yo fine ass."

Kayla was turned on by Block's approach. Not so much by his words, though she enjoyed his humor, it was more his presence that got her. Giving in to temptation, Kayla initiated the first move and kissed Block. Block reciprocated. Kayla dropped her arms around Block's shoulder and the other around the back of his neck. Block and Kayla blocked out the rest of world as they became lost in one another.

"Wow," Kayla exclaimed as they broke the kiss. "Dat brings back memories." She was taking down memory lane by the kiss. It had Kayla feeling nostalgic. She was finally able to give her body what she'd been missing. It had been desperately yearning for TLC.

"I hope dey good memories," Block teased.

They were having an excellent time enjoying each other company, until a Moe Wet bottle crashed over Block's left temple. The trajectory of the force caused the bottle to scatter and shards went everywhere.

"Nigga u got me twisted!" Wanda shouted. "Ova here lolli gaggin an' tonguing dis trick bitch down."

Block staggered from the impact of the blow and dabbed at his forehead with his left hand. Seeing his fingers covered in blood, he automatically reacted. Becoming enraged, it was like a bull being fomented by a matador dangling a red flag in his face. Without second thought, Block charged Wanda. Wanda tumble through a crowd of people onto the floor.

"U punk ass bitch," Block growled, pulling Wanda up by her weave tracks. "I'ma kill your stupid ass." Block had lost all focus and went into a state of blind rage. There was no knowledge to his actions as he rained a combination of wallop blows upon Wanda. He wailed her to she was near unconsciousness. Her cries and pleas fell to the death ear. He didn't care, he was trying to separate her body from her spirit.

"Please stop," Wanda begged for her life. "Ur gonna kill da baby, stop!"

The surprise news didn't disarm Block. It wasn't until two bouncers forced their way through the crowd and restrained him.

"Let me da fuck go!" Block screamed. During their entire fiasco, Kayla stood by not moving a muscle. She was paralyzed by fear. The course of actions Block took petrified her. "If u bitches ain't gotta death wish, I suggest u let me da fuck go!" Block continued the rant as the security extracted him.

"I suggest u take heed to what he saying before I blast your ass thru tomorrow thru da sun," Tree threatened, leveling his Glock 40 with a 30-shot extension at two security guards' chests.

"Man, we don't want no beef," the two guards mumbled in unison releasing Block from their grip. "We don't want no smoke. We just tryna do our jobs." Their eyes locked in fear on the end of the muzzle pointed right at them.

"I'ma give y'all ta da count of ten ta get da fuck out of my sight. Den I'ma get ta squeezin at'cha," Tree slurred inebriated. The Hennessey was taking effect. "One, two..." Skipping three, Tree squeezed a hot one into one of the bouncer's shoulder. He hit the floor clutching at his arm. Hurt and in a state of panic, he got up and scurried after his partner that didn't wait around to see if his partner was alright. He made himself scarce, running with the rest of the crowd whom stampeded out the jam-packed club as soon as the gunfire erupted.

"Ninja is u crazy?" Block chastised, coming back to his senses. "Come on, we gotta rise up out here before dem boys in blue show up." Block looked around and Kayla was still frozen in the same spot he'd left her demonstrating the fight, flight, or freeze response. "Come on, let's be out." He grabbed Kayla's arm and dragged her along. She didn't resist, she went along for the ride. "Fool u nuts. Dont'cha know mutha fuckaz be recording shit like dis on der cellphones? Or u didn't, take da time ta use your head."

"Man fuck dem bitch ass niggaz. U should be thanking me. Dem punk ass mutha fuckaz had'cha all hemmed up an' shit," Tree nonchalantly replied as they fled out the night club. "Dem bitch ass niggaz lucky I didn't send dey ass ta da sky."

"Fuck dat shit," Block dismissed Tree's irrational comment.

"Man, where da fuck y'all been?" Pimp asked, approaching them in the dark.

"Naw nigga, da question is where da fuck u been?" Tree countered. "When dat beef popped off, where da fuck was u somewhere cowering?" Normally Tree wasn't so cruel and verbally harsh to his crew, but the mixture of alcohol and weed had him feeling like it was him against the world.

"Fuck dat shit," Block conveyed once again, intervening into their near spat. Sirens began to wail in the distance. "We ain't got time fa dat shit. We gotta get da fuck up out of here."

"U can ride wit me," Kayla spoke up. She remembered she had her friend Connie's car keys as the series of cop sirens drew near. "Come on," she urged Block to follow.

"Look I'ma bout ta bounce wit shawty, I'ma get at'cha ninjaz later." While Block showed his boyz love, Kayla took off toward the whip. "Y'all ninjaz be safe. Hit me soon as y'all get ta your destination." Kayla heels clicked on the ground as she disappeared into the night. The clicking became fainter the farther she got away.

"Bring your ass on!" she shouted through the steal of the night. She couldn't fathom why she cared. This wasn't her problem; Block and his entourage had gotten themselves into this mess. But she didn't want Block to go to jail either. There was no way she would allow the law to prosecute him. She was loyal to those close to her. "Are u coming or what?" she yelled out of frustration. She unlocked the SUV doors and hit push start. The engine came alive just as Block appeared out the dark. Inside the ride, Kayla put the medal to the peddle, and the car sped off into the night...

***

Kilo had went downhill. He hadn't hit rock bottom yet, but he was heading toward a slippery slope that would finalize disastrous if he didn't regain control of himself. The white girl had gotten a hold on him, and once that happen it was damn near impossible to get your life back into perspective. He'd been using quite heavily. Ever since Stevo's death, he'd been lost in the sauce. He couldn't remember how or why he allowed the deep funk he was in push him into the arms of drugs. He had embraced them with loving arms, and now he depended on a hit to pick him up. He didn't consider himself an addict. He told himself time and time again he could put down the horn at any time; he just needed a fix to get through the day, not realizing his logic was the sole definition of an addict. Daily he hit the whistle; geeking on the very substance that destroyed black neighborhoods every day.

Kilo got out of bed and made his way over to his stash. With no remorse to what he was doing, he broke a piece of the crack he was supposed to be selling for Bando and stuffed it into a glass pipe. Sitting on the edge of his bed with a pipe in one hand and a lighter in the other, he blazed up and took a deep blast to the face...

***

"Bentley, sit still," Kayla ordered. "I'm tryna do dis. If u keep moving, u gone have croaked stitches. So, sit still before u be looking like Frankenstein," she jested. Block was perched on the edge of the sofa, while Kayla performed her erudite skill on him.

"Dat's eazy fo u ta say," Block said through clenched teeth. "Sssssss," he hissed and groaned to accept the pain he was experiencing. "U ain't da one on da other end getting stitches with no anesthetics ta numb da pain. Sssssss, shit," Block moaned, then gritted his teeth to stifle the pain.

"Ah, man up an' take it like a G," Kayla taunted. "U shouldn't have been beating up on pregnant women."

"If u gone judge me, I'll leave," Block angrily retorted, knocking Kayla's hands away and rising to his feet. "I don't need another mutha. An' I don't have time fo dis holyer den you B.S. u kicking. Dat stupid ass judgmental shit getting on my dam nerves."

"Stop!" Kayla grabbed Block's arm to stop him from storming off. "I'm sorry," she apologized, pleading with her eyes for Block to sit back down. "U can't leave like dis. An' calm down, we don't need'cha blood pressure up right now. Your blood flow won't regulate an' I can't stitch u up right." Block's anger dissipated at the soothing tone of her voice. Regaining his reserved demeanor, he returned to the couch. "I'm sorry, but dat gurl said she was pregnant. U should check on her ta a least make sure your child is alright."

Kayla words registered in Block's mind. Hearing the news Wanda was pregnant didn't faze him. He hadn't even considered the possibility the child could be his. Pondering the notion made him feel guilty.

"Yea, well, how do I even know dat kid mine?" he replied, trying not to put on he felt bad inside. "U don't know ole gurl like I do. She a stripper dat den rolled in da haf wit a lil bit of everybody. So, don't be jumping down my throat bout some chick u don't know." He refused to accept responsibility for his actions and tried placing the blame elsewhere. Although he felt bad, his pride wouldn't let him admit his wrongdoing.

"Excuse me, but don't try to make me seem like da bad guy here. I'm not saying I know dat gurl, but I do know u been sleeping wit her." Kayla wasn't no dumb broad you could tell anything to. She knew damn well Block had been sleeping with Wanda. Although she didn't know her personally, she knew women. Anytime a woman reacted in the manner Wanda had, there was a personal misunderstanding that made Wanda feel Block belonged to her. It was possible Block was misleading her. Kayla wasn't mad; whatever Block did before her was his business. "All I'm saying, is if u want ta be wit me, u need ta keep your groupies in check, an' keep your hands-off women. Cause u damn sure ain't gone be going upside my head. U got me bent if u think dat's da case."

This was clearly a classic case of domestic violence that all started for the lack of self-control. Block knew he had to ease Kayla's mind, but that would be next to impossible if he didn't step up to the plate and take full responsibility for his part in the matter. He couldn't continue to put the full blame off on Wanda. What was worth having was worth fighting for. Kayla was most definitely worth fighting for.

When Kayla finished giving Block stitches, fourteen in total, there was a large proportionate incision at center of his temple. The thought of what nasty scar it would leave behind didn't quite sit well in his gut. It made him feel some type of way.

"I know from an outside perspective dis must look really bad on my record," Block tried consoling Kayla the best way he knew how. In the process, he took her by the hand and pulled her next to him, so he could look her in the eyes as he spoke. "I know u expect me ta be charming, romantic, an' tell u everything u want ta here right now. Although it would be true, it would be so unoriginal. An' lacking originality isn't a trait I possess." Block searched Kayla's eyes for compassion and sympathy, but all he received was a stare of concern. He couldn't blame her for being alarmed. After what she'd just witnessed, she should. He had beat a woman, something any respectable young man was taught never to put his hands on any woman. Now here he was tryna explain the situation away like the average abuser would after he'd just beat his wife. Only solid foundation Block had to stand on, was he'd never violently reacted like he had toward any woman. Putting his hands-on females wasn't his pedigree. "I want u ta trust me... Ahh, wat am I saying?" Block questioned himself bowing his head in the process. "I mean, I want ta be wit'cha. I want u ta be wit me, near me. Growing old an gray wit u is da plan, if dat makes any since?" He watched Kayla's eyes become tearful. "One nite during one of our late nite telephone discussion, u asked me wat I wanted out of life? Den I didn't know how ta give a straight answer, but now it's clear ta me, I want u. U are my future, my life, my inspiration, my everything."

Kayla could no longer hold back the water works. The tears came gushing out like Niagara Falls. For so long she'd waited for a man to tell her how much she meant to him, but she'd never thought Block would be that man. What she felt inside had to be love. The way her heart fluttered, and breath slowed when Bentley was close was indescribable. If this wasn't love, then she didn't know what else to call it.

"Don't cry." Block wiped her tears away. "I'm sorry I ruined your nite," he apologized.

Kayla sniffled back her tears and produced a smile. "It isn't ruined. We can still make dis a special nite ta remember," Kayla said pulling Block close and placing her lips upon his. This was a rudiment inception, but all perfect endings don't always start like in the movies. The thing about love, is that it never ends how you plan it; it was funny like that. Love is unpredictable. It causes the most logical minds to drown in rivers of emotions trying to grasp a rational notion to its meaning.

Their kissing session soon became heated. It was the preliminary to the inevitable. Like beasts in heat, they ripped one another clothes off. Block laid Kayla on her back and placed her legs on his shoulder as he went down to taste her forbidden treasures.

"Mmmmmm," Kayla moaned out loud. An electric surge ran through her as soon as Block's tongue touched her clitoris. It felt so delicious the way his flexible tongue danced around her pussy lips before his stiff tongue ventured inside her walls. "Ooooooh gawd!" she screamed out while wrenching from side to side. The pleasures he was giving was unbelievable. She could feel the pressures building within as she neared an orgasm.

Block fucked his tongue in and out of Kayla for a while, then allowed his tongue to venture lower than he ever had with any other lady, and licked Kayla asshole. "Ahhhh!" Escaped Kayla's lips instantly while his pleasurable tongue ran up and down her anus. "Ooooh gawd, dat feels soooooo good," she breathed grabbing the back of Block head.

Block captured her clit between his lips once more. He knew she was on the verge of coming. He was an expert at reading body language. She was grinding her pussy against his face. Kayla went over the edge, shoving his face further into her crotch. Block held on for dear life as she humped his face. She came powerful and tumult. Block was scared the neighbors would call the police. When her climax subsided, she tried pushing Block's head away, but he knocked her hands away. "Nah," he whispered and continued to munch away until she was coming again soaking his face with her fluids. When he rose, his face was covered in her release. Kayla kissed him passionately before reciprocating the favor.

"Ohh my, wat have I gotten myself into?" she exclaimed, surprised. Block's ten inches stood straight up like a torpedo ready for launching. To her appreciation, she admired it, and relished the length up and down with her tongue.

"Soon you'll see," Block replied, although there was no need to elaborate because the question was rhetorical. Kayla was grown, and she knew full well what it was she was getting herself into. "Actions speak louder den words," he moaned as she engulfed him fully in the warmth of her mouth.

"Mmmmm," she moaned while sucking lightly around his bulbous head.

Block was enjoying Kayla's neck game. He stared into the beautiful light brown eyes while she did her thang. She looked so amazing while slobbing him down and staring back at him. Every time her head plunged down, she made an effort to take more of him in her gobbling mouth.

"Dam gurl, it's like u tryna eat me alive," Block joked.

Kayla smiled, determined to bring him off in her mouth. Fitting his whole thing in her mouth, she applied a technique she'd learnt her first year in college. She gurgled around Block dick and sucked him down her esophagus. The sensation combined with the hot moist compression of her jaws pushed Block over the edge, and he shot his load in her awaiting mouth. The first two globs forcefully blasted down Kayla eager throat and she swallowed. Suddenly pulling away, she pumped his missile a few times and was rewarded with another blast to the face. It dropped down her nose back onto his dick head and Kayla swallowed him back down her throat and sucked him until he was drained.

Block remained hard and Kayla was in heat. She rubbed his leftover cum into her breast like sunscreen.

Block took control, and placed Kayla on her hands and knees. Placing his meat at her center, he rubbed his dick up and down her pussy lips to lubricate himself with the flowing juices that covered her hillocks. Kayla was wet enough to go deep sea diving. Block plunged into her; her walls contoured around him, sucking him into her dark hole.

"Hhhmmmm," Kayla threw her head back and hummed. Block sunk his entire member into her. "Gawd!" she spat panting wildly. "Fuck me!" She lost herself in the pleasures he was providing. Normally, she wouldn't talk so filthy, but the way he had her feeling, she was open to anything. She didn't know if it was the liquor or what. She had only had three shots of Ciroc. Whatever it was, she wanted to feel like this forever. Block was fucking her so good from behind, that she gripped and bit the sofa leather. He was hitting all the right spots. It was certain he knew how to work it. Piston in and out, to the left and right. His dick game was on point. Every stroke kept her clawing at the leather and screaming in pleasure.

Block grabbed Kayla around the waist to keep her from escaping his pounding. With no escape, Kayla bit down hard upon the leather. "Mmmmm... Ahhhhh..." she moaned and screamed at once. The workout Block was putting on her was too much, and an orgasm ripped through her. "Yessssss... Dat's it!" She ululated so loud her lungs hurt. "Dat's da spot."

As she came, her walls contracted around Block. Her moans, wetness, and trembles coincided together, and Block erupted coital. "Ahhhh shit!" he shouted out while filling her insides. When he emptied his load, Block collapsed onto the couch trying to catch his breath. Kayla licked his ears, neck, and chest moaning and purring from their extreme hard love making. Kissing her way down his tattoo covered abs, she engulfed him once again. Kayla was insatiable. A raging fire blazed between her legs that Block had started, and she needed him to put it out...

***

Wanda woke up to the sound of the doorbell chiming. Groggy, she lifted her head off the pillow and looked at her alarm clock on the nightstand. It was 5:42 in the morning. The chiming bell made her head ring. Wanda noticed smears of dried blood in her pillowcase as she rose from the bed. She hadn't bothered to clean herself up from the savage beating she'd taken. She was still fully dressed, and her dress stuck to her sweaty body. The doorbell sound again.

"I'm coming!" she sonorously hollered as best as she could. Her throat was sore, and she cringed and reached for her neck to subdue the pain as she stumbled to the door. Opening the door, her sister barged in uninvited.

"Look at u," Porsha angrily pointed out, throwing her purse to the floor. "I heard what happen ta u last nite at da club. Dat shit all over social media. I couldn't believe it until I saw your face. Look at u, your a mess."

Wanda rolled her eyes and closed the door behind her overly dramatic, obnoxious sister. Sometimes she couldn't stand her big sister. She turned small matters into scrutiny, and she was always sticking her nose in other people business. It had been that way since their younger days.

"Don't start," Wanda contorted as she flopped down on the loveseat. "I don't need ta hear your mouth right now."

"What?" Porsha asked, bewildered. "Do u hear yourself right now? U should be opening' your mouth right now an' calling da police. Dat nigga beat u like you was a man. Have u seen yourself in da mirror?"

"Ahhgghhhh!" Wanda frustratedly cried out. Porsha was really getting on her last nerve. "Have u lost your mind? I ain't going to call no punk ass cops. Bitch I don't speak pig Latin. After all, I deserve dat shit. I shouldn't have never done wat I did, it's my fault." Wanda took blame, not realizing she sounded like an abused victim of domestic violence. They always made up excuses for the other person's actions; but Wanda didn't see it that way. Wanda saw the truth of the scenario. To every action there's a reaction. And what had happened to her was a sane reaction to anyone whom had been slapped over the head with a liquor bottle.

"U must be fucking crazy," Porsha exclaimed. Porsha couldn't believe what her ears were hearing. She didn't even have a consensus for ignorance. Some say ignorance is just a case of inexperience; but in her sister case, it was just bliss. Anger raging, Porsha snatched Wanda by her arm off the loveseat and dragged her to the bathroom.

"Let me go!" Wanda struggled to pull her arm away from her sister strong grip along the way.

"Look." Porsha pushed Wanda in front of the bathroom mirror. "Look at u. U still saying dis shit your fault. No dude never has da right ta put der hands-on u. U ain't his fucking slave. U a dam human being' dat don't deserve being' beat on like a punching bag."

Wanda lowered her head in shame as bloody tears poured from her face and dripped into the porcelain sink. The image that stared back was unbearable to see. Her nose was busted open, lip split and swollen, and her jaw and eye's looked like a disbursed airbag.

"U don't know da story," Wanda murmured in shame.

"Enlighten me, I'm all ears. I want ta know wat story u can possibly tell me ta justify dis horrific picture." Porsha tried hard to wrap her mind around her sister's notion, but it was impossible. Here was Wanda looking like a freak show straight out the Horror Story TV series, and she was making excuses for the unforgiving actions that had occurred to her.

"I started it," Wanda admitted.

"Wat do u mean u started it? Cause ta me, it looks like he finished it."

"I saw him in da club all kissy face wit another bitch, an' I snapped"

"An' u should have," Porsha tried righting her sister wrongs. "Any man who disrespects u, an' have da nerves ta be all up in another woman's face why u present, deserve everything he got coming' ta him."

"I disagree," Wanda couldn't second her opinion. No one deserved to be subjected to the treatment she'd inflicted on Block. "He didn't deserve fa me ta smash a bottle over his head. Plus, he didn't even know I was der. It wasn't his fault."

"It don't matter if he knew u was der or not. Now I agree u shouldn't have hit him wit a bottle, but it still doesn't give em a right ta be in some other bitch face when u an' him supposed ta be together." Porsha didn't have her facts straight. She wasn't aware Wanda and Block wasn't in an exclusive relationship. They just got together and fucked every now and then. The real reason Wanda had gotten fitting upset with Block, was because she had been trying to call Block to inform him about her pregnancy and he had been ignoring her attempts, sending her directly to his voicemail. So, when she had seen him up in the club with another chick, it had ignited her with jealousy. She took that as direct disrespect, and her anger had gotten the best of her

"I'm pregnant," Wanda blurted.

"An' u didn't take your narrow tail ta da hospital ta check an' see if dat child alright after last nite?" Porsha was concerned for her sister and her unborn niece or nephew's safety and health. "How far along are u?"

"I'm four weeks along, an' I can't go ta da hospital looking like dis. They ask questions, an' I don't wanna send da father of my baby ta jail."

"All u going ta da emergency room," Porsha forced the issue taking control. "So get'cha things, I'm taking u. We'll make up something ta save his no-good ass alone da way so da police don't get involved."

Wanda wanted to decline and tell her sister to back off and mine her own fucking business, but she didn't possess the physical strength to verbally or physically fight Porsha. So, she reluctantly forced herself over to her purse, grabbing her keys and phone in the process before embarking on their destination...

***

It was 6:15 A.M. and the sun beamed brightly over the horizon. A ray of beam shined bright upon Block's face waking him from his slumber. Covering his eyes with one hand, he stretched and yawned.

"About time u came around ta da living," Kayla greeted Block with a kiss. She stood over him fully dressed looking like a cover girl model. "I thought I was gone have to get'cha up wit a bulldozer."

"Wat time is it?" Block asked as he turned his back toward the open window to block the illuminating from beaming in his eyes.

"A quarter pass six," she enlightened, taking a glance at her Nike Fitbit. "Come on get up, I gotta get ta class. It's breakfast in da kitchen. I'm pretty sure U need it, after dat workout last nite. Gotta keep dat strength up."

"I got my breakfast right here," Block teased pulling Kayla onto the bed. She cackled at his silliness. "My strength always good." He palmed her ass. "U ready for another workout?"

"Boy stop, I gotta get ta school," she said, melting into his embrace.

"Why? I gotta enough school techniques, right here." Block kissed Kayla and she reciprocated.

"Come on, u gone make me late. I ain't got time ta redo my hair," Kayla protested. "I'd luv ta lay up an' ride dat thang all day, but I can't." Kayla got off the bed and went into the bathroom. "Anyways, wat's on your agenda today?"

Block slipped on his jeans and followed Kayla. He didn't enjoy being rebuffed, but he respected that Kayla was business oriented, and put her priorities first. Most men would kill to find a woman that was independent with oriented quality.

"Shit u know me, chasing dem dolla signs," Block answered her question then gargled some mouthwash and spit it in the sink. "Plus, I gotta go drop mom's city off some coins so she can pay her mortgage off. Dem blood suckaz been breathing down her back bout being' late, so I'ma relieve her of dat burden."

"Dat's nice. How Ms. Moore doing anyways?" Kayla inquired.

Block and his mother didn't share the same last name. He had taken his father's last name, a last name he resented. His father was a deadbeat that had walked out on him and his mother when Block was only 9 years old. Leaving them to fend for themselves. Ms. Moore took on a huge responsibility single handedly after Block's no-good father traded them in for a new family. By fourteen, Block was already in the streets hustling to put food on the table, something his father should've been doing. While in the trap, Block vowed never to follow in his father's footsteps. He was no role model to look up to.

"I ain't seen her in ages."

"She alright. She just beat cancer. Otherwise dat, she like any ordinary struggling mother in da hood."

"Dat's good, except for da part bout ordinary women struggles," Kayla sympathized. "I swear, no black women should ever have to endure da trials an' tribulations we strive thru every day." Kayla finished getting herself in an orderly fashion and turned to face Block. "When I make it, I'ma put together a nonprofit organization ta help all da women in da struggle. We all need a helping hand, an' I want ta extend mine ta give hope." Block smiled at her vision. He wondered how someone could be so exquisite and still possess a heart of gold. "How much your mother mortgage?"

"A lil bit of nothing," Block answered settled. "Nothing I can't handle."

"Don't be coy wit me. U can be open wit me Bentley," Kayla attempted, pushing Block to be straight forward with her. "Here I am telling u my future about how I'ma pay it forward to my community, an' u up here being shy wit me. Wat's up wit dat?"

"Nothing, I just don't think it's important."

"Why not? We just talking, u ain't being' interrogated," Kayla explained.

"Ain't I?" Block asked raising his left eyebrow. He was dubious of the conversation. He didn't want it to take a left turn into a quarrel because he wasn't forth coming.

"No, it ain't," she cured his curiosity. "I just want u ta be honest." Block knew that was what this was all about. She was testing him. He wasn't even mad at her; hell, she had every right to make sure she wasn't getting herself involved with the same type of man he once was. His mendacity is what had broken them apart once before. "Am I wrong fa dat?"

"Nah," Block assured. "U right, but I don't need u ta worry. I'm out here in des streetz doing my thang, an' I feel da less u know is fa da better," he explained. "I don't want u thinking I'm trying ta hide things from u, cause I'm not. It's just dat I want ta protect u, an' da less u know about my lifestyle, da safer you'll be. Just let me luv u, dat's all I ask. Can I do dat?"

Kayla pondered Block's words. He was right, she had no right prying into his personal business. Especially when they were fresh into the relationship, some things were sacred. Her insecurity was the main reason relationships fell apart. Love, trust, and respect were key to sustain a relationship.

"I approve of dat." Kayla wrapped her arms around Block waist. "I won't stop u from being' da man in dis relationship. A man gotta do what a man gotta do, an' I understand da street code, silence an' secrecy. U forget I ain't no square? My daddy was a gangsta too boo." Kayla smiled up at Block.

Block knew Kayla's father name was legendary in the streets. Smoke was his name, and he was a nigga everybody wanted to be, and everyone loved to hate. The hood respected Smoke like 2pac when he came through the hood in his fancy cars and his thuggish attitude that made all the hoes and hating ass niggas mad. Smoke was what you called the last of the dying breed. Standing true to the G-code, he wasn't afraid to put in work for the mob. He lived like a king in the streets until his time came and God called him home. Smoke was shot and killed back when Block and Kayla were in high school. Block still remembered how his death effected and crushed Kayla. It was a devastating blow to be dealt. But after the rain, Kayla didn't allow the murder of her father stagnant her goals. She put her head to the sky and chased her dreams with great determination and motivation.

"Nah I didn't forget lil Gangsta Boo," Block jested. "Come on, I need u ta take me ta my ride." Kayla did just that. When they arrived at his car, Block leaned over and kissed her. "I'ma get at'cha later," he assured.

"U better," she said, kissing him a final time. She honked the horn and blew him a kiss as she drove off.

Block hopped in his whip and chucked the deuces. He headed to his crib before he headed to his mother spot. He took $40,000 out his stash and stuffed it in a fanny pack he had laying around. $40,000 was enough to get the white man off her back and buy herself something nice. She deserved to splurge on herself for once. After all, she had always made sure he was provided with what he needed as a child. Now the roles had switched, and it was his turn to take care of her.

A half hour later, he pulled up in front of his childhood home and let himself in. He still had a key from when he once resided with his mother. He'd never given the key back and his mother had never forced him to either. Unspoken, his mother still enjoyed his company. She didn't mind him dropping by unexpectedly. As far as she was concerned, he was still the man of the household.

"Mom!" Block called out.

"In here in da living room," Brenda Moore replied. She was watching her favorite game show "The Price is Right" on Netflix. "Hey babe," she greeted Block as he entered. "Wat happened ta your head boy?" She noticed his injury right away.

"Oh nothing." Block reached for his bandage. A feeling of embarrassment washed over him. "Hit my head on da car door," he lied. For some reason, mendacity even made him feel incredibly ashamed. His mother gave him a knowing look as if to say I know you're manifesting a fib. Her dirty look made him feel like a teenager all over again. She had always been able to tell when he was untruthful. "Anyways, how u been?"

"U know me chow, blessed, saved, an' sanctified in da holy favor of Jesus Christ. I couldn't ask for a better relationship den wat I got wit my savor."

Block loathed when his mother got all holy and sanctified on him. It made him feel like church service filled with hypocrite's shouting and faking the holy ghost. Not saying his mother fit that category, but he just couldn't comprehend. After all that had happened to her, she was still head strong keeping her faith in a blonde hair, blue-eyed Jesus. That was completely absurd and unbeknownst to him.

"I brought u a gift." Block handed her the fanny pack. "Dat's something ta praise bout."

"Wat is it chow?" she curiously asked.

"Open it," Block insisted. "It's a surprise."

Brenda unzipped the pack to discover crispy one-hundred-dollar bills poking out the interior.

"Oh my!" Brenda exclaimed. "Where did u get dis? I know u aren't doing anything illegal." She automatically jumped to assumption. "U know God don't like ugly. U ain't got no bizness ouch der putting yourself in harm's way for me or nobody else. God got me."

"Momma... Momma," Block interrupted. "Ma, chill out. Just be easy. Dat money legit. It shouldn't matter anyways how I obtained it," he tried calming his mother concern. "Now u can pay off your mortgage an' buy yourself something nice. Live for a change instead of always worrying' bout bills an' overdue credit cards."

"Chow," Brenda patted his cheek. "U still have not come ta terms wit da laws of da land," she began her theological rant. "God didn't put us on dis planet ta have it easy. Whomever told u life would be easy lied."

"Ain't nobody told me dat. I'm just tryna make a way ta get u up out dis squalor," Block explained. "U deserve so much better momma. I wanna see u on top, an' not have to see u work all types of hours ta barely pay your bills."

"Yea, but at what cost?" Brenda asked, shaking her head. Block reminded her so much of his father. They were exactly the same when it came to the burdens of life. Weak is what she called it. They both wanted the easy way out. They forgot black people had done so much for so long with so little, that they we're now capable of doing anything with nothing at all. "Wat's it ta gain da world an' loss your soul? U don't need all da fancy things in life. Only thing u need is da luv from Jesus. When u accept him as your savor, he'll provide u everything u need an' more."

"I hear u," Block patronized. He'd grown agitated by the lecture. "But name one good thang dat your god den did for u? I don't see Jesus here right now. It's me standing here giving u dat money ta get dem white folks off your back."

"Boy hush up," Brenda warned. She was insulted by her son's ill words concerning the lord. "I want stand u speaking in vain bout my God. It's blasphemy, da only unforgiven sin."

"Ma I won't hush, cause its true wat I say. God ain't did shit fa u but allow da worst ta occur ta u. First, he allowed cancer ta attack u from da inside. Now your in debt," Block angrily spewed. "Don't get me started on when dad left an' all da hardships dat came barreling down on u. U know some things I can't believe u can stand der wit a straight face, an' say god give a dam bout u. God don't give a dam bout us. If he did, he wouldn't have put us on da bottom of da totem pole, why des white people got da world dancing in der hands." Quite frankly, Block was fed up with life's antics, and he wouldn't tolerate anyone trying to feed him fruits of the poisonous tree. Christianity was invented to segregate the people and keep slaves afraid of their masters. In Ephesians 6:5-6, Paul told the congregation, "a slave shall obey his master." There was no way Block could see himself worshipping a God that condoned slavery. His agnostic mind wouldn't allow it. "Look ma, I don't won't ta argue. I'm just saying I want be Jesus' puppet."

"An' I won't force u. It's your soul not mines, your da one who has ta stand before god on judgment day." Although she had succumbed to her son's decision, she still felt the need to place an array of guilt on Block's conscious. She always had a way to make him feel guilty, even when he knew he was right. "Remember da scripture said he would come like a thief in da nite. I just hope your ready when he returns."

"Ok ma," Block blew off his mother's last comment. She never understood God's word didn't apply to a heathen. Everything she preached went through one ear and out the other. "Ma I got some B.I. ta attend to. I just wanted to drop by an' give u dis so u could handle your functions. Take care of yourself, an' I'll see u later."

"Ok now, u be safe. But before u go, answer me one thang. Is dis money legit?" she reproached holding the bundle of money in his face. "An' don't lie ta me, cause even if I don't know, God know." She pointed up toward the sky as an indication of some unforeseeable force, God.

"Yea ma," he lied through his front teeth. "Now don't worry so much. Everything gone be fine. Just pay da bank an' do something nice for yourself. I know it's been a minute since u had'cha self a good time. So why dont'cha go out fa a change?" Block hugged his mother and gave her kiss on the cheek. She was a lot frailer than he remembered. Due to fighting the battle to rid herself of cancer, she had lost a tremendous amount of weight. He was concerned about her health. He hoped with the money, she could pay off what she needed to, and it would relieve her of the bottled-up stress. He just wanted her to start taken better care of herself. "Take care of yourself ma. I luv u," he said and headed on his way, leaving Brenda in the confines of a lonely house.

Brenda knew her son was into something he had no business. A mother knows. She cradled the money in her palms and thumbed through the bills. There was no way her son had accumulated the wealth legally. She appreciated the accommodation, but she knew the funds were made through some form of illegal activity. She didn't know what kind and didn't care to know; all she cared about was the safety of her only son. That thought alone brought her to her knees. She prayed to the heavens above to keep him protected through, the blood of Jesus Christ.

CHAPTER NINE

"Straight like dat, huh?" Dice asked Shay. They sat talking in his metallic blue 2018 Lexus RX 350L. She had just told him whom was responsible for trying to kill Tree. "U mean ta tell me dem ESG niggaz tryna move in on our turf?"

"Dat's wat I said. Dey been watching y'all for quite some time an' dey gone keep coming until dey move y'all round so dey can set up shop."

Shay placed a hundred on ten. What she spoke was an omission, so the jumper cables were necessary. If she didn't, Chop plan wouldn't play out accordingly. She hated she'd been forced to play the card. It was a dog eat dog world. It was either her life or theirs. That made it a relatively easy choice to make. On a selfish, self-preservation notion, she put herself first. When it came to destroying another person's life, she found it easy to damn that other person to hell.

"Tell me, why u just now telling me dis shit. Its been over two weeks since dat shit happen." Dice was right. He'd been aware of the attempt on Tree's life, because Tree had placed a 10,000 dollar reward out on the person's head who was responsible. "Where u get dis info from?"

"I got my resources," Shay replied. She had decided to keep her sources secret, even doe she knew she shouldn't't. Chop had violated her by defiling her in many disgusting, and repugnance ways. But yet, she still kept him behind the curtains. For now, that's how it would be. She had her own plans for Chop. "I just thought I'd run der plan by u, so u an' your people can handle dat bizness. I don't want ta see anything happen ta u, I don't know wat I'd do if I ever lost u." Shay should've received an academy award for her breathtaking performance. To top it all off, she got teary eyed to sell her winning act. "I can't live without u."

Shay's change of behavior through Dice for a loop. She was talking as if they were exclusive, which made him feel extremely uncomfortable. He didn't need the drama that came with fucking crossing the lines with no strings attached.

"Yea, I hear ya," he played it cool. With every fiber within his body, he tried his best not to tell her don't get it confused. They weren't in a relationship, and he didn't want to miss lead her, or give her the misconception that their FWB was anything more. "Here, I got something ta make u feel better." Dice unzipped his Saint Laurent's and reclined in the seat. "Gone be a good gurl an' get me right."

"No," she rejected. "Not right now." She frowned up odiously at Dice. "I can't believe u," she snapped. "I'm sitting here telling u my deepest feelings, an' all u can think of is your own sexual gratifications. How selfish." Shay sat back in her seat and folded her arms over her chest. "U must take me as one of your lil fluzzies u can placate wit an expensive shopping spree an' some dick whenever u call." Their relationship had not reached a new plateau as she had expected. She could see she'd been filling her head with false hopes and dreams. She had not moved into that number one spot. Dice still treated her like a groupie side piece instead of a trophy wife.

"Look, I ain't got time. If u ain't fucking, find somebody else's time ta waste."

"U never got time," she shot back. "U only call me when u want a nut. Wat'cha lady can't get'cha right?"

"Keep my wifey out dis. What me and her do ain't none of your dam bizness," Dice sneered. "Secondly, if u ain't fucking u can raise up out my ride. Time is money, an' wit u gurl I ain't making a dime."

"Really?" Shay exclaimed in disbelief. "Because I don't want ta fuck an' no longer be treated like a slut, u gone put me out? After all we been thru, dis da thanks I get?"

"Wat, I gotta draw u a picture? Rise up." Dice zipped up his pants. He had no intentions on ever calling her again. Somewhere down the line she had misconstrued the nature of their relationship. The fact that she thought they would ever be more then friends with benefits amused him. Everyone knew you couldn't turn a hoe into a housewife.

The plan she was trying to accomplish wasn't going as planned. Knowing she was no longer welcome, she grabbed her purse and got out the car. Angry, she slammed the car door with so much force, the window spider webbed. She didn't acknowledge Dice as he pulled off.

Inside her 2018 Maxima, she sat for a moment in deep thought. The man she thought she would be with after Bando's expiration date, had just dumped her. She knew she had to find a knight in shining armor to protect her from Chop's clutches. Otherwise she would be his slave forever. She had to find a way to kill two birds with one stone. Maybe she could pay someone to do her dirty work. Once Bando was out the picture, she would have access to all his wealth. It would be nothing to have Chop knocked off for a couple grand. Shay knew where Bando's stash was. In fact, she was the only one who knew its whereabouts. She smiled to herself, because his wealth was her undying dream...

***

Dice walked in his bedroom. Connie was propped up upon a bunch of throw pillows in nothing but her bra and panties. She had her cellphone in her hand, and she was texting away.

"Ay babe," she greeted with a smile. "Where u been? I been calling u all nite."

Dice shot Connie a dirty look. He was still upset about Shay's temper tantrum, and he wasn't in the mood for Connie's third degree. He was fed up and had had enough of women shenanigans for the day.

"What da fuck up wit u always questioning' me about my where abouts?" Dice snapped. He threw his duffle bag on the bed and started stuffing it with cash. "I'm nawt'cha child. U ain't always gotta be up in my bizness like u own me an' shit. Do I be up all in your shit when u out doing u?"

Connie stopped texting and dropped her Galaxy S9 between her parted legs.

"I'm not even gone feed into dat foul shit u kicking right now. I see u stressed out an' I'm horny as hell. So why don't u come over here an' release some of dat bottled up tension between these thighs?" Connie coquetted. She seductively rose from the bed and sashayed over to Dice. Dice stood to attention in his pants. She was a sight for sore eyes. Whenever Connie's clothes hit the floor, Dice eyes popped out of there socket. Connie was amazing, standing 5'2 and weighing in at 125 pounds, with the curvaceous measurements 34-24-42. Her aesthetic nude body would make a snail hard as the Thing from Fantastic 4. Not to mention, she was a beauty queen whom resembled Ella Mae. But Dice had business to attend to, as Connie proceeded to unzip his jeans, he kindly declined, and pushed her away.

"Hold up, be easy my lady. I got bizness ta handle" he informed zipping his pants back up.

"Bizness before pleasure?" she pouted. "Wat is it, u been laid up wit some other bitch all nite? Now u wore out."

"Gone wit aw dat drama," Dice warned.

It was money on Dice's mind; this was an opportunity he couldn't pass up. Block had plugged him. Dice would buy ten keys at 17.5 apiece. That was $175,000 in total. He couldn't complain, the prices were better than what he was currently paying. There was a $4,500 profit from his normal $22,000 he used to kicking out to the plug. And to be honest, the product he was getting from his current plug wasn't A1. Block had promised him the best white money could buy in the Midwest. This was a major step up the ladder. So, the ying yang Connie was kicking, she could save it.

"U always tryna hold up process wit your shenanigans, but always got'cha hand out when da money come in. U ain't never complaining when I be copping u dem fly ass ragz u be sporting. How da fuck u think I buy dat shit. So, yea, its bizness before pleasure," Dice spewed, checking Connie.

Connie was upset, and it showed on her face.

"Fuck it!" Connie shouted. "I'm tryna show my man some loving', an' u up in here talking like I'm da problem ta your cash flow. Well fuck u nigga!!!" she screamed and flounced off to another part of the home they shared.

Dice shook his head and continued on with what he was doing. He wished he had an excuse to explain away the emotional roller coaster Connie was riding. It was as if she was going through her monthly menstrual cycle, but that wasn't the case. Sadly, it was just another case of routine that average hood niggaz went through with their better half. To Dice, it was just another normal day.

Dice finished up his count and stashed the rest of the cash away before heading out. Connie was sitting on the couch. She was in a funky mood. It showed in her face as she set with her arms folded pouting.

"I know I ain't been showing u dat much attention, an' I know dat's not fair ta u," Dice tried to clear the air. Connie was his main dame, not just some hood rat he sled in and left up at the suite. So, he owed her that much to clarify things. "It's not your fault dat I'm out here in des streetz all times of nite, when I should be in bed wit u. I ain't got no excuse fa my absents, but u gotta understand I'm doing dis for u an' I, my lady."

"I know," Connie acknowledged. "I just get so bored an' mad u never here. I be wanting to spend quality time wit'cha, but when I try ta make dat clear, u push me ta da side," she expressed her concerns relating to their relationship. "I want ta spin sometime wit'cha. Are we ever gone have dat chance, or am I just gone be some barefoot wife pregnant in da kitchen?"

"Nah," Dice unintentionally laughed at her comment. "I apologize for laughing. I know it's not funny." Dice placed his bag by the door and sat next to Connie on the couch. "U just so cute when u get mad. I must admit, dat shit turn me on when u get like dis."

"Prove it," Connie said, climbing in his lap.

"I'd luv to, but I gotta make a power move right now. I promise once I get everything straight on my end, I'ma make sure your my first priority."

"U promise?" Connie asked like a little girl expecting her father to hold dear to his word.

"Yea, it's me an' u babe. Just be patient wit me." Dice lifted her back onto the couch. "Right now, I got ta handle dis, an' I'll be back in a couple hours tops."

Dice headed back to the door. He winked as he grabbed his bag heading out the door. Pulling his phone from his pocket, he called Block to inform him he was heading in his direction. At the same time, Connie picked up her phone and called one of the many guys she had stored in her call log as females. If Dice didn't want to give her no dick, she'd get it elsewhere from someone who wouldn't fail to adhere to her needs...

**

"Man stop jacking, u didn't smash da fine ass sista from da bar last nite," Tree tried to discredit Pimp. Pimp and Tree was posted up like streetlights in the hood talking shit as normal. "U always lying on your dick."

"Nigga please, u know I ain't flexing. My name Pimp," He asserted. His assertion was standard to defend his reputation.

"Wat da fuck your name got ta do wit dis?" Tree and Block laughed. Block was amused watching his boyz ridicule one another. It was humorous. Block never intervened when they got like this. Both Tree and Pimp had major love for each other, so Block knew there was nothing unreconcilable. Their love was bond. "Fool, we know who u are."

"Den act like it, cause u know I be smashing on da regular," Pimp insisted.

"I don't know nothing wit'cha jacking ass," Tree countered.

"Dat's why I took photos, ta prove niggaz like u wrong. I do dis shit fa mutha fuckaz who don't know my name speak for itself." Pimp pulled out his cellphone.

"Let me see dem joints." Tree demanded.

"Dam nigga, slow ya roll." Pimp swiped right numerous times until he came to the tell all photographs. "Here, eat'cha hart out. I had dat freak spread eagle fa ya boy."

Tree observed the presented photos Pimp had taken of the freak they had both shot their shot at the night before. Tree had been rejected by the thoty. Like a true player, Tree had rebounded, slamming it off the backboard by trying his luck with the bar tender. And in the end, it had paid off in a promising night of passion.

"Dis shit don't mean nothing. U probably photo shopped des pics," Tree refused to except the facts.

"Nigga fuck u," Pimp shot back. "Give me back my phone." He snatched his phone from Tree. "We know da real reason your bum ass be hating on me."

"Yea, wat's dat?" Tree asked.

"U da master of rejection," Pimp answered. Block bent over at the waist laughing, he was slayed by Pimp's remark. "U know it too, dat's why Block laughing. Cause he knows it's true. Da last time u had some pussy is when pussy had u. Your present girlfriend named Ms. Palmer." Pimp made a masturbation motion with his right hand at the end of his joke. They all shared a laugh at Tree's expense.

"U just clowning now. Cause I stay leaning into something like a hobo on da corner begging fa loose change." Tree thought he had said something slick, but it backfired on him.

"Dat's a bad analogy. Matter fact, a horrible one at dat. Only thing u been leaning into is dem cheeseburgers u been wolfing down," Pimp eased a fat joke into the equation. "Wat'cha think I ain't notice u getting fat? U starting ta round out like da bogy off da Mucinex commercial." Pimp had the whole crew howling with laughter. Pimp should've been on BET comedy. He was hilarious, but also truthful. Tree had started putting on a few extra pounds. It was building excessively around the midsection. It appeared he had a beer belly and he didn't even drink beers.

While Pimp and Tree continued gunning each other, Wanda pulled up in her bright red Honda Accord. Block's first intention was to ignore her, but he went against his childish intentions because they were immature. He'd been meaning to call and check up on her anyway, but his anger had hindered him from being the bigger person.

"Ay babe, can I talk to u?" Wanda rolled down her window and called. "Please daddy, I really need ta talk ta u," she whined.

"Look, I'ma bout ta go holla at ole gurl," Block informed his boyz rising from the stoup. "Make sure Dice get right when he roll thru. Also, he said he had something important on his mind, see what's dat about."

"I got'cha." Pimp replied. "Go handle your B.I. we got dis out here. Everything good over here fool," Pimp assured, then showed Block some love. Tree did the same.

Inside Wanda's compact car, Wanda beamed with glee. Her face was still slightly bruised over the left cheek, and the bag under her right eye was a purplish color. Besides that, she appeared fine.

The entire ride was quiet. Wanda pulled into an empty parking lot, but still, she refused to verbalize. She was silently staring at Block. For some odd reason, she couldn't bring herself to speak, so Block took the initiative to break the ice.

"So, wat is it u gotta holla about?" Block asked. Block adjusted to the size of Wanda's car so he could lean against the passenger door. "I can see u gotta lot on your byrd. So, speak your mind."

"I... I don't even know w... Where ta begin," Wanda stuttered. "I got much on my mind. I do know I've missed u." She placed her hand on Block thigh. Block cringed in disgust at her touch and pushed it away.

"Da beginning would be just fine. Why don't u start der," Block directed.

"Wat, I can't touch u?" Wanda took offence toward Block pushing her hand away. Her emotions had overridden her logical sense, and she had almost forgotten what it was she'd came there to accomplish.

"Look, get ta da point, an' stop wasting my time," Block redirected.

"I'm pregnant," Wanda blurted. She had wanted to tell him the moment she'd found out, but fate had taken a turn for the worse. Her sister had been breathing down her neck; bleeding her ear out, about why she shouldn't enlighten Block she was pregnant after what he had done. But Wanda was her own woman, and felt Block deserved to know he was going to be a father. He was entitled to know, because he had just as many rights as her. "Did u hear me? I said I'm pregnant."

"Yea I heard," Block answered unenthusiastically. "Wat else is new?" There was no interest in the information Wanda had already informed him of.

"Wat'cha mean wat else is new?" Wanda was vexed by Block's seldom attitude. She didn't like it, and if he kept it up, she would be on his ass like white on rice. "U bout ta be a dad, an' dat's your response? Wat else..." she couldn't finish her sentence coherently without blowing a gasket. Block's nonchalant manner toward the matter pissed her off.

"Check yourself before dis grasping conversation get out of hand," Block fairly warned. "I can see u getting mad, an' dat won't help da situation none. I'm tryna make sense of all dis. It's all happening so suddenly," He informed. "U can't expect me not ta have doubts doing wat it is u do."

"An' wat might dat be Block, huh?" she asked. She was offended by the shallow accusations he was implying.

"U know wat it is u do."

"Nah, tell me," she dared. "I wan't to hear u say it." Her bitch mood was in full effect. She was fired up from the conversation; so much so, she could feel the tips of her weave melting. "I know u ain't referring ta my dancing? Cause u knew wat it wuz before u laid up wit me in my bed. So, don't act brand new?"

"Yea u right, but I ain't gotta a problem wit'cha occupation. My concerns is da adventures your job leads u on. Ain't no telling how many clients den slid up in dat cookie. I know firsthand stripp'rs a bust it open for da highest bidder up in VIP."

Wanda's face frowned up with great disappointment.

"Nigga u acting like a real lame right now. Are u drunk? If so, get back at me when u sober."

"Look, I warned u once before ta check yourself. I don't like, ta have to repeat myself, so don't make have to again." Wanda's mouth had been getting way out of line lately. Block thought maybe it was due to pregnancy hormonal levels. Whatever it may be, Block knew she had better get herself in order. "Youve been talking all sideways out your neck lately. U better cease dat shit. An' as long as u liv's, u betta not ever fix your mouth ta refer ta me as a lame. I make shit happen on my own out here. So, keep dat shit out your mouth. Do I make myself clear?"

Wanda sealed her lips in the process of Block checking her. She was grateful to be dealing with a strong man, that wasn't afraid to put her in her place. Most dudes were afraid to show authority when she got out of line. Wanda acknowledged she was a hard woman to tame, and she needed a man with a backbone. Other men were weak links, and she ate them for breakfast. But not Block, he was the dominant type that didn't take any nonsense. The kind that didn't hesitate to put a bitch in her place. Wanda respected that quality and respected his demand.

"Alright Block, I'm sorry," she apologized, then continued to stress her point more settling before. "Aw I'm saying is u accuse me of laying up with otha niggaz, when I'm da one caught u wit'cha tongue all down some scank throat," Wanda explained in a reserved and respectable manner. "I ain't been laid up with no mutha fucka but u Block. I luv u, an' wood never do u like dat. But I don't get da same respect. U cheat on me, an' I'm supposed ta charge dat shit ta da game."

Block wasn't convinced. He knew the same bitches that claim she loved you, she'll set you up. There was an undying rule to the game, and the hood rats aren't to be trusted. They'll tell you anything just to get close to you.

"Don't try ta play me. How da fuck u charging something ta da game when u went ova my shit wit a Hennessey bottle?" Block scratched at the scar on his head. "An' ta top dis all off, how can I cheat on u when we only FWB, an' nothing more? Don't get it confused, cause u know wat it is."

"R u fucking kidding me right now? Am I being punked?" She couldn't believe how Block had categorized their relationship. "We been sitting da sheetz fa over two years now, an' u don't consider me more den dat? We still friend's wit benefits after u hit anyway an' everyway?" Wanda eyes glared with passion of hate. "So, wat title u give da lil hussy u was tonguing down like der was no tomorrow?"

"Dat's my wifey," Block answered, beaming proudly. "I don't know why u acting all confused like u don't know wat dis is between u an' I. But ta me, your nothing more den a good fuck an' a good time. If by some chance dat's my baby, den I'ma take care of it. Beyond dat, me an' u are no more."

Wanda found it hard to compose herself. Block's last statement had really struck a nerve, and before she knew it, she had reached out and hit Block in the mouth.

"Nigga fuck u!" she shouted hysterically. Wanda was overwhelmed with anger. "U got me all fucked up. U ain't gone play me like I'm one of these knock-off bitches out here. If I can't have u, nobody will," she threatened.

Block couldn't believe how much self-control he actually had. It took a whole lot to restrain himself to not react as he had the last time she had struck him.

"Wanda, dis conversation over," he calmly dismissed her. He could taste the saltiness of blood in his mouth, and he knew it would be wise for him to get out the car before he caught a murder case. "I'ma get out of here before I hurt your silly ass. Call me when u have da baby." Block reached for the door lever, but Wanda grabbed his arm in protest.

"Don't go," Wanda pleaded. There was a desperate tone in her sudden attitude change that reminded Block of an unstable lunatic. "Please, I promise I'll be good. Don't leave me," she continued. But her cries fell on deaf ears. Block snatched his hand away and stepped from the vehicle.

"Alright, if dat's how it's gonna be, u ain't gone ever see dis baby," Wanda yelled like a mad woman out the rolled down window. "If dat's how u wanna play it, let da games begin. I'm killing u an' dat bitch!" she threatened before smashing the gas, leaving Block standing in a vacant lot.

As Wanda's tires squealed across the asphalt, Block tried rationalizing how much time he'd spent getting nowhere. Looking at his Petek; he had wasted three quarters of an hour.. Dismissing the situation from his mind with no prejudice, he made a mental note never try to be civilized with someone that's incapable of rationality. Grabbing his cellphone, he pushed Tree's number in, and he answered on the first ring.

"Yo," he answered.

"Fam come get me. I just had another fight wit dis dumb ass bitch," Block informed.

"Wurd? Wat'cha beat her ass again?"

"Nah, nothing like dat. Just come get me."

"Alright, just tell me where u at. I gotta holla at'cha anyways. U ain't gone believe dis news Dice just laid on me."

"I'm on 35th an' Center," Block notified Tree of his location.

"Me an' Pimp on da way."

Tree's Durango pulled up ten minutes later, and Block hopped in the back.

"Wuz up, shawty left u on da curb?" Pimp questioned not soon after the door closed.

"Nah, I just can't deal wit dat drama," Block replied. Pulling a pre-rolled blunt from his ear, he sparked it and inhaled the gas into his lungs. "She got on some other shit, so I ditched her," Block told the tale by omission. "Fuck her, wat up wit dat news Tree? I hope it's good news."

"Depend on wat'cha consider good news," Tree spoke. "Remember dat shit dat happen ware a mutha fucka tried ta light me up like a x-mas tree?"

"Yea, dat situation dat I told'cha I'ma handle. I told'cha I got'cha," Block assured. He really hoped Tree wasn't gonna pester him on some minor shit they could catch off the backboard and slam dunk down the lane.

"Yea, an' I take your word on it. But remember dat fine ass side piece Dice be belly flopping on?"

"Yea." Block inhaled the gas into his lungs then exhaled through his nose. "What about her, what she got ta do with dat situation?"

"Well, she dropped da scoup on Dice bout whom sent da hit. An' I'ma fill dem ESG niggaz wit lead." Tree had already contemplated how he was gonna eliminate the enemy. "No nuts no glory, so I ain't standing down dis time. Dem bitch ass niggaz dug der self a ditch."

"Pump your brakes a sec, an' let me process dis info a minute." Block passed the bag over the backseat to Tree.

"Fuck dat!" Tree barked, taking a hit of Tree's. "Why u always tryna give des fuck boys second chances ta live? God forgive, I don't. I don't know nothing about ducking no action, all I know is weed, guns, an' ammunition, so I'ma give dem boys da blues."

"See, dat's da shit I be talking about. Your mouth always running wit diarrhea when u mad. Ninja use your head. I'm telling you dis for your own good. Relax, I know da leader of dem ESG ninjaz," Block enlightened. "Some ninja who go by da name Bando calling shots on der side of town."

"So because u familiar wit da clown, he supposed ta get a G-pass?" Tree questioned Block's logic.

"Never dat," he assured. "Hear me out, I gotta plan..."

**

Kesha reclined in a bubble bath uninhibited exploring her body without any hang ups or guilt. She'd been freer with her pleasures since G-Ball's murder. When G-Ball was alive, he had made her feel terrible for being open with her insatiable sexual appetite. It was times she felt as if she was in a nunnery full of Catholic school girls. She wanted to let loose and feel alive; not be all bottled up like some volcano waiting to blow. Now that Ball was dead, nothing would cumbersome her from giving her body what it deserved. Rubbing her clit, she pushed in Pimp's number.

"Wuz up gurl?" he answered smoothly.

"Why haven't I seen u since u know wat? U haven't even called," Kesha cut straight to the point. She was extremely horny and needed some dick like yesterday. Listening to Pimp's voice, she imaged bouncing up and down on his joystick in the soapy water.

"My hands been tied lil ma, an' I ain't had too much free time. I'm out here tryna get it in a major way," Pimp explained. His voice sent trembles through Kesha. Pimp's voice was sort of an aphrodisiac. "Plus, its been hot, if u know wat I mean."

"Yea, I know wat'cha mean boy. But I need u. Come thru here an' put it on me," Kesha coquetted. She was rubbing her clit vigorously now. She was overly aroused, and nothing would bring her hypersexuality justice except a hard pounding. "It's been a minute daddy since u put it down, an' I'm fiending for some of dat hammer. Come thru an' slang dat iron boy," Kesha moaned out loudly.

"Wat'cha nasty tail doing ma?" Pimp queried after a series of moans emitted through the earpiece.

"Playing wit dis pussy, getting it nice an' juicy for u daddy. Come get dis kitty cat, she purring for ya."

"Give me like an hour. I'm in traffic right now wit da fellaz. Once I handle dis on my end, I'ma slide thru an' bet it out da frame." Pimp rocked up listening to Kesha on the phone as she moaned it anticipation.

"Alright daddy. Don't take too long, I'll be waiting fa ya." Kesha hung up just in time as a mega orgasm tore through her...

***

"Wuz popping big homie?" Creep greeted Bando as he stepped in the trap. Creep was posted in the living room with a joystick playing Grand Thief Auto 5. "Wat brings u round des wayz?"

"Tryna find dat lil nigga Kilo. He been MIA for about three weeks now. U seen him?" Bando was losing his patience. He'd been searching for Kilo high and low. He'd even went to Kilo's mother's house, only to come upon yet another dead end. "I been hitting dat nigga line nonstop, but his lil weak ass keep sending me straight ta voicemail."

"Nah G, I can't help u on dat tip. We ain't seen him round des neck of da woods either." Creep really didn't care either. He was too entranced in the PlayStation 4. "A nigga thought u had him working another trap house. I wouldn't even worry doe. U know Kilo, his lil ass probably laid up wit some freak. He'll turn up somewhere."

Bando took heed to the faith Creep had concerning Kilo's loyalty. Too bad he couldn't express the same regards, Bando lacked in that department. Trust was the hardest thing to earn but the easiest thing to lose. Kilo was playing with fire, and when you played with the devil you got burned. Kilo had run off with a whole kilo of merch. The street value was estimated at $20,000; which was enough to get your mother whacked.

"I disagree, it's been 3 weeks. Dat nigga ducking, but dat nigga can't duck des hollows." Bando was dead serious. He was tired of excuses. It was a grown man's game they were playing, not one of the video games Creep had grown accustomed to playing on his free time. In the real world, there were consequences for your actions. You couldn't die and come back to right your wrongs. There was accountability between life and death. "At lease tell me u know where dat nigga Chop at."

"Yea, he in da kitchen wit Duck wrist twisting like its stir fry."

Bando headed into the kitchen. Along the way, he wondered how some things would never change. The game remained the same, but the players changed on a constant basis. Most of the newcomers gave the game a black eye; putting salt in the game when the rules became exempt to them. The dilemma he was peddling was a constant reoccurrence. It would always be niggaz in the game that figured he was a chief instead of an Indian. Bando would bet his bottom dollar that Kilo had conspired to branch off on his own with the key of merch. It was poor decision making; because niggaz didn't realize when you sold your soul to the devil, there was always a catch-22. There was always an ex post facto to running off on the dope man, and with Kilo actions, retaliation was a must.

In the kitchen, Duck was on the 1's and 2's rocking up dope, while Bando's right-hand man, Chop, did his thang, nodding his head to Jeezy Thug Motivation 101 album pounding from the house speakers.

"How u niggaz living?" Bando yelled over the loud lyrics spilling from the sound system.

"U know same shit different toilet," Duck replied. Dope boy magic was every day for him. He'd been hustling since the tender age of twelve. The streets had become his home when he had run away from home to get away from his drunk abusive father. Duck had suffered two long years of his father's physical abuse after his mother got tired of being a punching bag and left. She had left with some other guy leaving Duck behind to fend for himself. After his mother's departure, Duck became the main target of his father's drunken rage. The beatings he received lasted up until Duck became fed up. No longer able to endure the abuse anymore, he followed in his mother's footsteps and left home. Most find the dope game, but the dope game had found him down on his luck. "In dis bitch making da trap say A!"

"Dat's wat I like ta hear," Bando congratulated. Most of his trap houses were doing numbers, but none of them alone accumulated bread like the one Duck ran. Duck oversaw the drops point. Anybody that was big time on the East side, nine times out of ten, they were getting their product from Bando. Duck brought approximately a100 grand to the table every week, if not more. "Wuz popping wit'cha Chop?" he asked to feel his homie out.

"Shit, chasing des dolla signs as u can see," Chop answered. "We been in dis bitch all nite, an' a nigga dizzy ass a bitch from all dis snow. I'ma bout ta head ta da crib so I can caress my pillow for a couple hours." Chop finished wrapping the bricks and placed them in a Gucci duffle bag.

"Come ride wit me," Bando offered. "I need ta holla at'cha bout something. I'll drop u at da flat."

Chop rose and slung the bag strap over his right shoulder.

"Alright let's be out den," Chop said and grabbed his cellphone off the table along with his pistol that he stuffed in his pocket. "Duck, I'ma get at'cha in a couple hours. By dat time U should be done wit dis task, den we can handle dat other bizness, alright?"

"Fa'sho, u know my phone on 24-7. When u ready, just give me a ring. I'ma be up in here kicking Creep's ass in some NBA 2k18," Duck said over his shoulder amidst cooking up dope.

"Luv." Chop chucked the deuces then followed Bando. Chop placed the merch in the trunk of Bando's black 2016 Panoramic Porsha sitting on 22-inch Forgis. "So wuz up?" he asked while getting in the passenger seat.

"Wuz up wit'cha lil manes Kilo?" Bando hoped by some odd chance that Chop could relieve his mind from worry. Maybe Chop knew where Kilo was. "I been tryna contact dat lil nigga, an' I ain't been getting no response. So, I thought u might know something."

"I'm just as blind as u," Chop spoke. Chop hadn't seen or heard from Kilo since Stevo's funeral, and that was months ago. It was dubious for Kilo not to call or be in the hood on the regular, but Chop hadn't given that notion much thought. He thought maybe Kilo was still grieving or soaking on the fact he had went in his jaw. "Shit, I thought maybe u knew. I been hitting his line just like u. I been thinking about going ta his moms spot, but I been on da grind. An' I couldn't afford ta be side tracked."

"I know, but I need u ta put dis ta da side fa like an hour, an' see wat's good wit lil buddy. He got some merch of mine an' I wan't it back." As Bando cruised the streets, he peeped the scenery, keeping an eye out for Kilo. He was leaving the bricks unturned. Kilo could turn up anywhere, and when he did, Bando wanted to be the first on the scene. "If u can't find him, I wat'cha ta put a price tag on dat nigga head. U got dat?"

"I got'cha," Chop half-heartily agreed. He didn't want to see his boy harmed; he'd been knowing Kilo since puberty. In addition, he respected Kilo's mother like his own. How could he ever look Ms. White in the face again afterward, knowing he was the cause of her son being killed. On the other hand, Kilo was grown, so Chop couldn't keep protecting him. Kilo knew what ESG was all about; and ESG is where Chop loyalty laid. For the mob, Chop would wash his hands in Kilo's blood...

CHAPTER TEN

Heather sat across from Six in nothing but her Victoria Secret bra and panties. They both were at the glass dining room table counting wads of money. Heather's gold plated 3.80 Torres, twelve shots with a pearl handle was close, inches away and in arm's reach on the table. Heather was what most would refer to as a real bitch. That title didn't come easy, it took years of putting in work to sit on the throne fit for a queen. When she was introduced to the dope game, no one gave her respect in the hood. Simpletons couldn't wrap their heads around the fact she was a white girl that was on like the light switch. Niggaz already occupying the game looked at her like another slut with a butt, who was worth nothing more than a good fuck. They disrespected her by calling her Snow Bunny and Snow White. In relations to the dope game, she gratefully adopted the alias name Snow White, but she rejected the Snow Bunny reference. Referring to her as such would get you a hot one to the face real quick. Gunplay got her the respect she deserved in the streets. It all fell in place, when some low life scumbags thought her eye candy was sweet as bear meat, she filled their bodies full of lead.

One day, some niggaz in the streets had plotted to rob her and Nut ole lady Kimono for a nice score. But before the sting got a chance to get under way, Nut had gotten word through the grapevine. Nut couldn't allow what the haters was planning to happen. And even worse, he couldn't allow the scheming niggaz to live. So, he orchestrated a hit squad to eliminate the threat. But Kimono would have none of that nonsense that involved her man handling her functions. She loved Nut, but she couldn't have him fighting her battles. Her final call demanded Nut and his boyz to stand down.

Kimono didn't mind getting her hands dirty. It wouldn't be her first time and it damn sure wouldn't be her last. Upon execution to exterminate her foes, she brought Snow White along. She was a virgin, and Kimono had popped her cherry introducing her to a new game. Snow White remembered being nervous, but not scared. After they had body bagged the opposition, Snow White remembered feeling empowered, and in that moment, she had developed a thirst for blood. That's when she decided the murder game was far more lucrative and pleasurable than slanging dope. While her team remained slanging cane, she made a nice piece of change rocking niggaz and bitches to sleep.

"Dam gurl, I must admit u looking extremely sexy sitting der counting dat cash wit a gun," Six complimented. "I ain't never think I'd be so turned on by a chick wit a gun. Dislike some old James Bond shit."

Heather giggled then wrapped a bundle of hundred-dollar bills in a rubber band.

"U know wat else I'd sexy on?" she batted her eyelashes and licked her lips provocatively.

"Dis dick," he predicted. Six played right into her wanton nature. He knew her probably better than she knew herself. Six knew when she wanted to get her freak on. Sometimes she didn't even have to ask; her body language said it all, and he was an expert at reading it.

"U know it babe," Heather confirmed, then rose and sashayed over to Six's side off the table. Casually sitting on his lap, she whispered in his ear. "Now let me ride dat thang."

Six didn't need to be asked twice. He was already cocked and loaded for the performance.

"Is dat a gun or are u just happy ta see me?" she asked, wiggling seductively in Six's lap.

"U know I'm always happy ta see u but dis nine in my pants tryna kill dat pussy," Six retorted. He had rocked up in the process watching her prance toward him. She was beautiful in every way, and sometimes he couldn't help himself when she was near it was just a natural reaction.

Snow White smiled at Six's cheesy comment, then traced her tongue around his earlobe. A source of electricity shot up his spine. He loved it when she played with his ears. They were his soft spot. Heather knew how to rev his motor; his ears where the key to start up the engine.

Snow White smelt divine; Chanel radiated off his skin. The texture of her skin was emollient, it was like having marshmallows in the palms of your hands.

"Mmmmm," Six moaned gripping her ass checks. "U keep dat up, u gone be in for an all-nighter," he warned.

"Sounds marvelous," she marveled tugging at his earlobe with her teeth. She was well aware of what she was getting herself into. She absolutely adored when Six made her scream to the early morning. "Ain't nobody complaining but u. Now get ta it."

Six picked Heather up and placed her on the edge of the table and ripped her satin bra off in the process. With her bra discarded to the floor, Six pulled her thong to the side and dropped his head to her creamy center.

"Ooooooh, dat feels sooooo good babe," Heather moaned out when Six's tongue made contact with her clit. Grabbing hold of his freshly braided head, she threw her head back and enjoyed the tremendous tongue lashing she was experiencing.

Six sucked her clitoris between his lips before exploring lower to her forbidden territory. His tongue seeped between her walls causing her legs to tremble. She called out clawing at his head and humping desperately against his mouth. She wanted-needed the release that was building making her high.

"Oooh gawd!" she gasped and moaned as she came all over Six face. "Dat's it baby, I'm cumin. Ohh babe keep going." Six was smothered in her juices as she mashed her snatch against his face. Her thighs closed tightly against his ears, and her legs trembled tremendously as her orgasm washed over her and subsided in satisfaction. "Mmmmm, your tongue game is satisfactory," she moaned. Heather stuck her tongue in Six's mouth tasting her release on his breath. In a frantic, she unbuckled Six's jeans, and pushed them down along with his boxers around his ankles. Six's bulbous head pushed at her entrance. Scooting forward, her walls parted, splitting widely like the departing of the Red Sea as she accepted him inside her. Pleasurably, she kissed Six while gasping in short breaths. When Six's ship sunk to the bottom, she tightly wrapped her arms around him. "Gawd u fill me up."

Six retracted his piece until only the head was left inside of her womb, then slammed back home. Heather screamed his name while Six repeated the process, slamming into her over and over. She trashed around wildly on the table while being ravished. Speeding up his tempo, Snow White took a series of short gasping breaths while trying to run up the table. Six took hold, securing her shapely firm thighs so she couldn't escape, and commenced to a serious pounding.

"Ooooooh gawd," Heather continued to moan. She thrashed her head from side to side. "Please daddy," she begged, pressing her palm into his abdomen to prevent him from going to deep.

"Please wat," Six asked in between strokes. Heather couldn't answer, the fucking she was receiving had her in trans of absolute pleasure. "Wuz wrong, cat got'cha tongue? Now who complaining?" he teased.

Caught up in her own rapture, a momentum of orgasmic release, she held on for dear life, and accepted the trashing. She felt herself crescendo toward that awaiting release, closer and closer until she finally erupted. She gasped and screamed at the top of her lungs.

"Eeeeeeeh!" As she came, her fluids gushed forth leaving Six's pubic hairs matted in a creamy compound build up by copulation.

"Dat's right, cum on dat dick," Six edged her on.

Heater timed Six's eruption. When he was on the verge, she hopped off the table and took him in her mouth. It only took a couple of suckles from her greedy mouth, and he disgorged, sending his hot seed down her throat. The first few shots spilled down her throat, the next few shots blasted onto her tongue as she removed him and jacked him onto her quavering tongue. Heather savored his delicious cum. She loved the salty taste and slimy texture of it. Swallowing, she took the head of his pistol in her mouth and milked him for the rest of his cuisine. When there was no more left, Six grabbed his shirt and pulled up his pants.

""Where u going?" she asked on her knees, panting heavily.

"I got bizness ta tend to."

"Tease," she pouted. "U said I was in fa an all-nighter," Heather complained.

"Another time." Six headed off to the shower, leaving Heather hot, bothered, and frustrated...

***

Kayla tumbled onto her fluffy pillows sweating excessively hard. She'd just finished riding Block like in a rodeo.

"Real talk, ain't no slow motion in your blood. U just get on dis thang an' take off zero ta sixty real quick," Block joked, laying on his back looking at the ceiling. It was early in the morning, and he'd been awakened by Kayla fumbling and sucking him to attention. "No one would ever guess u are a lady in da streets an' a freak in da sheets. Wit dat innocent shy gurl persona, U could fool da pope."

"Ready for round two?" she asked while toying with his flaccid member. She had classes to attend that morning, but for some reason, she'd woke up hormones raging out of control.

"I can't," Block declined. "I gotta handle some B.I. dis morning." Block had recently acquired Niko's money in full. The trap had been clocking numbers and he was ready for another shipment. The team was now down to a measly two bricks. Not that Block was complaining, that was an extra $35,000 to be added to his bank roll. But Block was more interested in the big bucks,' his philosophy was go big or go home. "As a matter fact, hold on." Block grabbed his analog untraceable cellphone and pushed in Nikos contacts.

"How's it going? I've been expecting u," Niko answered in his strong accent. "Wuz up my mane?"

"I got'cha cash, an' I'm ready ta meet so we can discuss bizness," Block informed. In the middle of their conversation, Kayla took his dick in her willing mouth. "My people asking for more, an' I don't have da merch ta meet der request. I'm tryna expend, so when can we meet?"

"Sure, I'll text u da address where we shell meet," Niko agreed. "Bout noon, is dat ok wit'cha?"

"Dat's perfect. See u then," Block hung up the phone in a hurry. It had been hard for him to contain a steady voice without giving away what Kayla was doing to him. Her head was piston up and down at lightning speed. Every time her head plunged, she excepted more of him in her mouth until her lips ringed around the base line of his penis. While Kayla blessed him, he stared at her ripped derriere. Kayla was firm on her knees in the center of the mattress, which gave Block full access to her ass and pussy. Enjoying her superb head game, he fiddled with her clit.

"Hmmmmm," she moaned her approved satisfactory to his manually ministration. Kayla's body shook as a tiny orgasm washed over her when Block stuck his middle finger inside her and simultaneously manipulated her pearl at the same time. The double attention made her feel electrified; a source of power rolled throughout her body. Block was ready to cum. With his free hand, he locked his fingers in her hair pushing his hips forward. His dick pulsated then erupted in thick globs down her throat. Kayla swallowed with content. As she feasted on his sperm, she came violently, shaking and moaning around his piece. Her orgasm was mind blowing. It blew through her, leaving her body a wreck. Wrecked but satisfied, Kayla got off the bed and headed to the restroom. She couldn't afford to bathe in the afterglow of her body explosion, she had to get ready for class.

"Why dont'cha move in wit me?" Block asked. They had been spending a lot of inseparable time together. Most of the time Kayla spent nights at his house.

So, he figured why not make it official and transform his house into a home. "Wat u think?" Block had grown attached to Kayla and would adore coming home to her eternally. When she wasn't with him, he felt a void within.

"Where, here?" she asked astonished. Block's question had caught her off guard. Her and Block had fun, and it was no doubt she loved him, but they were on two separate courses in life. Kayla wanted to be a doctor, and Block was stuck in the game. Kayla wondered if two opposites could attract and stay together united as one.

"Yea here. Is der a problem?" Block was perturbed by Kayla's response to his answer.

"Nah, no problem. I just don't know wat ta say," she wasn't rebuffing his request. Kayla wanted to make sure they were compatible before making a solid decision regarding them living together.

"U could say yea." Block hoped that would be her response. The phrase would suffice.

"It would be easy ta just give in ta your demand. God knows I want too, but I'm not sure I fully understand da true nature of our relationship," Kayla explained. "I want ta know how u feel about me? Like why u choose me. I'm sure u got a flock of women u can have at any given time, but yet u want me ta live wit'cha. Please help me understand." Kayla was flattered to be chosen, but she wouldn't play nobody's fool. If Block wanted to be with her, he would have to make that clear. Because she wouldn't share him with any other women.

"I can feed U lines of wat you'd like ta hear all day, but I'd rather not," Block took the time to explain. "I can only give u wat's real, an' wat's real is I luv u an' want ta share dis world wit'cha gurl." If he was to sign off with a sentiment, it would be his sincerest. That's how much she meant to him. "Tell u wat, why dont'cha let me handle dis bizness, den tonight we go out an' discuss da possibilities of our future. How does dat sound?"

"Ok," Kayla excepted.

Once Kayla and Block had properly exfoliated and dressed, Block took Kayla to school. In front of Marquette University, he informed her he'd pick her up at home around 8 P.M. for their date. At the moment, he didn't have time to sort out their differences. There was money to be made. He had to head to the spot and collect the re-up cash and stash the rest. Saying their goodbyes, Block headed off in route to the trap.

When Block rolled up, Pimp and Tree were posted on the front stoop talking to one of the lil homies known as Two-G. Two was 19 years old and was one of the up and coming hustlers. Two had recently discharged from Ethan Allen school for boys, after Governor Scott Walker demanded the juvenile facility be closed. Two had served six years after shooting and paralyzing his stepfather to protect his mother from being domestically harmed. Two had woken up one night in pandemonium. The sounds of shattered glass and his mother wailing screams alerted him that his mother might be in danger. Knowing before of his biological father's mass incarceration for illegal distribution of firearms, his father kept a 357 Revolver stashed on the upper shelf of his mother's closet. Two rushed to his mother's bedroom and climbed on a chair to retrieve the weapon. The steal was cold in his cradled hands and the weight was massive, but Two didn't care. Downstairs his stepfather was crouched over his badly beaten, petrified mother who was balled in a fetal position. Her hands were thrown over her head to protect her face and head from his stepfather's walloping blows. Call it mortal instinct, Two shouted for his stepfather to get off his mother. He cocked the hammer back; the gun seemed like a missile in his small hands.

"I want tell u again," Two-G warned. His voice delivered in a child's manner that wasn't convincing. He was scared and trembling all over. Two's stepfather rose to his feet and slowly treaded toward Two in a menacing fashion.

"Nooooo, don't!" Two's mother mustered enough courage to scream. She hoped her utter screams would stop the drunken madman from attacking her child.

"Shut up bitch!" his stepfather growled. "Before I give u something ta scream bout." His eye glared red and he smelled of a brewery factory. "Dis lil mutha fucka think he grown an' can't stay out of grown folk bizness, so I'ma treat his lil bitch ass like an adult." His stepfather flipped over the living room coffee table in the process.

Scared shirtless, Two squeezed the trigger and sent two bullets through his stepfather's neck and chest. Thus, Two's name derived from such heinous crime. Incarcerated, he gained mad respect from his peers, but the judge had other plans in mind. Sentencing Two to 10 years; but Two had been released early when the facility was shut down.

"Wuz popping wit'cha fools?" Block greeted, showing the homies love.

"U know us fool, out here tryna make des coins accumulate," Tree announced, then pulled a bank roll from his pocket that was chunky with twenties and fifties. "Big bank rolls dat's how we roll," he quoted.

"I feel ya," Block agreed. "Speaking of money, go retrieve dem proceeds an' bring them ta me," he informed Tree. There was business to attend to, and Block was ready to expand. Once he ran the plan pass Niko, Block would summon the goons and move in on G-Ball's old stomping grounds. "Pimp, I need'cha ta roll wit me," Block enlightened Pimp when Tree headed in the trap. "I got a meeting wit da man at noon, an' I need someone who handy wit da tool looking over me."

"Why, wat up wit Tree?" Pimp questioned. "Fam a shooter."

"Yea, I'm aware, but I need fam elsewhere," Block explained. Tree was handy with the tool, but Block needed him at the trap guarding the merchandise, an' keep da vultures at bay. Block knew the streets talked, so he was pretty sure the streets knew he had that blue cheese for the low numbers. Block didn't need niggaz getting the wrong ideas and get their body separated from their spirit. "I need fam ta hold down da trap, an' make sure everything in order. Plus, u a fool wit da tool too."

"I do a lil something," Pimp boasted.

"Let me ride wit'cha niggaz," Two-G cut in. "It's about time I earn my slot." Two-G was trying to get a piece of the pie and live the American dream. "U know my big brotha ain't tryna share da wealth. I'm tryna eat an' get fat like y'all niggaz." Two-G's big brother Big-Mo was another around the way nigga who had his hands in a lot of doe, but for some odd reason, he had refused to put his brother on. For whatever reason, Block had not a clue.

"I see u out here an' acknowledge your effort. Dat's a plus," Block explained. "But right now ain't da right time. Let me get thangz situated an' den I'ma holla back at'cha. Till den, be patient, your time is coming."

"All dat sounds good, but I don't know how patient one can be before his bones start showing." Two pulled up his T-shirt in effort to show his bonny rib cage. "I gotta do something ta feed des starving bones."

"Wuz wit Mo?" Block inquired. Block knew Mo had a constant cash flow and was moving brick throughout the city. "I know he on. Why dont'cha holla a dat nigga an' see wat's good on dat end? Cause its shabby on dis end."

"Mane, fuck dat nigga, he out for self. An' quite frankly I don't show luv ta no one who ain't got luv for me. Dis a dawg eat dawg world," Two-G said. Block paid close attention as Two talked, he made a lot of verbal hand motions as he spoke. If it was one thing his mother taught him growing up, Jesus didn't come to bring peace to the world; before his return there would be wars amongst father against sons, mothers against daughters, and brothers against brothers. Hell, Cain was the world's first murderer, he slayed his brother Abel. "If it came down ta it, dat nigga can get it too. I'm tired of playing second ta another man. So, wat's up, u gone let a nigga eat wit'cha or not?"

For some reason, Block felt obligated to put Two on, but in a sense, ill willed about it too. The nagging feeling told him Two would only bring him more problems than he already had. But Block also knew that was to be expected; the more money the more problems. That's just how the game goes. Although Block knew there was no second chance in life, he went against his gut feeling. In the streets you had to take chances. The only way to prove a man's loyalty, was to give that man a chance to prove his loyalty.

"Alright, I'ma give u a chance," Block gave in. "I want'cha ta hold da trap down wit Tree ta I get back. When I come back I'ma get'cha right," he promised. Block didn't realize it, but he had just gained a trusted ally. "I'm giving u a chance yung blood. Don't make me regret my decision."

"Trust me u won't. Word is bond," Two placed the racks over his heart.

Tree lugged down compact duffle bags, and Block and Pimp took off in Block's beat up hooty.

"U sure u can trust lil buddy?" Pimp asked while cracking the window slightly. "I'm not too sure bout lil buddy."

"Me neither, but only time a tell," Block phrased a quick reply. Moments passed and they pulled up in front of a gated community. Checking the address on his cellphone, the surroundings was exactly how Niko had informed him it would be. Greentree housing was top notch. Mini-mansions filled the gated enclosure. As they rolled pass all the luxurious homes, they noticed all he driveways were occupied by some of the finest foreign vehicles. Aston Martins, Alfa Romeos, Porsche, Benz, Rolls Royce, and many other expensive cars were sighted along the way toward their destination. Block couldn't help but think how out of place his car must seem. Anyone could tell they didn't belong, and probably assumed they were up to no good. Luckily, they didn't have to worry about that scenario; cause unlike the ghetto, the streets were deserted, which was abnormal from what they were accustom to. They'd came from a place where man and child roamed the streets day and night.

"Dam your manes living big," Pimp exclaimed. He gazed up at the beautiful mansion. "Dis how I'm tryna be living someday. Dis crib fat wit a capital PHAT.

Block couldn't agree more. He was also in awe at what stood before him. Just like all the other homes, Niko's driveway also had eye candy. It was occupied with a 2018 Ford GT that cost Niko a pretty penny. Last time Block checked, the starting range for the beauty was $450,000. That was a half a mil ticket.

Walking up the cobble bottleneck walkway toward Niko front door, Block felt out of his element. It was if he didn't belong, which was a normal feeling he'd grown accustom to over the years. Anytime he left the hood, he started to feel out of place. Growing up in the heart of the streets had given him a handicap to all other existing regions.

It was a feeling he'd yet to overcome but hoped in time it would melt away like snowflakes in the spring.

Before Block could ring the doorbell to announce his presence, the door opened, and a massive armed figure stood before them. The man was one of Niko's bodyguards Block assumed.

"Come, u have to be patted down. Da boss awaits u," the strange figure ordered them inside. The man's aura came off as bit of a ghoul. His demeanor reminded Block of a Bram Stoker's *Dracula* motion picture. During the pat down, Niko's armed guard bumped Block' 40 glock, and tried to remove it from his persons. "No guns allowed."

"Wat'cha doing?" Block snatched his fully loaded weapon back. "U do know I was invited, right?"

"An' da rules still remain da same. No guns, no exceptions," the armed man asserted.

"Look here jolly Green Giant, it seems ta me dat u hard of hearing. If I can't invoke my second amendment, u tell Niko ta meet me at a different time an' place. Do I make myself clear?" Block made his demand abundantly clear.

"Der will be no need fa dat," Niko called down the corridor, interrupting the formulated democracy. "Cabo, escort our guess in." Without further ado, Cabo followed orders and guided Block and Pimp inside to an awaiting Niko.

"Welcome ta my humble abode. Why dont'cha guys take a seat," Niko offered. He had great hospitality. "Or have a look round my pallor. Mi casa su casa. I'll be back soon." Niko informed, then headed off to handle whatever task it was he had to.

"Dis joint tight," Block admired the home out loud. The inside interior matched the outside, that was something you rarely saw in the hood. The creme interior was complimented by gold. It was like a palace inside the spacious home. Wandering around, Block came across an encased glass tank. Inside was seven golden frogs hopping around their artificial enclosing the resembled a wild forest. "I see u find da Golden Dart frogs fascinating," an unfamiliar voice boomed throughout the room. Block turned to greet the mysterious male. "Dey were imported in from Columbia. One dart from des poisonous amphibians can kill ten men. Fascinating isn't it?" he asked Block and he nodded in agreement. "Know anything about poisonous frogs?"

"Nah, but I did watch something on da nature channel once bout a frog in da Arctic dat can survive frigid temperatures. It freezes itself in da winter, den unthaw itself out in da spring," Block responded, indulging momentarily in futile conversation.

"Now dat's fascinating, dont'cha think so Niko?" he asked rhetorically. "A frog dat can freeze an' unthaw is a miracle at work. Dat definitely beats u guys life story." The unknown man made an indication then tapped the glass. "Well, dat's enough concerning nature's life. Why don't'cha take a seat so u an' I can get better acquainted."

"Block, Pimp, Niko, and Mr. Apparition all took a seat at the round marble top table. It was like some true mafioso type shit.

"So, my friends, ta cure your curiosity, I'm da infamous Rock," Rock started in as soon as everyone was seated. "I took da liberty ta fly in ta meet u personally. Not for any fascinated reason like I have for frogs, but for a lesser reason as common as looking U in da eyes. U see, I'm a firm believer dat da eyes are da key window ta da soul. One will never know wat kind of man he's dealing wit until der eyes meet." Rock paused long enough to spark a Cuban cigar and inhale the heavy tobacco smoke. "Believe me when I say I've done all da extensive research on u, an' your record is squeaky clean..."

"So, wat are u saying, dat u trust me?" Block interrupted with an eager and impatient question. The question took Rock by surprise, and he took the severity of the question in before giving a solid reply.

"Trust is da hardest thang ta earn an' da easiest thing ta lose," Rock replied, conveying sincerity in his strong accented words. "When u emit trust, der is a value dat must be set. An' u must clearly enumerate in specific trust values your searching for. Just because I trust u wit my work, don't mean I trust u wit my life. Product can be replaced, but my life is a different matter. Ain't no second chance in life."

Rock was a rich, dark skinned Cuban, who sort of resembled Pitbull in a sense with his slim build and bald head. The only difference was, Rock kept a well-groomed beard, unlike Pitbull who kept a babyface. Rock was an old soul, and the more he spoke, his words resonated with wisdom.

Block opened his ears to tote the game up. Block knew if he wanted to make it far in the game, he had to take heed of what the old head was giving. The old heads had been around the world and back; they'd seen it all before. Plus, some of the best leaders were first followers...

***

"Finish bagging des Oz's up. I'ma bout ta go upfront an' handle some bizness wit Trish," Tree informed Two. "U think u can handle dat?"

"An' some," Two replied in a short phrase of words. "Do u an' I'ma do me homie."

"Alright," Tree bent off, turning the sound system up along the way. He cranked Jeezy trap album "Recession" up enough to drown out the tattle tale sounds Trish would be making. Tree had to be careful. If word got back to the hood he was knocking down a hype bitch, his player card would surely be revoked. So, he made sure what him and Trish was carrying on stayed behind closed doors.

"Ay babe, u ready for your daily dose?" Trish asked. She was stretched out on the sofa wearing nothing but a T-shirt and panties. Her bare thighs showed. Uncrossing her juicy thighs, then re-crossed them.

"U know wat it is, u ain't even gotta ask. Just get your ass in da room an' drop dem draws." Tree pointed at the corner side bedroom, while unbuckling his Louis belt buckle. "Nigga finna put big folks in your life." Tree followed behind Trish. As he watched her ass switch beneath her dingy T-shirt, he stroked his semi-hard dick. In the bedroom, he pushed Trish over the mattress and ripped off her satin thong panties.

"Oooooh daddy," she moaned as Tree penetrated her from behind. "Sssssss," she hissed and bit her bottom lip. His dick game touched every part of her. She felt like Kesha Cole with love all over her. They'd been fucking daily since their first encounter, and she couldn't get enough. She'd had to admit, she had found a new profound high, and she was turned out.

"U like dis dick dont'cha?" Tree asked, ramming into her. Their shared passion had left Tree oblivious to the outside world. He had no clue the whole time he'd been getting his dick wet, Two-G stood outside the crack door watching their every move.

Two-G was disgusted and shocked at the same time at the fiasco unfolding before him. Scarred by the scene, he walked back into the kitchen. Two couldn't help but to think how weak ass niggaz always played themselves out by thinking with their dicks. All the money Tree was getting, all types of groupie bitches would eat a boss dick. But instead, Tree was going out like a sucker by sticking his thing in a hype bitch. That, Two just couldn't understand. Two wondered if he should divulge what he'd discovered to Block? There was no way Block would believe him. In all honesty, claiming accusations so damning could get Two killed. So common sense led him to keep his mouth sealed.

Meanwhile, while Tree was fulfilling his sexual gratifications trying to get a nut, the back door came crashing in, followed by a loud explosion.

"Milwaukee police department! Get down on da flow!" The swat team announced as the smoke from the flash grenade started to settle.

Two, unfazed by the tactics, swept most of the dope off the table into a duffle bag. Refusing to go back to jail, he ran into the bathroom, and escaped out of a side window. He would never let them take him alive, that was for certain. Throwing the bag over his shoulder, Two climbed out the window. Climbing to the roof, Two tossed the bag to the rooftop of an abandon building, and followed behind. It wasn't a far jump. Landing softly on his side, he scrambled to his feet, and fled down a flight of stairs where he disappeared into thin air.

Tree wasn't so lucky; captured, he struggled desperately to free himself from twelve.

"Stop resisting!" Officer James yelled, while kneeing Tree in the rib cage. Tree had been caught in the worst manner, literally with his pants down. Embarrassed by the ordeal, Tree obeyed and refrained from resistance. He just wanted the circus act to cease...

***

"Come open dis dam doe," Moski ordered into the phone. "Got me standing out here looking all crazy an' shit fa your nosey neighbors ta see. Get'cha ass down here." Moski disconnected and waited for Shuana to open up the door. When she did, she stood before him wearing a white halter top that hugged her breasts for dear life. Her nipples protruded through like high beams on a convertible. Moski gave her a once over after their brief embrace. As she walked ahead of him, Moski licked his lips in anticipation, staring at her ripe behind. Shuana's booty moved like jello in her red booty shorts. Soon Moski would put a name on it. It had been quite a while since he'd last put a stamp on her ass, and she was due for postage.

Shuana smiled over her shoulder. "I see u looking, wat'cha gone do?" she invited him to her goodies. Shuana knew the effect she had on man. She'd discovered the powers early, at the tender age of 14. It was when she had caught her stepfather's wandering eyes lingering over her ripe body. They were alone in the living room while her mother slaved away in the kitchen to fix them a hot meal. Shuana had just come home from a track meet. She hadn't bothered to shower or change, she'd run straight home after practice still in her skimpy blue boy shorts and tight fitted T-shirt she wore to train in. Her blossoming body showed vividly in the treads. After that day, her stepfather Kenny started hitting on her. She didn't rebuff him either, although she should have. She allowed his advances to carry on until they had both crossed the forsaking lines of carnal. She was a horny teenager who had needs, at least that's what she told herself. Plus, for 30 years old, Kenny was handsome. For two years, up until Shuana's sixteenth birthday, Kenny and her carried on a torrid affair behind her mother's back. Shuana would fuck and suck Kenny wherever. One day she sucked Kenny's dick in front of the television while her mother slept inches away in a recliner chair. Behaviors as such carried on until her mother busted them red handed in the act. Kenny had Shuana bent over the entertainment stand, ferociously fucking her from behind, when her mother walked in. She'd arrived home early from work to find the shock of her life. Shuana's mother threatened to contact the authorities and have Kenny imprisoned for statutory rape. But in the end, that never happened. Instead, she had thrown Kenny and Shuana out in the streets. Shuana was forced to go live with her auntie until she graduated and was old enough to get a place of her own. To the very day, Shuana and her mother still hadn't spoken. Her mother wouldn't even acknowledge her existence. In the cruel words of her mother, she didn't have a whore daughter.

"U know I puts it down," Moski bragged. He then pulled out a pre-rolled blunt from the pockets of his True Religion jeans. "Come here an' let a nigga poke," Moski palmed her posterior and gave it a firm squeeze. It was soft to the touch and felt like pudding in his hands.

Shuana returned the caresses, jacking his hard dick through his jeans. "Some ones happy to see me," she whispered in his ear, then trailed her tongue gently around his earlobe. "U think u can keep em like dat?" she inquired about his stiffness. "Why I freshen up a bit."

"Baby, I can do magic," Moski pretentiously appraised himself. "Hurry up now, don't have a nigga waiting. Time is money shawty." Moski took a seat on the loveseat while Shuana headed off to the bathroom.

While Moski relaxed smoking, Shuana was up to her old venomous, conniving ways. She turned on the sinks faucet as she dialed in Sco's number on her cellphone.

"U ain't gone guess who I got cooped up at my place," Shuana murmured into the phone.

"Who Trick?" Sco asked. "I ain't got time for da 21-question game. Speak your mind, or forever hold your peace." Sco was being sardonic. Sco was a businessman, and he didn't have time for futile antics. His patience had run thin when it came to Shuana. Her hourglass was seeping out of time. There was only a matter of time before he put a bullet in her head. He knew she had played a role in his right-hand man Blaze's death. It didn't take a rocket scientist to figure out she was responsible. The way his guy had been gunned down in front of the trap house, Shuana might as well been caught with the smoking gun. Everyone knew Shuana's pedigree. She was a low-down dirty type that would sleep wit the enemy and sell her mother out if it benefitted her. Shuana knew Bando and Sco were arch enemies They'd been shooting and killing each other people for years over some old beef that hadn't froze over. Sco didn't have full proof, but his sixth sense told him Shuana was involved.

"Bando's foot souja Moski," she answered reluctantly. She wasn't a big fan of his disrespect. Quite frankly, she was missing her patience as well. Ever since Sco and his entourage had forced her to set up Bando and his crew, Sco had been real foul at the mouth; using expletive language to address her. Sco's cognomen had no barren. Everyone knew her forte and how she rocked. Even doe she did what she did to get Blaze knocked off the face of the earth, she felt Sco had no right to call her any other name then the name her mother gave her at birth. "Wat do u want me ta do?"

"Wat da fuck u mean wat I want'cha ta do?" Sco spewed in frustration. "Do whatever sluts do. Suck an' fuck him. Do whatever it take. Just keep dat nigga der until me an' folks arrive."

Shuana's line went dead before she could reply. Left with no other choice but to do what she had to, she sprayed on some D&G perfume then bailed out the bathroom. Unconsciously unaware of her surroundings, she collided into Moski who waited outside the door cradling a 32-snub nose in his hand.

"U scared me," she said nervously. She was frightened out of her wits by Moski, but she tried not to let it show on her face. "I thought u was still..."

"Shut up bitch!" Moski cut her off. He knew she was up to no good. "I'm da one asking questions from here on out." Moski's once calm demeanor had changed from admiration to pure savage. There was a psychosomatic derange look in his eyes that made Shuana fear for her life. Shuana felt her boy shorts moist, but not from arousal, it was pure unadulterated fear. "Who was u in der on da phone wit?" he growled through clenched teeth. Shuana was stuck between a rock and a hard place. She didn't know whether to answer truthfully or mendaciously. Either way, he would probably kill her. There was no doubt in her mind that he had just overheard her on the phone. "Well?" Moski waited for her reply. "Cat got'cha tongue? It sure seem u had a lot ta say in der," he pointed at the bathroom. "So, wat's it gone be? U gone tell me, or I'ma put a bullet between dem pretty lil eyes." Moski raised his black revolver in a menacing fashion and placed it right between her eyes.

"I was on da phone wit my girlfriend," Shuana lied. She hoped she could by some chance save her life. A tear escaped the corner of her eye in pseudo sympathy. "We was just..."

Shuana was silenced by a forceful slap before she could get the full sentence out of her mouth. Moski knew she was untruthful. He had heard every word she had conveyed over the running water.

"Lies!" Moski barked while cocking the hammer back on his cannon. "I heard u bitch!" he shouted like a mad lunatic. "Now u want me ta kill u before dem weak ass niggaz get here, or after? Its your choice."

"Please don't!" she begged for her life, prostrating at his feet. Moski loomed over her like Juneau the God of death. "Please, I'll do anything."

"Dat's da pathetic plea I here from so many before I clean dey clock. I thought u would be different, but I was wrong." Moski scratched his temple with the muzzle of his gun. "One thang dat's for certain, is u will die."

"Please!" she cried. She didn't realize her pleads satiated him. Moski was what clinicians would diagnose as a sadist. He found pleasure in others pain. She cried profusely when it became abundantly clear she was going to die. Pathetically, she clawed at Moski's pants leg. "Do I have to die? I'll do anything."

"Shut da fuck up cry baby bitch, an' get da fuck up!" Moski snatched Shuana up by the roots of her hair and dragged her into the living room with his pistol pointed at her head. "For starters, you'll wait ta our company arrives, den you'll invite dem inside like a good hostess."

"Ok," she agreed blindly. Moski shoved her down on the floor. She was trash, so he treated her as such. She had not the slightest clue the extent of the verbal contract she'd just signed. Moski's machination specialized in yellow tape. He had plotted a pogrom, which she would witness before her own demise.

A rap came at the door. The hit squad had arrived to put Moski down like an old diseased dog. Inside the mind of a killer, Moski hoped he had enough munition to take em all. He was unaware how many guns and men waited for him on the other side of the door. Regardless, Moski was ready to ride with six, and be carried by six if that was the case. Whatever the outcome, Moski would stand and die like a soldier in war.

"Clean yourself up an' open da dam doe," Moski ordered, then leveled his pocket rocket at Shuana's face. "An' u better not let them know I'm behind dis doe. I swear ta gawd I'll face time your shit."

Shuana dried her wet eyes with the palm of her hand, then opened the door to her domain. Sco was unaware he was entering purgatory, where their souls would remain.

"Where he at?" Sco asked stepping into the foyer.

From where Moski stood, he had a clear advantage point. He could see Sco's partner looming in the shadows from the other side of the door. The man already had his gun out, ready for action.

"He in da room," Shuana misguided by pointing toward her bedroom. "Y'all be careful. Don't be messing up my crib." Shuana had mastered the art of deception. They didn't even detest stranger things.

Sco was the first in, and his gun slinger Pistol followed in tow. As soon as Shuana shut the door, Moski stepped out of the dark shadows and brought the butt of his gun down over Pistol's cerebellum. He went down like Smoking Joe Frazier in the third round. He was out cold.

"Wuz up bitch ass nigga. Dis wat'cha came for," Moski surprised Sco from behind. Facing his enemy like a man, Moski didn't even give Sco a chance to register what was going on, he sent two to Sco's face, and stretched him out next to his partner Pistol.

"Ahhhhh!" Shuana let out a wailing scream. She had never witnessed a murder. The piercing screech caused Moski to stick the barrel of his snub nose in Shuana mouth and plaster her brains on the walls. Her body slid down the wall leaving a trail streak of fresh blood.

Moski then kicked Pistol in the face a series of times. He kicked him until he revived consciousness. "Wake your bitch ass up, so I can be da last nigga u see."

As Pistol slowly opened his eyes, Moski sent the remaining trinity into his face. The hollow points turned Pistol's face into cranberry sauce. Moski then fled home laughing to himself. Another unsolved murder...

***

Two-G ran into the home he shared with his baby mother and slammed the door behind him.

"What's wrong wit'cha slamming doors like u crazy?" Jordin nagged. Two flopped down on the sofa and tried his best to ignore her. "U gone wake da baby wit all dat damn noise. I just put him ta sleep, an' u aint' gone help me rock his cranky ass back ta sleep if he wake up."

"Gone wit all dat," Two dismissed her complaint. He was breathing hard and perspiring heavily. So much so, it soaked through his clothing. "Go get me da phone."

"Tyrone, what's wrong?" she questioned using his real name. She had an eerie feeling about the state Two was in. She had never seen him like he was at the moment. "An' what's in da bag?" She eyed the Nike duffle bag curiously. She thought maybe the bag pertained to the situation. All she knew was Two was sweating like an athlete and looking around all nervous like he'd stole something.

"Mind your damn bizness, an' do as I say," Two snapped. "Go get me da phone Jay." He stared at her coldly. "Yo ass act like u don't know how ta act some mutha fucking times."

Jordin huffed out of frustration, then flounced to retrieve the cordless phone. They still had a landline, because they couldn't afford to pay a cellphone bill on the salary they were living on. Jordin was the only one in the household bringing in any source of income. Two had been out on the streets for over a year now, and they had a third mouth to feed. Jordin never complained about their living condition, or, that Two didn't hold any employment. She loved him and wasn't the type of bitch that tore down her man because he was down on his luck. She was a real bitch that believed in building anew. She was with him whether rich or poor.

When Jordin returned with the phone, Two took it, and kissed her on the cheek to show his appreciation before rushing out of the room.

"Hello," Block answered. He and Pimp was in traffic on the road to riches.

"G, we got hit," Two informed Block of the mishap while pacing back and forth in a panic. "Mane, I don't know wat happen. Da boys came busting in..." he rushed through his information, stumbling over words along the way.

"Hold up, who dis?" Block asked with caution. The number didn't register on his display. The number was unfamiliar.

"Dis Two nigga!" he breached hard into the phone.

"Look, I ain't gone talk over dis phone. Where u at? I'ma swoop down on ya."

Two gave Block his location, and ten minutes later, Block was honking the horn.

"Baby," Two called stepping back into the living room. "I'ma see u later. Sorry bout yelling at'cha earlier. I applaud u for wat'cha been doing, an' puting up wit a nigga. U my super women." Two tried to make up for his inconsideration.

"I know babe," Jordin assured. She understood the struggles of a black man. She had watched her father endure the same trials and tribulations when she was a young girl. So, she knew sometimes shit could get hectic for a nigga. "U be safe out der." Jordin grabbed her fo-nickle from under the sofa and placed it upon Two waistband. She kissed him, indicating her forgiveness. "It's better ta have it an' not need it, den ta need it an' not have it," she quoted.

Two smiled at his B.M.'s gutsiness. "Dat's why I luv your crazy ass." Two kissed her again while gripping her firm backside through her pajamas. "See u later." He grabbed his bag and headed out the door.

Outside, Two jumped in the backseat and tossed the bag over the front.

"Wat's dis?" Block asked skeptical. "An' ware Tree at? He ain't answering his fone."

"Dat's aw da dope I could grab before dem smurf boys came charging in da spot," Two explained. He wasn't sure how much merch he'd slid into the bag, but he was sure it was most of it." As far as Tree, I don't know was cracking. When dem boys came in, I jumped out da window and took flight." He kept to himself what he'd witness.

Block searched through the bag. He was surprised how real Two was. Eyeballing the merchandise, it was clear most of the dope was all there. He approved of Two's loyalty. Two didn't have any real ties to him; he could have taken the work for himself and claimed the police confiscated it. Block realized real honor and gave major props when due.

"Dis all der?" Block asked.

"All wat I could grab," Two enlightened. He wasn't disappointed Block had questioned his loyalty. In fact, it was Block's right to do so. This was only Two's first day on the job, and coincidentally the police had raided the spot. If Two was in Block's shoes, he would have done the same. "I told u ta give me a chance ta prove myself, an' dat's wat I did. I'm a man of principals an' honor lies in my word."

"I feel dat. Look, I'ma need u ta lay low until we get everything situated, an' find out wat's up wit Tree." Block was looking out for Two and the crew's best interest. Block couldn't risk having Two out on the streets right now, especially when the police had just hit the trap. It was hot, and the law might be planning a sweep. He wasn't certain, so Block took safety precaution. "Here, u take dat. Dat's u." Block tossed back the bag as a gift. "Dat's royalty fo loyalty. I'ma program your number in my phone, an' get at'cha in a couple days. Here take dis too." He handed Two a wad of bills. Two took the money graciously and smiled. It had to be about five stickers wrapped tightly in a rubber band. "Be easy."

"Fo'sho." Two showed Block and Pimp love before getting out the car. Two-G didn't know what he had done to deserve this much love, but whatever it was, he planned to keep it that way. Because loyalty is compensated by royalty...

***

Bando and his team were all having a good time up in Jean steppers nightclub. The team celebrated pouring up libations and blowing gas. They were celebrating Moski's success on knocking Sco's dick in the dirt. Bando couldn't explain the thrill of pride he felt when Moski had told him he'd just pushed Sco's shit back. That was great news. Now that Sco was out the picture, ESG could expand. Bando was on some get down or lay down shit like Benny Segual in State Property.

"Cheers ta our boy Mo for giving us access ta new regions ta reign over." Bando raised his Ace of Spade bottle in the air. Eastside, Creep, Chop, and Shay all did the same to celebrate Moski's honor. Duck was somewhere in the club sack chasing.

"We salute ta dat," Chop acknowledged, toasting his Remy bottle with the mob.

While the team was living it up partying, Chop had deviant intentions. Shay was sandwiched in between Bando and Chop in the VIP section, and Chop had his hand up Shay's short Givenchy dress playing with her pussy. No one notice the deceitful act unfolding right beneath their noses. Shay was enjoying the risky attention. The trill of getting caught excited her. It was both a mixture of fear and pleasure that made her creme on Chop busy fingers. Leaning over, he whispered for Shay to meet him in the bathroom, then slid out the booth. Not long after, Shay followed suit.

"Six bottles of Ciroc, an' a bottle of Nuevo fo da lady," the waitress, Sherry, announced while setting the libations on the table.

"Hold up," Bando grabbed Sherry arm preventing her from leaving. "We didn't order des."

"Compliments from da gentleman a couple tables down," Sherry explained.

Bando released Sherry's arm and she scurried away.

Bando looked in the direction the waitress had directed him. There alone sat a brown skin brother who resembled Jaheim. Bando picked his mind for a facial recognition but couldn't seem to place the unfamiliar man. Bando had never saw him a day in his life. So, he pondered why he sending him bottles. Bando thought the nigga must be on some gay shit. The mysterious man raised his bottle when he acknowledged Bando.

Bando excused himself from his table and went over to see what was on the nigga's bird.

"Wuz up?" Bando approached, poking out his chest in case ole boy wanted some smoke. "Why u sending bottles ta me an' da squad? U on some gay shit or something?"

Bando's choice of words must have been hysterical, because the man replied with a hearty laugh.

"First, let me say I'ma gangsta an' only way I slide is on a bitch. Secondly, I sent da bottles as a calling card." Six cleared the air, extirpating any sideways assumptions. "Dey call me Six, an' I'm new in town. Word is u da man out here in da Mil, so I thought we could do some bizness," Six stroked Bando's ego.

Bando gave Six a once over before responding. He had to admit Six was fly head to toe in Gucci. But Bando's antennas stood up on alert. The calling card gesture was an odd way of an introduction, an' Bando wasn't so sure Six wasn't twelve.

"An' u just knew ta find me here?" Bando expressed his skepticism. "I'm curious as ta know how u knew ta find me up in da club late nite. Dis ain't no normal routine for me an' da team."

"I didn't know u was up in dis joint. Believe me dis was strictly coincidental," Six tried to explain the caprice of the situation without blowing his cover. "When I arrived in town, I asked round bout some local big timers an' your name popped up. Just so happened I decided ta kick it thought ta see wat fine thoties Mil-town had, an' just so happen, I ran into u."

"Where u from?" Bando asked. Bando was sure there had to be some truth to Six's words. Six spoke a different lango from Milwaukee niggaz. It was most definitely Midwest. Maybe Chicago, or Gary, but definitely not Milwaukee's.

"I'm from Gary. Da hart of da streets," Six claimed. Little did Bando know it was a tell by omission. Six was born in Gary, Indiana and lived there until his mid-teen years, then his family relocated due to all the gang violence. "Mutha fuckas eating over der like every day, steak an' potatoes."

"So, wat brings u des way if u eating so good over dem ways." Bando was no nincompoop. Bando knew most of the time niggaz parted ways from the city or the G was because they were running from something or someone. Maybe it was them hitters or the law. Whatever it was, Bando wanted to know.

"I'm looking ta expand. I gotta bizness proposition fa u ta consider."

CHAPTER ELEVEN

───────

Block's phone rung and he answered.

"Wuz popping?" he asked, taking a pull from the gas him and Pimp were smoking on.

"Ay cat daddy," Connie purred into the phone. "Why dont'cha come thru here an' let me bounce up an' down on dat Pogo stick fo a while? Dis pussy hot fa u daddy," Connie pleaded for Block to adhere to her request.

"Gurl, u know dat ain't gone happen," he rebuffed her proposition. "U know I fuck wit'cha gurl Kayla. An' anyways, u my ninja Dice lady. So, we can't be creeping round like dat no more."

"Why not?" she retorted. "Dat shit never stopped u before from taken me down. Now all da sudden u talking about I'm Dice's gurl. Negro please, beat it wit da jokes," Connie smacked her lips. She was trying to lay guilt on Block's conscious, but little did she know it wouldn't work. "So, what's up, u gone come thru or not?"

Block was tongue tied. Connie was right, they'd been sneaking around behind Dice's back for a little bit over a year now. Ever since they reconnected, when they'd ran back into one another by surprise one night at the club, Block had been putting pipe in her life. But the past was the past. Things somehow felt different now. Everything was falling in place in Block's life. His money was stacking up, and on top of that, he had the woman of his dreams. What more could a boss ask for but a condo on the beach. Kayla made him happy, and that was enough.

"Yea I know, but things gotta change," he told Connie. He didn't want to hurt her feelings, but this was the way things had to be. "It was different wit u. Now I got Kayla, an' I don't want ta hurt her."

"Don't tell me dat bum bitch got u whipped? Dat bitch ain't got nothing on me, an' she most definitely can't ride dat dick like I can," Connie bad talked Kayla. But she didn't care not one bit. Connie couldn't even decipher why she kept Kayla naive ass around. Kayla was so caught in the illusion of her educational books, that reality of the world had become obsolete to her. "See dat was da reason I didn't want ta give u her number in da first place, because I knew u would fall in luv wit dat weak ass bitch."

Back when her and Block reconnected, Block had inquired about Kayla, but Connie had lied, saying she didn't know Kayla's whereabout. But when he had gotten ahold of Kayla's contacts without her assistance, Connie did like any supposedly friend would do, and pushed them together even doe she didn't agree of the nature of their relationship.

Connie liked fucking other bitches' men. Knowing they was taken, made the sensation of the coitus way more satisfactory.

"Now look at'cha finna miss out on da best thang dat ever happen ta u over some bucket head bitch."

"See dat's ware u got it all wrong. Because Kayla da best thang dat ever happen ta me. An' if I ever hear u disrespect her again, I'ma slap da taste out ur mouth," Block checked Connie, putting her in her place. He couldn't stand to hear Connie talk ill of his future wifey like she had. Kayla didn't deserve any of it, she had become a victim by circumstances. "Me an' u are no more. Don't call my phone, an' don't come thru. None of da two. Just stay your distance if u know wat's good for u." It was funny how love could change a person perspective in life. Because of Connie he'd had bodied a nigga. Now he wanted nothing to do with her.

"Nigga if u leave me now, you'll be sorry u ever fucked me," Connie spewed a venomous threat. "I mean I'll make your life a living hell. You'll wish u was dead before I'm done wit'cha," she made sure he understood the full weight of the threat. There was no idol or emptiness in her words. She would hold dear to her word if Block didn't adhere to her demands.

"Do wat u have to." Block took no heed to her and hung up. He figured she was only venting and needed time to clear her head. Time heals all, and so he thought time would do them both justice. But little did he know, he'd just made a grave tragic decision.

Soon as he hung up, his phone chimed again.

"I said stop calling my damn line," Block answered in a hostile manner.

"Calm down, it's me bay," Kayla clarified. She was at dismay and thrown that Block had answered the phone as he had. "Don't bite my head off. U ok? Dang."

"My bad Kay, des dam pest keep calling my phone harassing me. I just lost my cool, dat's all," he lied by omission. He couldn't tell Kayla the pest was her best friend, or so-called best friend. He wanted to tell Kayla the truth. She deserved to know, but he knew the truth would hurt. And how could he explain the very thing that had split them apart many years ago. Block knew that would be the straw that broke the camel back. "Never mine me, how u doing wit'cha fine ass?" Block queried about her day.

The fact that Block put forth the effort to check on her needs and feeling before his own made Kayla smile from ear to ear.

"Nah, don't try ta butter me up so u can slide on my good side," she faked like she was upset. "Why didn't u hold true ta your word, an' come get me last nite for our date? U had me get all dolled up waiting on u, but u never showed."

Kayla wasn't mad at Block, maybe a bit disappointed, but not mad. She knew Block didn't intentionally stand her up, Block wasn't the type.

"Damn, ma," Block scratched his head searching for an excuse that would explain his carelessness. "My bad, Tree got knocked last nite an' I forgot. I got caught up in da moment, but I swear I'll make it up ta u."

"U better," Kayla assured. "I hope dis ain't how our future gone look. If so, I'ma brake your heart. Dis fine ass brotha I seen at Subway on my way ta school offered ta take me on a date. I might just take him up on it," Kayla pulled Block's chains. Cheating would never cross her mind. She was a real bitch that kept it real with her man know matter what.

"U better be playing. I'll beat u an' dawg ass," Block half wittily joked. The tone in his voice was serious. He would kill over Kayla and set the world ablaze if it meant they could spend eternity together. "Matter fact, I'ma go slide down on buddy ass right now, an' let him know its many thangz in life he want, like money, cars, an' clothes, but dis ain't one of dem."

Kayla cackled at Block's silliness. She knew he was playing around, but also knew by his actions, he would take on the world for her. That was a quality she loved most about him; he was sweet in the sheets with her, but a beast in the streets for her. Truly she loved Block always and forever.

"Look doe, me an' my man out here hitting des corners tryna tie up some loose ends," Block informed Kayla. He didn't want to cut their conversation short, but he knew he had to. It was for the better good. "Tonight, I promise, I'ma make it up ta u. I'ma take u ta do something nice, den I'ma beat dat pussy out da frame."

"Alright, u better hold dear ta dat, or I'm going wit Mr. Subway."

They both laughed. It was humorous because Block knew she wouldn't lower her standards so low to date a sandwich slanger. Kayla wasn't no Subway hoe.

"Be here, I ain't playing Bentley," she proclaimed. "Luv u."

"Luv u too, kisses." Block hung up feeling quite joyful.

"Kisses, smooches," Pimp mocked, blowing air kisses. "Old Peppy La'pew ass nigga. I never thought I'll see da day, but ole gurl got'cha whipped." Pimp flicked his wrist in a popping motion. "Wat's next, u gone be singing "Let's Get Married" by Jagged Edge?"

"Fuck u ninja," Block laughed while stubbing out the roach in the ashtray. "Soon u gone meet dat one, an' she gone bring u ta your knee's an' have u begging fa marriage."

"Maybe so," Pimp didn't deny. "But I ain't gone be getting off no phone talking about kisses. Dat's some white gurl shit." Pimp had just set the world back by almost 80 years with his sexist-racist joke. But they didn't care, they chuckled because it was funny, not because of the content that could cause irreparable damage to the public views.

"Whatever fool. Let's go plant our flag an' claim dis territory," Block said, getting out the car and placing his forty on his hip. Block had been scoping out G-Ball's deck for some time. Now it was time to execute his plan and shack trap. It was about expansion. Rock had giving Block his wish, and expanded his shipment 20 plus 30, that was a total of 50 kilos he'd be pushing on a regular. In order to be king, you had to reign over vast territory, so now it was time for the takeover. It was time to let Ball boyz know there was a new ruler.

Block and Pimp approached a squad of hoodlums posted up on the porch getting money. From the car, Block and Pimp had watched numerous hand to hand transactions. So, it was obvious they were doing numbers.

"Can we help y'all niggaz?" a scruffy looking new breed nigga asked. He looked rough like he'd seen better days, just not now. His hair was disheveled and matted together, and his beard was a scraggly mess. He was a poor sight to see in his low budget wear that looked as if he had purchased them from lost and found.

"Yea, u can start by selling my work," Block replied, simultaneously pulling out his 40 caliber. Its appearance produced a quantity of fear from Mr. Scruffy A.K.A Lack of Detergent.

Two queues fled from the porch. Pimp let off a shot after the pair, and one went down.

"Anybody else wanna be on track an' field?" Block asked staring into the steel of day. No answer, there was complete silence. "Let me know so I can add your body ta da collection." Still no reply. Scruffy stood before Block shaking by the ordeal. He tried to compose his signs of fear. "Pimp, finish dat lil ninja off over der, so des ninjaz know I mean bizness."

Pimp walked over toward the nigga he'd dropped. Buddy laid on his side harnessing his wounded leg in his hands. When Pimp started toward him, he tried scrambling to his feet, but there was no use. The pain was too much to bear. As Pimp stood over him, he pumped three shoots in his chest, and put ole boy lights out.

"From now on, dis my deck, an' y'all ninjaz work fa me." Block claimed his turf...

***

Tree sat uncomfortable in the first district interrogation room. Two plain clothes detectives entered the room.

"Hi, I'm Homicide Detective Michael Corbind an' dis my partner Sandra Felts," an officer that resembled Charlie Murphy off "Paper Soldiers" introduced himself and stunning partner.

Their presence had Tree paranoid. Homicide detectives didn't investigate gun and drug cases. If they were there, Tree knew it was for a reason.

"Would u like ta talk ta us?" Corbind asked. Corbind copped a squat on a metal stool next to his partner. He and Det. Felts expected a reply, but Tree didn't respond, only gave a cold stare in return. "Dat's ok yung man. U don't have to talk, we'll do all da talking for u." Corbind neatly stacked three paper folders in front of him on the wooden table. Tree wasn't sure of its content, but whatever they contained within, would determine his fate.

Det. Corbind cleared his throat before resuming his interrogation. "Your a popular guy. U seem ta get many likes on da web," he conveyed fake admiration. Tree twisted up his lips at the corner. He knew bullshit when he heard it.

Tree wasn't hip to the internet like the rest of his generation. He didn't even have a webpage, so whoever the police were looking for, he knew it couldn't be him.

"I can see your in disbelief." Corbind made direct eye contact. "Should we show him wat we obtained?" he directed his question toward Det. Felts.

"Why not? He seems like da exhibitionist type," she returned. This was the first time she'd uttered a single word since the inception of their interrogation.

Tree couldn't help but to stare. Felts was a gorgeous woman, with rich mahogany skin, full lips, and hazel eyes that sparkled beautifully off the reflection of the light. Her hair was reddish brown in an Andrea Day style, and her body was in tip top shape like the number eight. Tree would most definitely smash.

Det. Felts passed Corbind the tablet she possessed. He made a few swipes to the right, then placed it in front of Tree. Tree stared at himself in disbelief. There he was the night he'd shot the bouncer at

Victor's. Never in a million years did he think his rash actions would come back to bite him in the ass.

"Dis video made u famous. It went viral, gaining u more den a 100 thousand likes. Aren't u proud?" Corbind asked in a sarcastic manner. His extemporaneousness really exacerbated the hell out of Tree. "I tell u, me an' my partner was thrilled. So thrilled, we obtained a search warrant, after we received an anonymous tip ware, we may find u. We just had to meet U. Not ta mention how fond we were when we found out u were a serial killer."

"Serial killer!" Tree blurted. Astounded by the accusations, he could no longer hold his tongue. They were tryna pin a murder rep on him. "I ain't killed no mutha fucking body."

"He talks," Det. Felts patronized.

"Yup, he does. Corbind agreed. "Didn't think we'd get a word out him so soon." He laughed. Corbind had seen this many times before. There wasn't many that kept their tough guy act up when their livelihood was at stake. "I guess it's like they say, a lip is sealed until u apply a hot poker to da owner's ass."

"U pigs funny. U ain' got shit on me," Tree continued to play naive. He knew he was in deep shit. That Drako they'd found had two bodies on it. One he'd committed, and another he'd played a role in. But he didn't have no rap for the law. Tree had to get on the phone and contact a lawyer, so he could get the boyz off his back. "U mutha fuckas in here fishing. I ain't gone let'cha place no hooks in me, I'm smarter den a sea bass."

"Believe me, we're not tryna hook u. We're just tryna inform u wat we have an' wat'cha up against." Corbind calmly spoke. You could tell he'd been through the routine many times before. Because he had mastered the arts of a pig's fashion by trying to get in the subject head. "U see, upon our raid, we recovered 56 grams of a controlled substance, a scale that contained residue, an' numerous corner cut baggies. But dat's minor, an' I'm sure da D.A. would throw dat out known da murders will trump all of the above." Corbind opened the first folder. There were numerous photos of the crime scene. "Da first occurred approximately three months ago. Here's 17-year-old Steven Jones." Corbind slid a photo in front of Tree. "Secondly, we have Derrick James an' Benjamin Lamont. We know u didn't kill Mr. Lamont, because da casings recovered from da crime scene doesn't match those of da gun we found. So, we know u had an accomplice," he informed, pushing the rest of the photographs toward Tree, but he pushed them onto the floor.

"Wat? Pig please, u didn't even find dat gun in my possession. Dat crib ain't mine," Tree hysterically jumped out of his seat. "I want my lawyer. Take me back ta my cell!" he shouted and kicked over the chair he was sitting in.

"Well, it seems we've come ta a dead end here." Det. Corbind and his partner leaped out of their chairs on guard. They were afraid of being attacked. "Officer Grant, u can come escort Mr. Frederick back ta his cell," Corbind yelled for reinforcements.

Officer Grant rushed into the room, and roughly pushed Tree against the wall, before placing him in handcuffs. Tree didn't even protest. He was used to those who took an oath to serve and protect using unnecessary force. Back in his enclosed habitat where he was caged in like some animal at a petting zoo, Tree paced the floor in deep thought. He was down bad, but he refused to let the white man jam him up and stick him with a life bid. He had to do something, because there was no way in hell he would spend the rest of his duration locked in a jail cell. His demarcations had been met, and there were no boundaries above loyalty. He refused to get out of jail free on some Master Splinter shit. Standing true to the game, he would do his time like a gee, and stand tall.

Tree stood over the commode and looked up to the ceiling as he anticipated to urinate. The first splash forced him onto his tippy toes. A sharp agonizing pain tore through his urethra that caused him to hiss in pain and grab his dick head trying stop the tormenting pain. With no luck at stopping the flowing urine, he let go. As the piss passed through his hole, he cried out like a bitch. "Police!" He shouted...

***

Block dropped Pimp off beside his hooacty.

"Be careful my ninja," Block warned Pimp before he was halfway out the vehicle. "U an' Six, we all we got now dat Tree been pinched," he spoke with much sorrow.

Pimp empathized with Block's pain. Pimp and Tree was like joined twins at the hip. Tree was his brother from another mother, and Pimp would never let anything come between the love, honor, and respect he had for Tree.

"Keep ur eyes open an' pilled ta da streetz. We on another level now, an' des vipers can't wait ta sink der fangs in ya."

"U know I always keep my grass cut so I can see da snakes," Pimp said, leaning back inside the ajar door. "Plus, I keep dis burner on me, an' finger always itchy, feel me?"

"I feel ya my ninja," Block nodded his head. "Look, I'm bout ta be up out of here doe. I gotta handa some B.I before I go swoop my baby up. One luv." Pimp closed the door, and Block threw up the rakes and smashed the gas.

It was real on the streets. At least to Pimp it was. Less than an hour ago, he had just sent a nigga ceiling down the river. Another mother in mourning, he thought. His hands were always dirty; in fact, he couldn't remember the last time they had been clean. Unclean hands had been the story of his life ever since he was 16, way before life removed all the innocence. Pimp couldn't remember where his infatuation with guns derived from. There was no need for them. The foster family that had adopted him and Tree was a good wholesome couple. They were Christian folks. The kind that ate, slept, and devoted their lives to the holy scripture. Through it all, they never tried to force feed their beliefs down Pimp and Tree throat like all the other monotheism Christians. Pimp and Tree had a choice of free will to believe or not. Guns was a natural instinct for Pimp. From games they played in the orphanage like finger guns to cops and robbers. Pimp could always remember adoring being the bad guy that toted a big stick. And thus, his love for guns began.

One day, Pimp was up the street from his home with some neighborhood teenagers. A pair of twins named Dre and Biggs, and their sister Crystal. It was Crystal's fault that he had gotten his hands dirty in the first place.

Pimp had asked her to connect him with someone he could buy some weed from. For her service, he promised to hit her with a couple nicks. When the oz arrived, Pimp weighed the loud on a pocket scale, only to discover the pack didn't weigh right. It was short, only weighing 24 grams, which was four grams off. Pimp told Crystal to call ole boy back so he could straighten Pimp out, but she claimed he wasn't answering his phone. That when it hit Pimp like a ton of bricks; he knew Crystal or her brothers had pinched some off the top. So, he informed Crystal until ole boy returned to straighten him out, he wasn't giving her anything. That didn't sit well with her. She became hostile on some fake bravado beef and started threatening Pimp. She told him she would destroy his people's home, cut their tires, bust out their windows, etcetera, etc. And she wouldn't stop until she was paid. Instead of Dre and Biggs being rational and telling their sister to quit with the ying yang, they got involved and tried to shake him down. So, Pimp gunned them down in cold blood. It was sort of like Billy The Kid, where he'd developed his thirst for blood after his first kill.

Dre was the first to get his shit pushed back. He didn't even see it coming. Dre had tried to corner Pimp between the washer and dryer in their basement. Pimp produced a millennium 9mm from his pocket and sent a hot one straight through Dre head. *Bop!* Dre's blood splashed all over the place, then exited through the back and lodged in the basement wall.

Biggs was next. He stood frozen from shock of his brother's death. Pimp fired five shots into Biggs's chest cavity. Crystal tried to run, but Pimp caught up to her at the bottom of the staircase. *Bop, bop!* He fired two. One went through her upper torso, the other through her neck. Crystal's body fell forward and slid backwards down the stairs. Pimp wiped his fingerprints off the appliances and gun and dropped the gun next to Crystal's corpse. Pimp knew it had to be a gruesome site for their parents to find their children slain like casualties of a cartel war.

When the authorities came to question Pimp, he stayed quiet. He never told a living soul, not even Tree.

Pimp started his car. As soon as he pulled into traffic on his way to Kesha's house, his cellphone rung. Pimp checked his display and frowned. He had never seen the number before.

"Who dis?" he answered.

"Boy stop acting. U been tryna hit dis pussy fa years. Now all da sudden u tryna act like u don't know da voice of da sparkle of your eye," Wanda pretentiously conveyed. "I shouldn't even dignify dat wit a response, but I wan't ta give u a chance ta live out dat lil fantasy of your's," she offered him the sea food platter.

"How in da fuck did u get dis number?" Pimp was confused. They had never exchanged numbers. He remembered when he had tried to get at her and get her seven digits. She had rejected him for Block. Now all if the sudden, she was calling, and that didn't sit right with him.

"I have my wayz," she replied, but didn't reveal her sources. Between her and God, she'd gotten his digits from some freak Pimp used to fuck on named Keke. Wanda had met Keke while she was gossiping up a storm in the hair salon. Keke was telling everyone how Pimp had wined and dined her and fucked her so good that she had tears in her eyes when they were finished. Just like a number written on a bathroom stall, Wanda coaxed Pimp's number out of her. "Just know I get wat I wan't when I want!"

"Oh, so I get it. Since my manes kicked u ta da curb, I'm da next runner up." Pimp saw right through Wanda charades. "Stop playing gurl. If u want a nigga ta come thru an' blow your back out, just say so. Otherwise I got money on my mind."

"Dat's exactly wat I want," she undeniably replied. Not dignifying what he'd implied about Block kicking her to the curb. Although it was factual, she just didn't have time to revisit the past. She had much more important things on her mind, and she knew how to scratch the itch. "Come thru right now an' get dis juicy pussy. I'll be waiting for u." She gave Pimp her address and left the next move in his hands.

Pimp made an illegal u-turn in the middle of the intersection, almost causing a pile up. Kesha would have to wait for another time. Pimp had always wanted some of Wanda's chocolate factory. Now, she was offering the opportunity, and he damn sure wouldn't miss his chance for Kesha. It was just like Yo Gotti had said, "God forgive me cause, I pray for the pussy." Now Pimp's prayers had been answered.

Pimp arrived at Wanda's flat and rang the doorbell. He was breaking the bro code by fucking on his man's sloppy seconds, but he didn't care. Block wasn't fucking her, so Wanda was fair game, and he didn't give a fuck how Block felt about it.

Wanda opened the door wearing nothing but her famous birthday suit and invited Pimp inside. Her look seemed to do the trick, because before the door shut, Pimp was all over her. He pinned her against the wall in the foyer and stuck his tongue in her mouth. Wanda reciprocated while unbuckling his belt and pushing down his jeans along with his boxers. She got down on her knees and sucked him into her mouth avidly with animalistic lust. She devoured Pimp in one gulp. Pimp's ten inches wasn't a problem, she had mastered the technique of swallowing big sticks...

***

"Wuz da deal Pickle?" Chop answered his phone on the first ring. It was his man Pickle off the south side. "Only time u hit my line is when u got something good fa me. So, holla at me." Pickle was the man to see when you needed fire power. He was an arms dealer, and he could get anything at your request.

"Nah fam, I got something better den wat'cha thinking," Pickle said, adjusting his Ray Bans on his face. "Aint'cha looking for dat nigga Kilo?"

"Yup, wat's up?" Chop asked, somewhat trilled. They'd been looking for the Kilo for about a month. "U know ware dat clown at?"

"Even better, dat nigga right in front of me, an' he got dat bitch Connie with em," Pickle informed. The news brought joy to Chop's ears. Pickle had found two of the most wanted people alive. That was like killing two birds with one stone. "Ya boi looking bad to, all strung out an' shit."

"Fuck all dat, just keep dat nigga der ta I get der," Chop demanded.

"Alright but hurry up. Ya boi just went in da dope spot across da streetz, an' I don't know how long I can stall em," He said stepping off the porch. " I'ma go rap wit dat freak Connie."

"Whatever." Chop hung up and grabbed his cannon and keys off the entertainment stand. "Come on Moski, let's ride out," he summoned Moski. Chop's body language gave off the vibe that some beef was about to pop off. Moski lived for drama, so he hunched his shoulder, took his 9Torres off safety, and followed Chop out the door.

Half hour later, Chop's box Chevy sitting on 30-inch Dalvin's came to a halt behind Kilo's candy painted green Camaro sitting in 26-inch blades, and Chop hopped out with his stick.

"Ware dat bitch nigga at?" Chop inquired. He then pushed Pickle out the way and snatched Connie through the open car window. She screamed and struggled, so Chop slapped her over the head with his pistol to shut her up. "Shut da fuck up before I shoot your fucking face off bitch. Mo, go drag dat bitch nigga out here."

"Hold up y'all," Pickle pleaded. "Be easy, y'all niggaz gone make da block hot like dat. Let me go get him," Pickle asked out of respect. Chop respected Pickle because he was always plugging them, but his request fell to the death ear. Chop overlooked Pickle's absurd request. Chop didn't give a fuck about making no block hot, he was a hot boy.

"U heard wat I said Mo, go get dat weak ass nigga," Chop ordered. "Now back ta u bitch, I should blow your fucking face all over dis pavement." Chop shoved his 4-10 down Connie throat. "Yea, suck dat mutha fucka like u accustom to." Connie was too afraid to utter a sound. Instead she whimpered and cried a river as Chop inserted and retracted his gun in and out of her mouth. "Filthy bitch, u ain't shit. I don't know wat my manes seen in your stank ass."

"Wu...wuz dis all bout?" she managed to mumble around the chunk of steal in her mouth. "I... I didn't do an... anything," she sobbed.

"Shut da fuck up. Ain't nobody tryna hear dat shit." Chop tightened his grip in her Shirley Temples. "An' quit acting dumb, u know wat dis bout. Bitch, u da reason my manes dead. Now u gotta pay da pipper."

Connie was horrified. The foreign situation had invaded her life in a matter of seconds. She had never been confronted by such imminent danger, and she didn't know what to do. There was nothing in life that could have prepared her for this life moment. Although she felt worthless, she would remain strong. She didn't know if she had the strength to, but there was one thing for certain, she wouldn't give her captor's the satisfaction of hearing her beg for her life.

"Punk ass trick." Chop disrespected her as he dragged her across the rough surface of the concrete. He forced her in the back seat. "Bitch u better not make a sound, or I swear ta gawd, I'll decorate da back-seat wit your blood," he threatened and slammed the door shut.

Moments later, Moski came out the house with Kilo at gun point. He shoved him in the backseat along with Connie and Chop fish tailed off the scene...

***

Block rolled up in front of Kayla's residence in a fully loaded black 2018 Cadillac CT6. The whip sat on 24-inch factory skates, with mirror back tents that hid Block from plain view. It felt good to be a gangster. Block was feeling himself as he stepped up to Kayla's front door and rapped twice. Block blew in the palm of his hands to make sure his breath was fresh. He was smelling and looking good dressed down in Mauri.

"Ay boo!" Kayla exclaimed opening the door and jumping in his arms. She was happy to see him, and she rained kisses all over his face and neck. "I miss u so much. Dont'cha ever stand me up again."

"I guess its true wat dey say," Block smiled and quoted a phrase. "A lil anticipation makes da heart grow fonder." Block wasn't the romantic type, but the mood was right. "Since I'm receiving dis kind of affection, I'ma stay MIA more often," he joked.

"Don't make me kill u."

Block couldn't take her serious when she looked so innocent. Kayla smiled up at him with her infectious smile, and Block couldn't help but return her smile.

"Here, des for u," he said and extended a bouquet of yellow lilies toward her.

"For me? U shouldn't have." She took the bouquet. "Let me put dem in some water before dey die," she said, taking a whiff of the flowers while heading back inside the house. "Come in, I'll just be a moment. I gotta grab my shoes an' my purse. Den we can go."

"Dat mean about an hour, right?" Block jest. "Normally when women say it'll only take a moment, dey leave us man impatiently for enough time fa us ta study fo are S.A.T.'s."

"Shut up stupid," Kayla laughed while heading into the kitchen to nourish the lilies. "U want anything ta drink?" she asked.

"Nah Kay, only thang I need is u."

Kayla placed the flowers in a vase with some water and ran to her room to put on her creme Dior's. The shoes matched her Christian Dior blouse. Kayla gave herself a once over in the mirror. Everything was well put together, and she was killing e'm. The way her ass set up in her black Dior jeans would make niggaz and bitches eat their heart out gawking over her.

"I'm ready babe," Kay announced stepping into the living room with her Dior clutch in hand. "How do I look?" she asked for a second approval. She already knew she looked fabulous, but she just wanted to hear Block say so.

"Worth a million photos an' million words I never said," Block said licking his lips. She was mesmerizing, and Block was glad she was his. "Da way u look, we should just skip dinner an' head straight for dessert." Block stared at her lustfully thinking he could eat her alive.

"Nah negro. I spent to long ta look dis good. U gone take me out," Kayla grabbed Block's hand and pulled him toward the door. She was flattered that he was ready to devour her, but he wouldn't get the nookie tonight without treating her to an enjoyable night out. "If u ever want to get in des jeans again, u better come on." Block laughed. He swore she acted like Mrs. Pickett sometime. The apple hadn't falling too far from the tree.

Outside, Block opened the passenger door and she got in. New car smell invaded her nostrils as her butt contoured to the plush leather.

"Nice car," Kayla admired. "Wat did u do wit da other one?" She wasn't being nosey; she was just making small talk.

"I junked it," Block indulged her. "It was about time I got my whip game proper. Dat other trash looked like Godzilla's lunch."

Kayla cackled. It was funny cause he had never lied. With all the bullet holes in the frame, it looked just as he had described.

"Plus, I figured dis ride more suitable for a king ta chauffeur his queen around," he smooth talked her. "So, lean back, an' enjoy your carriage ride."

Block put on some slow jams as they rolled through the streets, and Kayla reclined to get comfortable. Cheryl Lynn and Luther Vandross' song, "If This World Were Mine" emitted through the speakers, setting the mood for a night of thug passion.

"Oh, dis my song," Kayla exclaimed when the song came on. "Dis song so beautiful, just listen," she told Block, turning up the volume so she could sing along.

On cue, he stopped the car in the middle of ongoing traffic and parked under the night stars. Block blared the music and stepped out and opened Kayla door.

"What are you doing?" she asked nervously as Block extended his hand for her to take.

"Giving u da world. Come let's not spoil da moment," Block smiled charmingly. Block unpredictability flattered Kayla beyond belief. Not wanting to spoil the mood, Kayla took his hand, and he led the way.

In the middle of East Capital, they merged and moved to the rhythm of Luther's soothing voice. Kayla was lost in the moment. A source of all kind of feelings ran rapidly throughout her body; so many, she couldn't identify her emotions. There was only one emotion she could identify without a doubt, and that was love. She loved Block without doubt. There would never be another man like him. He had giving her a lifetime memory. How could one ever forget a night under the night skies, where their man took their hand, and danced with them in the middle of the intersection to their favorite song? Forever she would remember it was them against the world.

"Bentley, I luv u," she spoke softly into his chest. "An' ta answer your question, yes, I'll live wit u. I wan't to spend many more wonders wit u."

Overall of the traffic commotion and the melody of the loud music, she noticed Block's heart rate change. As she spoke the words, he'd been waiting for her to speak, his heart beat urgent rejoice. Kayla had made him the happiest man under the sun.

"An' from now on, everyday da world will be yours. I'd kiss da grown u walk on," Block informed sincerely. "Da nite has just begun, remember, I promised u da world. Come on so I can hold dear ta my word. I have a surprise for u." Block led her back to the car as the song ended. "Close your eyes an' no peeping," Block proposed and closed the door.

Kayla didn't obey. When the car was in motion, she peeked through the slit of her fingers, and Block swatted her on the arm.

"I said no peeping," he warned.

"Ok," Kayla huffed. "Where are u taken me? Don't I have da right to know."

"Not right now u don't. Your in my world right now," he said, and Kayla kept her eyes covered until they made it to their destination.

"May I uncover my eyes now? "She asked impatiently. Anticipation was eating her alive inside; she thrived to know what other surprises Block had in store for her.

"Sure," he provided permission. "Behold your new world," Block showcased when she removed her hands from eyes.

There was no way Kayla could declare the vision before her a reality. It was like a dream come true. Here she was with her dream man, and he was providing a dream home. She was thrilled and ecstatic at the same time. The euphoria gave her such a high out of this world, she never thought she'd return to earth.

"U like?" Block queried. He was enjoying the bewildered stare depicted on her face.

"Do I like?" she replied rhetorically. "Dat's an understatement, I luv it," she chimed with glee. She was like a child experiencing the wonders of McDonald's for the first time. "But how can u afford it? Its gigantic," she inquired about the humongous home.

Kayla had never seen anything so miraculous. This was a sight she'd only had a chance to view in Home magazines, but never did she think she'd be witnessing such a beauty off paper. And to think it was hers was unbelievable.

"It was a gift," Block answered truthfully. It had been passed down to him after he'd expressed his admiration of the opulent mansion to Niko. "Let's go inside, I've prepared a delicious spread fa us ta enjoy." They entered the palace turning the page to a new chapter in their book.

CHAPTER TWELVE

Block's ringtone woke him. He rolled over and unraveled himself from Kayla's embrace. They had had a wild night of mutual passion, and he hated he have to disengage from the comfort of her arms. He never wanted to let her go.

"Hello," he answered groggily why rubbing the built-up crust out of his eyes.

"Dey got her man," Dice cried. "Dey got my baby. I don't know wat ta do." Dice world was currently in shambles.

"Ninja, wat da fuck u talking about?" Block was confused and a bit disturbed by Dice's emotional call.

"Dey go Connie. Dey got my baby Block mane," Dice groaned painfully, he was heartbroken.

Block's heart was too callous to sympathize with his homie. He didn't give a damn about Connie or what had happened to her. Inside, Block was crying tears of joy, she was just one last bitch he had to worry about.

"Wat?" Block acted concern. "Meet me in da hood, I'm on my way."

Block hung up and got dressed. Kayla was still out cold, sleeping like the beauty she was. Before leaving, he wrote her a concise message and placed it along with a surprise gift upon her pillow.

He hit the deck half an hour later. Everyone was surrounding Dice to console him. It was always something, and it was too much for one man. Block thought money would be the root to solving all his problems, but that was fiction. The more money, the more problems. There was always something, this or that, that stagnated his happiness.

"Wuz popping family?" Block greeted the masses, showing love to Pimp, Six, Dice, and Two-G. "I thought I told u to stay ghost for awhile?" he confronted Two.

"Mane save dat shit for another time an' different place," Dice snapped, and pushed his phone into Block hands. "Look how dey doing her mane."

Block took the phone to see what it was that had Dice all worked up. What he saw made him shy away, and he wasn't squeamish. Whoever had sent the video, had recorded them torturing and pulling Connie's finger nails out with pliers.

"I got dat shit dis morning. I had ta wake up an' watch da luv of my life in dat state, an' I can't do shit about it."

When Dice verbalized his hurt, Block's heart softened. He didn't give a damn about Connie, but it pained him to see his boy in pain, he'd known Dice since middle school. Although Block had done some low-down dirty shit, and fucked his bitch, it didn't mean he had any lost love for Dice. What had transpired between Block and Connie, was going on way before Dice had come into the picture. Dice had fell in love with the chick Block was loving on, and not loving. When Dice fell head over hills for Connie, her and Block had been fucking on and off for years. Block just didn't have the courage to tell Dice once he found out Dice had giving his heart so fast to Connie, because Block didn't want to see his man hurt like he was now.

"So, wat's up, did dey request a ransom?" Block inquired. He was trying to figure out what was the purpose behind the whole situation, and most of all, who was behind it. "Who u think behind dis?" Block handed Dice back his phone.

Dice didn't reply. Connie's abduction made his life have no purpose; it was her who made him whole. His spirit had sunk to rock bottom, and without Connie, he knew he would never experience the highs of life.

Block realized he was scourged. His boy Dice was fighting to hold on to what sanity he had left.

"Dawg, let me speak wit'cha a moment," Six whispered in Block's ear. Six felt he needed to run the information by Block before he disclosed it to the team.

"Wuz hood?" Block questioned as he followed Six away from the team. Block was curious to know what was so important that Six had to pull him away to talk discreetly.

"I had ta pull u away cause I couldn't divulge dis info as an collective. At lease not yet, Dice not in da right state of mind," Six explained. Block understood Six's motive. It was sensible in regard to the matter at hand, so by taking Dice's mind in accountability, Six had did a considerable deed. "I made contact wit da nigga Bando. It was quite easy, almost too easy."

"Ok, so wat's up wit dat?" Block asked. He was satisfied with Six's positive results. It meant Block was one step closer at accomplishing his endeavor he'd set out for. And hopefully, Tree was back on the street, so he could rock Bando to sleep. "So, wat? Ole boy embraced u like one of his?"

"Not yet, It's a process. I supposed ta be getting up wit him today an' show him some of da goods a nigga got. Dem niggaz so stupid, dey believe I'm from out of town scouting fa local hustlaz."

"Wait a minute," Block spoke suddenly. "Do u think ole boy an' em behind dis mess wit Connie an' our mans?" Block rubbed his chin as he brained stormed. He had an eerie feeling. Remembering the night, he'd gotten into it with them ESG niggaz, he also remembered Connie was in the club that night. Before he had flat lined Stevo, he remembered Connie being hugged up with lil buddy. Something told him Connie had been kidnapped as a result of his actions.

"I don't know." Six was not too sure about the entire ordeal. When the drama behind Block and ESG kicked off, he was still in the big house. So, he could only speculate. "Wat'cha think?"

Block hunched his shoulders. He couldn't give a for sure response, because he only had a hunch. But it was a strong hunch.

"I don't know, but let's keep dis under way." Block squared vital deeds away that could save Connie's life. He'd rather sacrifice Connie life, because if she was dead, she couldn't make good on her threats. "let me get back over here so we can abrade dis ninja pain away. Keep your eyes open round dem ESG ninjaz."

"Fa'sho," Six assured.

Big-Mo creme cheese big boy Yukon sitting along 30-inch DUB's came to a screeching halt, and Pimp and Six drew their irons in record time. They were ready to burn something.

"Witch one of u clown ass niggaz got my lil brotha out here peddling dope?" Big-Mo hopped out in front of Block trap house on business along with his right-hand man, Crusher.

Crusher was an ugly nigga who stood a towering 6'5 and weighed 340 pounds even. Crusher looked like he crushed stones for a living, but that didn't frighten Block. Block had the heart of a lion.

"Bitch ass ninja, wat'cha talking about?" Block cut right to the chase and threw his hands up. Block knew what Big-Mo had come for, and it wasn't to talk. Block had mad heart; win, lose, or draw, he was trained to go. "U better get back in dat bucket an' slide up out of here before I knock yo bitch ass out."

Big-Mo stepped to Block's face, but he stood his ground and didn't budge. Big-Mo was twice Block's size. At 6 feet and 300 pounds, he made Block look like Mini-Me. But Block had not a single ounce of fear, he believed the bigger you are, the harder you fall.

"Hold on bro." Two stepped between Block and his brother. They were grilling each other down. Block was ready to rip Big-Mo head off his shoulders, and if his brother wanted some action, he could get it too. Wasn't no favoritism in Block's reign of fiery. "Bro I'm grown, an' u ain't got no bizness coming round here up in my bizness. U niggaz had a bag but didn't help me when u seen me down. Now u mad cause fam fuck wit me. Do me a favor an' make like da Flintstones an' pat your feet." While Two was trying to calm his brother down, Block blew Big-Mo kisses, as an indication he was sweet.

"Watch out wit all dat." Big-Mo growled and shoved Two out of his way. "So, wat up bitch nigga?" he said, stepping back in Block face.

Block's first blow rocked Big-Mo on his back heels. It was unexpected when Block's right hook connected with his chin. Mike Tyson said it best, "everybody got a plan until they got hit."

Shaking off the faze, Big-Mo charged at Block swinging wildly, but none of his blows landed. Block bobbed and weaved Big-Mo blows. Block was much quicker than Big-Mo. Crusher tried to jump in, only to be meet by Pimp's cold steel to his temple.

"Dis ain't dat type of party playboy," Pimp warned. He had a big 40 with a 30-round extension that stuck out the bottom like the soul train line. "Make another move, an' I'ma put your face on a T-shirt."

Crusher was defeated, so he stepped back and threw his hands up.

Big-Mo was wheezing for breath and sweating profusely.

"Yo bitch ass tired huh?" Block asked while landing a combo to Big-Mo's jaw. A left, right, and an upper cut. "I'ma talk ta your bitch ass why I whoop your ass, just like your momma used too," Block said as Big-Mo charged at him again. Block stepped to the side and caught Big-Mo with a mighty right hook that sent him sailing to the ground. Instantly, Big-Mo scrambled to his feet. "Dont'cha ever come round here like u some G," Block continued his assault.

Block's taunts sent Big-Mo rage boiling over. Getting ahold of Block, they wrestled for a moment. Taking control, Big-Mo used his massive upper body strength, and body slammed Block on his shit. They rolled in the grass struggling for position, but Big-Mo ended up on top.

"U ain't talking shit now, huh?" Big-Mo breathed heavily, slamming his right elbow into Block's jaw.

Block fought desperately to get out from beneath the blob, but the mass of Big-Mo was unmovable. Big-Mo threw another punch, and a haze of darkness cascaded over Block. That's when somehow Block found Samson strength, and pushed Big-Mo off of him. Block staggered to his feet and shook off the daze.

"Fuck dat shit. I'm not finna keep fighting your big ass," Block said flouncing toward Six. "Fam give me da face popper, I'ma burn dis fat slob," he warned snatching Six 9 Rugor.

Big-Mo and Crusher became track stars and wobbled as fast as their wide bodies would allow them to their respective truck. Block let off a gang of shots, but none of them hit his attended target. Big-Mo smashed the gas, and the truck leaped forward as bullets perforated the back end of his truck. As the truck sped away, Block squeezed the trigger until the 9 was empty...

***

Connie was divested and hog tied. She laid on her side on the hard, cold basement floor, with Flex-Tape over her mouth. As Moski and Chop stood above her urinating on her body as if it was a urinal. They had beaten her and worked her over badly. They had worked her over pretty badly, and their urine stung like hornets when it contacted with the open wounds, she'd substantially obtained from the torment she had endured. She flopped around like a fish out of water begging for them to stop, but her pleads only antagonized them more. They were enjoying themselves, laughing, and shaking hands as they released their liquids upon her.

"Now bitch, u ready ta talk?" Chop asked.

Connie was mortified by their debasement, but she still nodded her head. She would have done anything to make them stop.

"Mo, go check on dat nigga Kilo," Chop sent Moski off. When he was gone, he ripped the tape from Connie's gullet.

"I told y'all I didn't have anything ta do wit Stevo's murda!" Connie cried. They had beaten the dignity out of her. She had been beaten and scalded with hot boiling water that left third degree blisters all over her body head to toe. Plus, all her fingernails had been removed by pliers, she had been humiliated beyond any self-respected human being when they had pissed on her like a minor starring in a R. Kelly home video.

"Shut your fucking trap. I'm tired of da fucking lies. If u lie ta me one more time, I'll rip your fucking tongue out. Do I make myself clear?" he asked, smiling maniacally at Connie.

"Yea." She agreed in a fate whisper. She was frightened of Chop, and she didn't want to do anything to aggravate him.

"U don't know me dat well," Chop informed. "But I know u very well. In fact, I took da initiative ta send your man a video of me torturing u. U look so beautiful when u holla an' scream. I wish I could rewind da hands of time so I can do it all ova again," he meandered off the course of topic.

Connie had paid him no mind. She couldn't believe Dice knew about her truculent torment. At the worst time in her life, she wondered how he was taken all this.

"After Stevo's death, I went thru extreme extent putting da pieces of da puzzle together tryna place whom could be responsible. An' believe it or not, da entire picture surrounds u."

Connie had no idea what Chop was talking about. In fact, she wasn't even supposed to be at the club that night. Her and Dice had had a big argument when he had discovered she wasn't at Kayla's.

"I don't know..." Connie whimpered.

"I want ask u again ta speak only when spoken to," Chop raised his hand over his head again, and Connie flinched. Her fear gave him confirmation of her cooperation.

"Now who was dem niggaz u was up in da club wit?"

Connie was conflicted in confusion. She wasn't sure if it was a trick question so he could strike her again, or if he wanted her to be straight forward. Regardless, she chose not to answer.

"Back ta dat huh?" Chop despised her silence. He picked up a box cutter that was stored next to the bloody pliers they'd used to remove her fingernails. " I got something dat a make u talk. A disfigurement ta da luv bud should do da trick." Chop threaten to cut off her clitoris. Placing the blade at the outer side of her vagina lips, he made a thin incision.

"Aaaahhhhhh!" she screamed. "Ok...ok, I'll talk," she promised. Tears clouded her eyes, and she tried desperately to run away to subdue the pain, but it was no use because her legs had been zip tied together. "Wat do u want ta know?"

"U know dam well what I want ta know." Chop snarled. "Who killed my nigga?"

Connie still wasn't sure; she didn't know who killed Stevo. She wasn't there, nor did she arrange for his assassin. Making an inference, she only assumed it was Block Chop may be inquiring about.

"I don't know much about him," Connie weaved a tale. "When I see him, it's normally at da Pfister Hotel." Chop didn't care about her futile relations, but she provided the fact to shape her pseudo story into something believable. She was making up the tale because she didn't want to get Block killed, she had something else up her sleeve. "But I know ware u can find his lady at." Her plan was to give them Kayla on a silver platter. She figured if she got Kayla out of the way, she could have Block all to herself. But before she put her diabolical scheme into effect, Moski came back into the room.

"Bando want ta see u," Moski advised Chop.

"Hold dat thought," Chop said, and placed the tape back over her mouth, before he and Moski exited.

Chop meet Bando in the cellar where Kilo was tied to a wooden chair in the center of the floor. He had been beaten so horribly, his eyes were swollen shut, nose broken, and his front teeth had been knocked out, along with three broken ribs.

"Did dis piece of shit tell u where my dope at?" Bando questioned Chop. "I hope u got something out of him cause he looks like death worn over."

"He claimed he smoked it all," Chop told.

Kilo had went down the drain after Stevo's killing. Drugs had become his blanket because he couldn't cope with it. So, he used white to cloud his perception of reality.

"When we caught em, he was in da dope spot copping den. Ta be honest dat shit fuck me up. I couldn't believe my eyes," Chop explained. Chop couldn't believe Kilo had allowed the very substance that had destroyed black communities since the 80's tear him down. Kilo wasn't the person he once knew. The nigga he knew always stayed fresh like a space cadet and would never indulge in drugs. Chop felt this was a sequel to the "Body Invasion."

"U smoked up my shit," Bando exploded in rage. "A whole fucking brick?" he shouted, then started beaten Kilo over the head with the187 pump action in his hands. "Punk ass nigga, I trusted u. I gave u wealth when u was broke. Bitch I was your gawd!!!!" Bando brought the gun down repeatedly over Kilo's cranium, until he was a bloody mess, and blood poured from his skull like an over flowed sink faucet.

"Clean dis mess up, an' get rid of dis piece of shit," Bando ordered, wiping his bloody hands on his black T-shirt. "Let dis be a lesson ta both of U niggaz," he warned, looking at Chop and Moski with an ice-cold stare. "Don't play wit my loot."

Bando left the room, leaving Kilo's bloody corpse and minatory word incised in the depths of Chop's and Moski's minds...

***

Kayla disgorged into a wicker basket that was on the side of the bed. This was the third time that morning she'd experienced morning sickness. Rushing to the bathroom, she rinsed out her mouth and brushed her teeth. She was concerned. Her monthly period was almost a month in a half late, and the nauseous vomiting had become a daily ritual. Kayla feared she might be pregnant. God how she wished that wasn't the case, she had to focus on her studies, not raising a baby. She always figured when she had a child, she would be able to give the baby all her undivided attention, and right now she couldn't spoil a baby with the attention he or she so rightfully deserve. Kayla loved Block, and by his actions, she knew the feelings was mutual. But love wasn't enough, she was determined to have a career, and a baby wasn't predestined.

"Oh my gawd, snap out it gurl," she told herself, then threw some cold water over her face. Before she became pervaded pessimistically, she would take a pregnancy test and find out the results first. For all she knew, it could be a case of stomach flu.

"Bentley?" she called out heading back into the bedroom. She noticed his side of the bed was empty, but there was a note on his pillow. Grabbing the kite and key from off top, she read the billet-doux. "U looked so beautiful in a Jag,

> I thought u deserved your own.
>
> Follow the roads of Hershey
>
> Kisses..."

Kayla glanced at the trail of Hershey's Kisses, and smiled to herself. Kayla followed the trails through the home she still couldn't believe was hers. Arriving at a closed door that lead into the garage, she opened the door to discover a candy apple red 2018 F-Type Jaguar wrapped in a bow. She couldn't believe her eyes as she ran around to the driver side. To her surprise, a card was wedged in the crevice of the door. The message read:

> "Now that I have kissed the
>
> ground you walk on, will
>
> you Marry Me?"

Tears cascaded down her face, she was overwhelmed with emotions. Block was full of surprises. The fact that he treated her like a queen, warmed her heart. How could she say no to a man that made her feel like the only woman in the world?

"Yes, I'll marry u!" Kayla shouted into the void. "Wherever u are, I'll marry u!"

Whoever said fairy tales didn't exist wasn't telling the truth, Kayla was a living example...

***

Tree scampered into the Milwaukee County Jail day room. After three long days being interrogated at the police district, finally, the worst was over, or so he thought.

Tree needed to use the phone. The police had violated his rights by not providing him a call within a 72-hour period. Twelve was mad he wouldn't cooperate and squeal on his team. He held dear to the first rule, which was silence and secrecy. Wasn't no trophies for being real, loyalty was a way of life, not just a word.

Before Tree relieved the phone from its cradle, he unconsciously grabbed his junk through his orange county pants. It felt good to know he wasn't burning. Thanks to antibiotics, he had been able to rid himself of the gonorrhea he'd contracted from Trish. He made a mental note, more like a vow, to kill Trish if he ever saw her again.

With his mind made up, Tree picked up the phone, and called Block...

"Yo," Block answered his phone.

"U have a collect call from, Tree," an automation voice informed. "If u except, press one."

"Yea, I except u weak ass computerized bitch," Block said why pressing one. "Wuz popping my mutha fucking ninja. We out here an' missing u mad crazy," he greeted once his call went through.

"Glad ta hear dat big homie," Tree accepted. He was glad to be appreciated and missed. Especially, after the maggot ass police had condemned him to a dimly light and freezing room for three days. "I'm still Tree Stump ta I D.I.E., how you living?"

"Mane, da world got my shoulders strong. Shit crazy out here. After u got knocked, some ninjaz kidnapped Connie, an' I had ta put my foot in Two's big brotha's ass earlier today," Block explained the everyday struggles, trials, and tribulations of a gangsta. "U know its da same shit different toilet. But enough about me, wat dem crackers talking about?" Block wanted to know what was up with his hitter. He had to get Tree back home by any means necessary, even if he had to spend a bag on attorney fees.

"U know da usual trumped up charges. Des cracker jacks tryna stick me on a triple homicide, felon in possession of a firearm, an' possession of a narcotic," he explained. "Where u at right now? My nigga Pimp wit'cha?"

"Nah, I'm in traffic on some solo dolo shit. Tryna get back ta da crib so I can spend some quality time wit my wifey."

"Wat'cha living together now?" Tree asked in disbelief. He was tripping the way Block was talking. The Block he knew was a playa for life, not no suit and tie type nigga. Like Jay Z, he would be forever macking. "I only been gone 72 ours, an' u talking like u married. Wat'cha drunk or something?" Tree was the first to cast stone and spew judgment. But during their colloquy, not once did he mention he'd contracted gonorrhea from Trish's nasty ass. He didn't understand the definition of you shouldn't throw stones if you live in a glass house.

"Yea, something like dat." Block decided not to inform Tree he'd proposed to Kayla. For two reasons, one Tree wouldn't understand, and secondly, he didn't know Kayla's reply yet. "We out here making big boy moves, so in da process, I made a big boy move ta move my lady in," Block enlightened. Block wasn't afraid to tell his boy his true intentions with Kayla. With being his friend, Tree should understand. When you're a child you do childish things, but when you become a man, you put away the childish things. Block was on his grown man shit, and he didn't have time for childish games. "U know grown man do wat dey want, an' boys do wat dey can. But back ta u, u got a bail yet?"

"Nah, not yet. But look, a nigga do need a lawyer. I still got a nice stash put away..."

"Never mind dem dollaz, we gone get'cha an attorney. Everything gonna be alright, alright?" Block cut Tree off in mid-sentence. "Save dem coins fa when u touchdown. Why u down, da family got'cha. Just keep your head ta da sky."

"U have one-minute left," the automation chimed in, indicating one minute remained.

"Look, tomorrow I'ma go holla at an attorney ta see wat's good," Block spoke fast. "An' a ninja gone send u some coins. Call me tomorrow, Pimp a be wit me den. Stay true."

"Always," Tree assured, then the line went dead.

Block drove up to his two-story home. Kayla's F-Type was parked in the driveway, which meant she'd found her gift.

Block was glad Tree had called. Tree's voice was upbeat, which meant he was fighting the powers that be, and not letting the system break him down.

"I'm so glad your home." Kayla beamed leaping into Blocks arms. "I got some good news." She informed raining kisses all over his face and neck.

"Argh, take it easy," Block moaned his discomfort.

Kayla jumped out of his embrace and looked at him strangely. Block's shirt was covered in blood.

"Don't tell me ole gurl got at'cha again," Kayla joked.

"I see I'ma have to beat your smart ass, huh," he returned, while tackling her to the plush carpet, then started tickling her mercifully. Kayla cackled uncontrollable. It was just like old times sake. When they were younger, Block used to tickle her nonstop.

"No, ok, stop, I quit!" she pleaded.

Block ceased the torment, and they laid entangled side by side with Kayla breathing hard, trying to catch her breath.

"Nah, it ain't nothing ta worry about," Block explained. "Just a misunderstanding. U know typical guy shit," Block told the mild version. His business was his business, and the fact he might have a possible war on his hands, was his business, not hers. Block knew Big-Mo was a killer, so he was sure he wouldn't sit on his hands or turn the other cheek. Block was sure Big-Mo would retaliate; he just didn't know when. "Wuz up wit dat good news u wuz telling me about before u attacked me at da door? I see I'ma have to stop coming thru front doors cause u like ta attack me at the entrance."

"Whatever boy, u know u luv dat shit, so stop fronting," Kayla stood correct. Block enjoyed her displays of affection. What man wouldn't want his woman greeting him like it was their first time they met, every time they met? A man would have to be blind, crazy, and cripple to turn down ardor adoration.

"Bentley, I'm pregnant," she blurted. She tried to read Block's expression through his eyes, but his stare was blank. While Block was gone, she had went out to purchase a pregnancy test. And it turned out, she was pregnant.

"Yea, I'ma be a dad?" His eyes lit up with pride. He reacted how Kayla had hoped he would. She didn't know what she would do if Block didn't want to support her or didn't want a child. His reaction let her know everything was going to be ok. Block took her in his arms, and kissed her passionately, why rubbing Kayla stomach. "All snaps, I'ma have a lil son ta be stunting like his daddy. Yes, he is," Block bent down and cooed at her soft tummy.

"Nuh uh, move stupid." She playfully pushed Block head away, giggling at Block silliness. "How u know it's gone be a boy? It could be a gurl Dat's gone be stunning like her momma She said rubbing her stomach in a circular motion.

"Don't nobody want ta grow up looking like your ugly self," Block joked. "He gone be handsome, not grotesque."

"Ugh, get away from me." Kayla pushed Block away, pouting like she was mad. Block saw right through her persuade and grabbed her in his arms and gave her a kiss.

"Still fronting, u know u da most beautiful Goddess on dis green earth," Block reassured. "An' I luv u. Wat do u say ta my proposal? I can't let my child be born no bastard," Block had wedding bells in his head. He hadn't gotten her a ring and proposed in the traditional manner society was accustom to. He figured if she said yes, they'd go get matching tattoos on their wedding finger, or a diamond embedded under the skin in a more contemporary fashion.

For a response, Kayla gave him a hug and a deep kiss. "Does dat answer your question?" she asked gazing into his eyes.

"Not really, I'ma lil slow I need a lil more convincing."

"Your wish is my command," she obliged, straddling Block...

***

Freeza leaned against the wall with his feet kicked up in a Red Lobster booth. He'd just devoured a scrumptious lobster tail, steak, and potato.

"Damn dat hit da spot." Freeza burped then picked the leftover meat from his teeth with his pinky nail, simply ignoring the toothpicks that set in plain view in the center of the restaurant table.

Snow White watched in disgust and disapprobation. The nerve of some people she thought. Freeza was a man of no class; although his pockets were lined with blueberries, there were just some things money couldn't buy, like etiquette. Manners are a trait your parents had to install in you, and it was plain to see, Freeza's guardians had lacked in that department.

"I hope u good an' full, because u gone need your strength for tonight," Snow White stroked his ego. She knew Freeza was a sucker. He thought he was gang-gang, but in reality, he was a goofy. She placed her hand in Freeza's lap and stroked his manhood through his Gucci jeans. "I'm so hot inside, if I don't have u, I'll burn alive from within."

"Gurl, u ain't never had a nigga like me," he said, laughing jollily like Santa Claus. His laugh fit him perfectly. Freeza was a heathy size dude, but he wasn't ugly. In her opinion, he favored DJ Khalid. "Matta fact, let me pay dis bill, so we can get up out of here. Waiter!" he shouted across the diner. The ghetto fabulous outburst drew attention from the customers, who all turned in their direction to stare. Snow White was so embarrassed by Freeza rude displays. "Wat?" Freeza challenged the spectators. "Wat'cha looking at? Turn da fuck around an' eat'cha food, before I act ugly up in dis bitch," he warned.

Freeza's horrible attitude turned Snow White off. In many ways, he would never compare to her man. Six was a thug and a gentleman.

Niggaz these days had no sense; they had no idea what it took to turn a woman on and keep her there. Most men thought cause their pockets were fat, they could have any women they want, like they was God's gift to earth. News flash she thought, women that only dated for the loot was gold diggers. A real woman didn't appeal to what a man had in his pocket; she appealed to the man.

After Freeza picked up the tab, he left the waiter a wealthy tip, and they migrated toward their destination.

"Damn gurl, u so fine, a nigga can eat u alive," he complimented in a miffed way. "I must admit, when Niko told me he had dis breezy dat wanted ta holla at me, I was reluctant, cause buddy be fucking on thoties. But u, u on a whole nother level. U blow my mind." Freeza made an explosion sound effect, using hand gestures to magnify an example.

"I've been watching u for a long time, an' I couldn't wait ta get my hands-on u handsome," Snow White lied. She didn't know Freeza from an ant in a hole. This was strictly business, and she couldn't wait to be over with it, so she could get back to her life. "U so fucking fine, I can't wait ta get ta da hotel. I'ma ride u like an equestrian," she affably pinched Freeza's chubby cheeks.

When they arrived at the hotel, they rushed straight to their room Freeza had reserved. They was like teenagers, kissing, pawing, like they couldn't get enough of one another. Snow white pushed Freeza onto the bed, straddled him, and snapped the buttons on his Gucci button up as she snatched it apart.

"Dat's how I like dat shit, rough," Freeza breached, huskily gripping Snow White's ass. She kissed him and nibbled her way down his chest.

"I'm glad, because dat's just how I like ta give it," Snow White disengaged from atop of him, and grabbed some tweed rope she had stored in the confines of her purse. "Tonight, your gonna reach a new height. I got something for u."

"All u kinky, just how I like em." Freeza didn't object to her tightly binding him to the bed post. "Me an' u gone have a lot of fun. I can luv a gurl who into experiencing new thangz."

Snow White removed his jeans, leaving him in nothing but his Polo boxers, before tying his legs to the frame also.

"Believe me, u ain't never experienced wat I got in store for u," she assured.

"Dat's right, tease me, please me. Tell me wat'cha gone do ta me."

"I rather show u," Snow White pulled a hypodermic syringe from her purse. Freeza became wide eye, and started to struggle against his binds the moment she climbed back on top of him, and removed the syringe cap.

"Wat'cha doing? Wat's dat?" Freeza panicked and screamed for help. "Help! Somebody come get dis crazy lady off me."

"Just relax, it'll all be over soon." She injected the needle into Freeza's neck and squeezed a deadly proportion of Fentanyl into his blood stream. Instantly, his body started to convulse and foam at the mouth. He would be dead in a matter of seconds. His death would be fast and painful, but his murder would never be linked back to Niko, who had arranged his death. Niko had received information from a mole he had in the Federal Bureau, that Freeza was a C.I., and was turning state evidence. So, Niko arranged for him to be hit...

"Oh, dis dick feels soooo good!" Wanda moaned in pleasure while riding Pimp backwards cowgirl. His baton was bringing her great satisfaction. They'd been going at it for approximately 30 minutes, she had bust multiple nuts back to back.

"Dat's it gurl, jump up an' down, have da holy ghost on dis mutha fucka," Pimp said, pushing himself into her every time she plunged downwards. "Oh, shit," he groaned and stiffing, grabbing her accelerating hips, as he filled her with globs of his cum.

"Agghhh!" she moaned. His semen had triggered her own orgasm. "Yes baby, oooooh weeeee!" she howled collapsing on her side. She had lost all control, and her body spasmed uncontrollably. "Damn boy, if I knew u could do it like dat, I would've told u to come get dis pussy long time ago," Wanda breathed as her climax subsided. "U make a bitch feel like a born-again virgin."

"Yea, all dat," he dismissed her admirations. He wasn't fond of her glorification. Now that he had got his rocks off, an egregious feeling of guilt made him feel like shit. He liked Wanda, but he also knew he was foul. "Ain't nobody ta blame fa your decision making. U choose Block, an' now u see he can't luv u like I luv u."

"Nah boo, it most definitely ain't da same," Wanda boasted. Pimp was a straight shooter, and she had to admit, he was right. Pimp filled every crevice and orifices like Block had never. Not saying Block was small and never satisfied her, Pimp was just more efficient with his dick game. "I'm just tryna figure out how I'ma be able ta get u ta come thru here, an' make me feel like dis on da regular?"

"U know my number," Pimp replied. There was no telling how long he would allow this to continue between the two. They been getting together for weeks now, but soon he felt he would have to rectify himself and ameliorate the strength between he and Block's friendship. "I'm only one call away."

"Yea, but I'ma need u ta do something else for me," Wanda became serious. She knew she had Pimp right where she wanted him. His eyes couldn't hide the truth; she knew he would choke a stick and kill a brick for her.

"Anything," Pimp agreed eagerly, not realizing he was making a deal with the devil.

"I need u ta kill Block"...

CHAPTER THIRTEEN

Block awoke to the sound of rattling pans, pots, and the delicious smell of fried sausages and eggs. As he set up in bed, a dubious feeling washed over him. He couldn't explain it, but he couldn't shack the eerie feeling. Something told him to be careful.

Kayla stood over the stove preparing breakfast when he entered the kitchen. The aromas of scrambled eggs, sausages, and biscuits lingered in the air.

"Ware u all dressed up, ta be dis early?" Block inquired about her attire, wrapping his arms around her waist, then kissed on the back of her neck.

"U know I gotta be at school," she replied. "Den I'ma go ta my apartment an' pack a few thangz." Kayla turned the stove off, dumped the preparations on a plate, and turned to her fiancé.

"I don't want'cha ta go. Let's stay in fa today," Block requested, pushing his groin against Kayla's abdomen. He was hard, and Kayla could feel the solidness of his manhood on her stomach. "See wat effect u have on me?"

Kayla knew exactly what effect she had on him, but she had to get to school.

"Nah uh, u had your fun last nite. A bitch still sore down der. Your not finna destroy my walls before dis big head child of yours come out," she quickly maneuvered away from Block embrace. She knew if she stayed in his arms, he would eventually charm her into a quickie.

"Alright, since da cookie jar ain't open, is da head still in play?" he wittily requested. If you can get the top, the bottom shall follow.

"Ugh, wit your nasty self," Kayla laughed. "Now eat your breakfast dat I spent all morning preparing. I need ta finish getting ready for class. When I get home later, u can have it anyway u want it," Kayla promised, placing Block's food in front of him and giving him a morning kiss.

"However, I want it huh?" Block asked with a deviant smile plastered across his face. "I'm tryna get into it right now."

"U just don't give up easy do u?" She asked a rhetorical question because she already knew the answer. He was relentless.

"Nope," he returned. Kayla drove a hard bargain, when she had made up her mind, there was no use in trying to negotiate. Knowing he had reached a dead end, he threw in the towel. "Go get ready Kay. I gotta go handle some B.I. anyways. But I'ma hold u ta your promise. Maybe I'll do it ta ya tied ta da ceiling tonight."

Kayla chuckled, and started to walk away, but Block grabbed her around the waist, and pulled her into his lap. He kissed her, and they stayed that way for quite some time, until Block's hands got fresh, and she pushed them away.

"Nah uh," Kayla murmured. "Flattery will never get'cha nowhere," she said, patting him on the chest before switching away.

Block laughed to himself, because she knew him so well. He could never get anything by her. While Kayla was getting beautified, Block took the time to call Pimp.

"Wuz popping Pimp?" he greeted, taking a bite from his sausage links. "Today da big day, u ready?"

"I was born ready, I'm to ready," he retorted. "I'm on my way ta da hood right now ta catch dis action. U know early byrd gets da worm."

"Dat's wat's up," Block assured. "Dat ninja Tree hit me up yesterday, an' he asked bout yo fool ass."

"Yea, wat he talking about?"

"Nothing dat I don't believe he won't come from under." Block had faith in his words. He couldn't see Tree doing life. Tree wasn't built for that shit, he was built for the streets. "Dey dangling a few bodies ova his head, but dat shit ain't gone stick. I'ma go holla at dat lawyer dat got Six out, an' see wat he talking like."

"I'ma go wit'cha. We gotta get bro back out here. It ain't da same since he been gone," Pimp groaned. Tree absents had Pimp fucked up inside. He missed the hell out his boy, and he wouldn't rest until he got Tree back home. "Feel me?"

"Yea I feel ya," Block reassured. "But I just called ta see if u wuz ready, I'ma hit'cha when I'm on my way. One luv."

"Fa'sho, struggle," he replied then hung up.

As Block was finishing his food, Kayla came back into the kitchen and kissed him before she headed off.

"Call me latter, I luv u."

"Ditto," he replied as she left...

***

That afternoon after class, Kayla cruised across town to her apartment complex. Along the way, she tried to call Connie, but she didn't receive an answer. Kayla had started to worry; she didn't know what was going on with her girl, she'd been trying to reach Connie for two days, but she had gotten nothing but the voicemail. It was unlike Connie not to call. Connie had made it a habit to call at least once a day. But knowing Connie, she had probably found her a new sponsor, and was laid up somewhere. That was the only theory she could summon to rationalize why her phone was off.

When Connie was out screwing around, she would turn her phone off, so Dice couldn't contact her.

As she turned into Hillside projects, she felt a sense of relief. She was glad she had beaten the odds and was able to make it out of the squalor. It wasn't many who done such. Between 70 and 80 percent of the ghetto black men and women either ended up in jail or dead. Under those extreme conditions, she was glad not to be a statistic. Now only thing she had to do, was get her mother out the slums.

As she went into the complex and began to pack, she called her mother to share the good news...

***

Chop and Moski sat staked out. Things were just how Connie had detailed them things would be. Kayla had come from school and straight home. The time had come for him to get revenge and avenge Stevo.

"Get'cha phone out," Chop demanded while tying a black Paisley scurf around his face. "I'ma put dis shit on YouTube, so dat bitch ass nigga know dis wat'cha get when u play wit ESG."

Moski cringed at Chop's ignorance. It was the sort of reckless behavior that got niggaz and bitches indicted every day. Against his better judgment, he pulled out his phone.

Kayla came out the apartment talking on her cellphone to her mother and lugging her traveler's suitcase.

"Yo Kayla!" Chop called as they approached. Fright washed over her as she turned to be confronted by the two masked gunmen. It was too late to run. The unknown males already loomed upon her. The only thing she could do was utter a shriek as Chop raised his blue steel 357. "Dis fo Stevo," he said, then fired a trilogy of shots. *Bop, bop, bop.*

The first bullet lodged in her left eye socket. The other two blew off her ear and ruptured her heart. Kayla was dead before she hit the pavement. Chop and Moski fled the scene, leaving behind the faint sounds of a mother's cries that emitted from the cellphone that was mingle in the blood next to Kayla's dead body...

The End!

Also Available by Bagz of Money Content

Live by It, Die by It (By: Ice Money)

Mercenary (By: Ice Money)

The Ruler of the Red Ruler (By: Kutta)

Block Boyz (By: Juvi)

Team Savage (By Ace Boogie)

Team Savage 2 (By Ace Boogie)

Available at Bagzofmoneycontent.com and most major bookstores.